WADE IN

THE WATER

WADE IN THE WATER

A Novel

NYANI NKRUMAH

AMISTAD

An Imprint of HarperCollinsPublishers

WADE IN THE WATER. Copyright © 2023 by Nyani Nkrumah. All rights reserved. Printed in the United States of America. No part of this book may be used or reproduced in any manner whatsoever without written permission except in the case of brief quotations embodied in critical articles and reviews. For information, address HarperCollins Publishers, 195 Broadway, New York, NY 10007.

HarperCollins books may be purchased for educational, business, or sales promotional use. For information, please email the Special Markets Department at SPsales@harpercollins.com.

FIRST EDITION

Designed by Bonni Leon-Berman
Image on pages iii, 1, and 101 © Tina Bits, Shutterstock

Library of Congress Cataloging-in-Publication Data has been applied for.

ISBN 978-0-06-322661-6

23 24 25 26 27 LBC 5 4 3 2 1

For Mansa Nkrumah, with love

PART ONE

CHAPTER 1

Ricksville, Mississippi, Summer 1982

There weren't many people I loved when I was eleven, but I loved Mr. Macabe. I knew he couldn't be my daddy because he was too old, but I always thought of him as my granddad even though I'd never had one. Mr. Macabe said his blindness gave him the second sight. That he could see deep into souls. I didn't believe him one lick.

"I go to Sunday school," I would say sharply to him, "only God sees into souls."

He would grin back at me, his partly toothless smile reminding me of my seven-year-old cousin, Devin.

I ran all the way down Ricksville Road to get to Mr. Macabe's house at number 2, feeling the last memories of school fade with every step I took. I wanted to keep that feeling going all day, so I dawdled by Cammy's house, wishing she hadn't gone away to her father's somewhere up in Indian Reserve country, and dodged around that half-naked crazy Sammy who shouted obscenities at anyone who came within his sight.

Finally, I was at Mr. Macabe's.

Mr. Macabe lived on the right, five houses down from mine. I walked up the porch stairs and up to his front door. I pushed the door open and went inside and there he was, sitting in that old wicker chair. I went right up to him like I always did and stared into his milky eyes, willing him to open them and see me. He was wearing a dirty, torn, pale blue shirt.

My eyes swept up and down to scrutinize his skinny frame, taking in the overgrown gray beard that partially covered strong carved-out, oak-colored features, and finally settled on his worn and calloused feet. Every inch of him was as familiar as the red dirt that filled the potholes on our street.

"That you, Ella?"

"Yes. It's me, Mr. Macabe. Just wanted to tell you that we won the Ricksville mud battle this morning." The mud battle happened only in May, a few days after school ended, and it had to have rained enough for the soil to get so sopping wet that we could scoop it up like clay and mold it into balls. The battle was one side of the street against the other, and every child between the ages of four and fourteen had been outside hurling mud balls.

"Heard you all a-hollering this morning. Couldn't even sleep in. Must think I'm deaf, too."

He took his time packing tobacco into his pipe, and I stood by his side, close as I could, while he finished.

"How're your legs doing?" I asked.

"Still not working as good as they should, Ella. You've been asking me the same question since you were six."

"Because I'm still waiting on God. He'll fix those up good as new, same as your eyes." I looked at him again, wishing that what I believed would just flow from my eyes into his brain.

"Ella, why you always waiting on a miracle? Those don't come by here often, you know."

"I know God can make many miracles," I said. I was tired of having to convince Mr. Macabe that if he believed hard enough, he would see. He was so old, you'd think he would know these things by now, but no, I always had to tell him.

"Have you seen Fats around here?" I asked.

"Why you all keep calling that boy such a horrible name? What if people started calling me blind old Mr. Macabe? Would that be nice?"

I wanted to tell him that everyone *did* call him blind old Mr. Macabe when they were talking about him, but I didn't want to make him mad because then Mr. Macabe would raise that cane of his and bring it down every which way about, and you'd have to duck just in case it hit you.

"He was just here, not ten minutes afore you, looking twice as muddy."

Fats was my second-best friend, after Cammy. Everyone called him Fats, even his ma. Every single part of his body was round, from his full soft bulging lips to his pudgy rolling belly. Fats was the color of sandpaper, but when you looked carefully, that color seemed to depend on which part of his body you were looking at. His face was like butterscotch, all smooth and warm, but his belly, hanging out over swim trunks, was pale and pasty, like the underbelly of an octopus, while his arms and legs were a chocolate brown.

Mr. Macabe reached and took my thumb out of my mouth and put his hand in mine. I could feel the calluses in lumps and bumps under the hardness of his palm. I could never figure out how he knew the minute my thumb was in my mouth. He had long grown tired of telling me that I was too old for that, and I'd get rabbit teeth.

"You all right, baby girl?" he asked me. "Things all right at home?"

I nodded.

"Leroy's still away?"

I hesitated, not wanting to say anything because maybe Mr. Macabe had that second sight that made him sense things no one else did, but in those seconds I waited, Mr. Macabe's voice was back again, sharper. He was now leaning forward, looking through me, trying to see deep into my soul again.

I kept it out of his reach, buried it way, way down.

"Is he back?"

"No, he's still away." I managed to keep the wobble out of my voice.

"That man's been away almost nine months this time." Mr. Macabe seemed to be talking to himself again.

He leaned back in his chair.

Leroy, my stepfather, was Ma's husband and the father of my sister and brothers. I knew he hated me. Couldn't stand to look at me.

I wanted Mr. Macabe to go right on talking about something else and not try to look into my soul, so I said quickly, "You going to be all right?"

"Yes, don't you worry that pretty head of yours over me. Just hand me a clean shirt."

I went to get Mr. Macabe a clean shirt and came back with his favorite gray shirt with the white collar.

"Want me to fix you a sandwich before I go?"

"That would be real nice. There's a piece of bacon in the fridge and some bread on the counter. Make sure you wash those grubby hands first."

I fried up the bacon and made the sandwich.

"Now, what's your new word for the day?" he asked.

"*Preposterous.*"

"My, my, my. That's a handful for a little girl. You know what it means?"

"Yes," I said, rolling my eyes to give him some sass. "It means ridiculous, absurd, foolish, inane."

Mr. Macabe could hear that sass right in my voice, but he only shook his head and said, "You keep it up, hear now?" He stretched out his hand, and when I grasped it, he pulled me close to him for a quick hug.

I ran down the street. Past the tiny, mostly rented clapboard houses that made up my neighborhood in the black part of town; past the big old sign where if you squinted you could just make enough sense of the peeling red paint to read "Town of Ricksville, MS, Population 8014"; past our neighborhood liquor store; past Fats's house at number 6; past Cammy's at number 8 until I reached the smallest house on Ricksville Road, number 12. It was a slightly lopsided house that you could just about tell used to be yellow. We lived in the poor, all-black neighborhood of South Ricksville, which, on our classroom map, was south of Main Street.

Years back, in 1964, Main Street and most of its stores had been burned to the ground in retaliation for what happened near Philadelphia, Mississippi, when the Ku Klux Klan had killed those young election workers turning out the black vote. All that had put in stone the open resentment between blacks and whites, and even though the white owners had rebuilt, we kids almost never ventured north of Main Street into the white part of town. Those lines, drawn in the sand between north and south, stayed unchanged over the years. Every child in Ricksville knew where they were supposed to be when the sun set. If we were sent to get something from the larger grocery five blocks into the north side, the moment the glow of the sun started to retreat, our feet had better be on North Perry. If darkness was moving in fast, we would have to run at full tilt—only when we hit South Perry could our feet slow down, and our hearts steady, and our lungs fill with air. Then we would settle into a stroll, because from there it was a straight shot from Perry to Woodlawn, Woodlawn to Grace, and Grace to Ricksville, and then we were finally home.

CHAPTER 2

Princeton, New Jersey, January 1981

She wore a white dress, one of those pretty cotton sheer dresses. She had felt like wearing a summer dress today, but it was freezing, so she had it on over her warmest wool turtleneck and her thickest leggings. The dress was sleeveless, gathered at her narrow waist. Pearly buttons ran down the front of its length, just stopping short above her ankle. She was all fingers and thumbs as she tried to button it up quickly. She slipped on her black boots before stopping to glance at herself in the mirror. Her father, who preferred her all dressed up the older she got, would have approved of the dress, all southern and demure. But he wouldn't have liked the shoes, nor the turtleneck.

She never was one for mooning in front of mirrors, but she took a glance at herself out of habit. She knew what she was: nondescript. She had shoulder-length straight brown hair, brown eyes, and pale white skin that burned easily in the sun. An everyday person that barely afforded a second glance. She made up for that with a well-placed belt, or shoes, something that would cause them to take another look, if not at her face, then at the rest of her, which she knew was very well proportioned.

She would be late, and she couldn't afford to be. She paced up and down the tiny apartment searching, first for her black cross-body satchel, her coat, her journal, which she took everywhere with her, then her ruler and pens, and finally her watch, which she hurriedly shoved in the bag. She didn't stop to grab anything to eat but almost ran down the stairs, jumping over the steps two at a time, till she was at the bottom. Ten minutes of brisk walking and she was almost there. Relief at the sight of the massive dark brick administration building ahead of her slowed her down a notch. Two minutes later, she pushed through the large spring-loaded doors and immediately could hear them even before she saw them, a raucous crowd of students, the din of their excited voices filling the hallway. She joined the line in front of a long desk behind which sat four ladies, each busy registering second-semester classes, papers and books strewn all over the desk in front of them.

"Is Dr. Livenworth's class still open?" she called out, even as she stood eighteenth in line.

"Wait your turn," someone said behind her.

She turned and stared into a set of hazel eyes. It was an undergrad. Lank brown hair, needing a cut. She made an impatient gesture.

"What's so important about getting a class with Livenworth anyway? Heard he's a terrible grader. A guaranteed C or below."

She had no time for him. She ignored all the babies, or so she called them. Those eighteen-year-olds who were at least fourteen years younger than she was. She was a graduate student, but certainly older than most of the graduate students in her year group. She screwed up her face in concentration. She considered buying someone's spot in the line, but she had not thought to bring cash with her. She had to get into this class, The Rise of the Black Working Class in America. Her advisor had said it would help her as she began her thesis research on the impact of the black migration and the civil rights movement on southern society between 1940 and 1980. She had become more and more liberal since college, fully immersing herself in the diverse environment of NYU, where she had been an undergrad, and now at Princeton her friends were a mix of every race, creed, and color under the sun, as were her interests. It was deliberate, and her thesis topic was just as deliberate as everything else she had done since she left the hospital.

By the time she reached one of the registering ladies at the table, there was only one spot left in Dr. Livenworth's class.

She almost wept in relief.

CHAPTER 3

I looked down at the state of my clothes after the mud battle; Ma would surely give me a hiding. So I left my shoes at the door and went upstairs to wash. I changed, put my dirty clothes in a bucket and gave them a good scrub on the washing board, like Ma had taught me, before hanging them to dry on the line outside.

I sat on the front step, reluctant to head back into the steaming house. It was getting dark, and the sinking sun gave the clouds a heavenly golden-red aura. I reached up and waved to God, who I could just see by his wispy beard. I didn't need a Bible or preacher to tell me God was there; all I had to do was to look outside, past the buildings and the roads that humans had created, to the magnificent magnolia trees that spread out on their own, branches outstretched as though the trees were praising God. Then, finally, I would look up, way up, past the clouds, past the edge of the earth, almost into the Third Heaven.

"Hello, God," I whispered. "It's Ella again."

The clouds moved and God's mouth opened into a wide smile. I smiled back, taking in the gentle breeze and the responding rustle of the leaves. God was passing by in the wind.

"Please make another day just like today," I asked silently.

I never got an answer, because just then I heard the shuffle of Ma's feet down the road, heavy with weight and tiredness. I ran to help her carry in our evening meal—a bag of leftover chicken and fries from Nate's Diner, where Ma worked. The last stretch was downhill, but she was still breathless from the steep climb where Grace meets Ricksville Road.

"Ma, please give me the bag . . . Ma . . ."

Ma's mouth twitched a little, but she said nothing.

"Ma, give it over."

Ma handed me the bag, and I ran past her, wishing that someone could do something about her sore legs. I flicked on the lights, dumped the bag on the table, and took out the place mats to set the table.

Ma finally came in. She moved slowly past me and stood heaving by the kitchen counter. She opened the bag and began putting chicken pieces and mounds of fries onto the paper plates, and I took them in turn and carefully set five heaped plates on the small kitchen table by the window.

Finally, she turned.

I waited, knowing that she would now speak.

"Get the others."

She never called me by my name.

I was the sin that she couldn't wash out.

I went out the front door and yelled, "Kitty, Callun Thomas, Stevie! Ma wants you!" I waited ten seconds and bellowed out their names again, hard. Stevie came first, running from behind the house, carrying a baseball bat and gloves. He was thirteen, almost fourteen, two years older than me. C.T., the baby and only four years old, trailed behind him. Kitty, who was sixteen and the eldest, was always late. I left Ma to deal with finding her and banged the door shut. Then I scooped C.T. into my arms. He was a bit slow, but he was the sweetest boy I knew. I ruffled his soft light-brown hair and rubbed my face on his cheek.

"You're so pretty," I said.

"No!"

"Okay, handsome. You're the most handsome boy in the world."

C.T. smiled, a big broad toothy smile. I took him to wash his hands, and by the time I got back into the kitchen, the others were all there. Three heads that looked like Ma and Leroy: soft light brown curly hair; vanilla-hued skin and almond-shaped green eyes. They were so pale they could almost pass for white, except for the curls in their hair and the slightly generous set of their mouths.

I sat at the end of the kitchen table, dark as an oil spill, looking like a cuckoo in their nest.

Becky, my ex-best friend, had taken me behind the woodpile four years ago when I was seven and whispered that I was illegal and that my real father was an Army man with short steel-wool hair, coal black, just like me, who had stopped by Ma's house while her husband, Leroy, was away on one of his long trips. "Just long enough to hang his coat before he was gone," she had added, with her ma's snide smile.

"Illegitimate, not illegal," I had corrected, furious enough to strike her dead. I hated her from that moment on, and I planned an exacting revenge—hacking off all the hair on her baby doll with the open-and-shut eyes. I swore I'd never talk to her again, and I never did.

Ma spent most of the meal with C.T. on her lap, feeding him like a baby even though he was old enough to use a fork. She was breathing better now. Her hair, pulled into a bun for work, now hung loose and luxurious down her back. As soon as she was done with C.T., she put him down on the floor. Kitty put her arms around Ma, and as she did so, Ma's face became soft and relaxed, like putty. I wondered what it would be like to have that effect on people, on Ma.

Kitty was pretty, slender, and waiflike with wide-set eyes, a button nose, and long wavy hair. Ma had once said that looking at Kitty was like standing beside a blue ocean and gazing over the sunset. In our house, we knew that she mesmerized Ma and Leroy with her beauty and her dainty flounce. Somehow the rest of us had escaped her spell.

Stevie saw me looking at them and winked. He was tall for his age, and handsome, except he had big old buckteeth. No one made fun of his teeth, though, because he was the smartest kid in town. Ask Stevie anything about math, physics, or engineering and he would talk you into an unexpected nap. He wolfed down his dinner as usual and waited for Ma. She was who we all yearned for, and Stevie and Kitty constantly fought to be first place in her affections. But we were never able to forget that it was Kitty who was to be Ma's ticket out of the poor side of Ricksville. Ma was going to get Kitty married to a lawyer or doctor up in Atlanta, one of those Morehouse graduates who was looking for a beautiful wife. Never mind that she couldn't divide eight into fifty-six without having to recite the entire eight-times table.

"Do you want some more food, Stevie?" Ma finally noticed Stevie's empty plate.

"Yes. Ma, you sure can fry up some chicken."

"Yes what?"

Ma was a stickler for good manners. She didn't want us disgracing her in public. She wouldn't let anyone forget that although she had sunk this low, she hadn't started out this way.

"Yes, please, Ma. We're in the finals for the baseball tournament, Ma."

Ma turned her attention fully away from Kitty and smiled at Stevie. "We'll be there," she said. "I told Nate there was a chance, and he said he'd give me the day off if it happened."

"Ma, we won the Ricksville mud battle today," I said loudly.

No one spoke.

My words hung in the air and disappeared. Kitty kept picking at her food, and Ma was wiping C.T.'s nose, her eyes keenly on him.

Stevie twitched in his seat.

Why did I even try? How could I have been so stupid? What an idiot you are, I said viciously to myself. What a stupid, ugly idiot. I looked past Stevie. Caught the pity in his eyes and hated him for it. Hated his legitimate birth, his fair skin, and that he was still loved despite his buck teeth.

The silence grew and held.

"You mean our side of the street won?" Stevie's voice was raspy, and too loud.

I felt nothing but shame. I didn't need rescuing. I could rescue myself.

"Yes," I said flatly.

"We never won before," he said.

I shrugged, wishing he would just shut up.

Ma pursed her lips. She turned and lifted C.T. into her arms and carried him off to be cleaned up.

"Hey, Oreo," Stevie said softly.

"What?" I answered meanly.

"Don't worry about it."

I stared at him blankly, as if I didn't know what he was talking about. Hated the name that many outsiders thought was a sweet, pet name. Only I knew it was Leroy's particularly sly way of branding me, so I never forgot that I was the illegitimate child of his wife, a constant reminder of her infidelity, neatly sandwiched between his legitimate children. Only I knew how deep it went, for didn't we all know that the paste in the middle of the cookie was white, when I was as opposite to that as you could get? How could I forget even without the nickname, looking so different than they did? But that was never enough for Leroy.

I willed my tears to slide back into my eyes by thinking how much I hated them all.

And my lovely day shattered and crumbled into dust at my feet.

CHAPTER 4

Philadelphia, Mississippi, Early 1953

She was white and was never allowed to forget it. But she wasn't quite the right type of white. Wasn't blond, or blue-eyed. Just the mousy brown of an ordinary white person. Her mother always told her that her hair was near white when she was born. It had taken two years for it to turn a pale blond.

"You were so adorable. Like a cherub," her mother would say wistfully. "Skin like cream, eyes the palest blue-green. You took after me then." Her mother always paused after saying this, as though she didn't want to relinquish the image. "Then your father's genes kicked in and now look at you, all that beautiful hair and eyes turned brown, just like your brother." Then, perhaps feeling guilty, her mother would add hastily, "Well, at least you still have your beautiful skin. You need to stay out of the sun, or you will burn. I keep telling you that." She must have heard this almost every day of her life, right up to when her mother died.

Yet she remembers a time of being out in the sun all day, hatless. It was a time when her mother didn't care or had other things to occupy her. She doesn't remember her mother much during this time. All she remembers is running barefoot outside, and someone, Bessie, their black cook, calling her name, running after her, swooping her up, smooshing her laughing face against that soft round mountainous chest before swirling her around and around. It was a chest she returned to time and time again: when her stomach hurt, or when she felt lonely, or when her brother, Randy, was tormenting her. Bessie would swoop her up, kiss her with a big resounding smack, and put her under her skirts, where she would stay, quiet as a mouse, as Bessie hummed and sang as she washed the clothes in the tub, till Randy disappeared. She would then crawl out from under those skirts and Bessie would say, laughing, "Go on with you, chile. I gots work to do. Don't think I got time to play games with you," and then she would wink at her.

"Don't go encouraging that chile," Mary, Bessie's helper, would say, scowling. "You know how they be. One minute all cute and babyish, and the next like the very devil take them over. Look at that Randy over there. See how quickly he turn? Wasn't but five years ago he was sucking on your breast, and now can't barely stand the sight o' you. Sooner spit at you than say hello."

"This one's different. I knows it."

"This one's just the same as her ma. You just slow, Bessie. How many of them babies you raised?"

They were always talking about her and her ma, but she wasn't sure what they were saying, just that Mary looked mad, but she always looked mad, and Bessie, well, Bessie was just Bessie. She put her thumb in her mouth and listened awhile more before going to pull on Bessie's long skirt.

"I'm tired."

Bessie immediately sat down on the kitchen chair that was pushed against the wall. Reached up and pulled her across her lap, so that her head was resting on that mountain of pillows. She relaxed into Bessie's soft flesh.

"Sleep, chile."

CHAPTER 5

Nate's Diner stood right in the center of town on Main Street, an oddity because it was the only black-owned business on the white side of town.

If you were on Main Street, you could not miss the brand-new Greyhound Bus Station, nor ignore the delicious, greasy fried chicken smell that wafted in and out as Nate's doors opened and closed; so tempting it made everyone waiting for the bus wonder if they had time to slip out of line to grab a quick bite to go before the bus driver shouted, "Bring your tickets, step up, bring your tickets."

And if you decided to make a run for it, all you had to do was follow your nose, and it would lead you across the road and half a block up, right to the red neon sign. Ma was the tall, heavy-set woman you saw behind the counter fixing and wrapping sandwiches or burgers or sometimes frying crispy chicken wings and fries. She worked afternoons six days a week at a job that she said was way beneath her.

"My mother would turn in her grave," she'd often complain. When I asked Stevie why, he said it was because Ma's father was a white lawyer, and her ma was a mulatto seamstress. I didn't know what it meant then, but from the proud way Stevie said it, I knew it somehow made Ma better and more genteel than everyone else.

◈

I did chores for Nate on Saturdays, mostly helping him clean the diner and earning three dollars for my trouble. It was Nate who had bandaged my knee at age five when I was too scared to go home and tell Ma that I had jumped off Kitty Hawk Bridge, right into the Big Black River because Fats dared me.

For many years, Nate's Diner used to be called Catchedy Groceries, white-owned and the town's only family grocery store. It was the only store that had not been burned to the ground during the Ricksville riots of 1964 that followed the murders of the civil rights workers later called the Freedom Summer murders. Joe Catchedy had died in 1971, and eventually, with pressure from an incoming grocery chain, his ailing wife sold off its contents and closed the doors. The store had stood empty over two years until the townsfolk finally talked about pulling it down. Nate later told Ma that someone started a rumor that the store was infested with termites, "damn near about to topple down and maim someone," while others talked about what an eyesore it had become.

Then, early one spring morning, while the white town council members met to discuss the dilapidated store at their monthly town council meeting, Nate, who was in those days the town drunk, walked unsteadily to Mrs. Catchedy's back door and demanded to see the old lady. Meeting resistance from Lucille, the black housekeeper, he forced his way past her to the door of Mrs. Catchedy's sickroom. In the darkened room, he gently took off his hat, made his apologies, and humbly whispered that he would like to buy the store. It was later said that Mrs. Catchedy had looked him in the eye and said, "But you're a drunk, Nate. Nothing but a drunk nigger."

Nate had slowly moved forward till he was right up close to the bed, and there he had whispered some words, all the while his head bowed and his eyes not even meeting hers. According to Lucille, who had stood at the door trembling with fear at the thought of what the crazy black man would do, Mrs. Catchedy, who hadn't gotten out of bed in a year, waved her over and, with the use of her walker and guiding hands, Lucille on one hand and Nate on the other, walked clear across the large hall to her husband's study and handed Nate the papers. Paid enough for it over the years was the rumor, for those white folks were all about business right to the very end.

I heard Miss Claudia, who was my friend Cammy's ma, say that a few trouble stirrers slyly hinted that there was some bizarre sexual relationship between Nate and Mrs. Catchedy, but she said that was the nonsense talkers, since it wasn't so long ago that you could get strung up for just looking at a white woman. Others said that Nate must have threatened her with all kinds of bad things, but Stevie, knowing Nate's kind nature, merely said the old lady sure knew a good business deal when she saw one, especially when it reached down and bit her in the ass.

Whatever it was, it was said that this was the beginning of the new Nate. He never touched another drop. Sure enough, every Sunday morning, you would find him cold sober as could be, sitting on the front pew at the AME church at the corner of Ricksville and Pike. On Sunday afternoons, townsfolk heading home from window shopping in Louisville town center would see him making his way to Mrs. Catchedy's, walking with a spring in his step, cool as you please, right up those marble front steps of her big mansion. Once I heard Ma saying that black folk never would stop gossiping about that. Even though they all done grown used to the sight with each passing year, they still gossiped, shaking their heads, wondering what made Nate think he was good enough to stride through those rose-colored front doors, just like he owned the place.

This particular Saturday morning, I ran through the rain all the way down Ricksville, up Grace, took a right on Woodlawn, and finally reached Perry before crossing over to Main. I hurried past the Wilkinson Hardware Store without looking in, because everyone knew that they didn't serve blacks and everyone's ma said we were not to go near there or we'd get such a whupping our butts would be aflame for a week. I swung open the door to Nate's and quickly went to the back and put on an apron. Then I got out the mop, broom, and dustpan and filled a bucket with soapy water.

"This floor here is real dirty, Nate," I said, mopping away.

Nate was tall, with a high forehead, light brown eyes, and thick, smooth brown skin. He was looking at me impatiently, momentarily distracted from spicing the chicken he was about to cook.

"Sure is. A dirty floor store is a profitable one. Means people are coming in and out. Just make sure you mop up real good. It's been raining and folks' shoes are muddy. Now, back to work, Ella. Today's a busy day."

I cleaned in silence for the next half hour, giving the floor all my attention, getting on my hands and knees to scrape the gummy sticky mess off the linoleum with a knife. Afterwards, when the floor was clean and shiny, I washed my hands and sat at the counter, watching Nate fry the spicy batch of chicken for the Saturday noontime rush.

"Nate?"

"Yes?" Nate was focused on dipping chicken thighs into a bowl of flour mixed with seasoning.

"Sure you couldn't be my father?"

He abruptly stopped what he was doing, dusted his floury hands over his apron, and turned around so he was facing me. After a moment, he walked up to the counter and looked at me wearily.

"Ella, what is wrong?"

I shook my head. "Nothing. Just checking."

"Okay, you ask me if I am your father at least three times a year, and if I remember correctly, you even asked me once if I was an angel. An angel, Ella?"

My mouth wobbled and I concentrated on counting the number of chicken pieces on the table to hold back the bucket of wetness that was always behind my eyes, trying to seep out.

"You know the answer is no. I'm just a single man with no kids, just a lot of chicken to fry."

His face softened. "Why does it matter so much that you have no daddy? I never had one. Not one who would acknowledge me anyway." His eyes looked sad for an instant. Then he shook his head and continued, "Half the kids up Ricksville Road don't often see their fathers. How often do your brothers and sister see Leroy? That man's always gone. Eight months in Alabama, six months in Arkansas, here for a few months, then he's gone again. It's what we do down here, Ella, men trying to chase down money to keep body and soul together."

I didn't answer, holding in the volcano trapped inside my chest.

"What happened to God?" he said. "I thought you told me the last time that He was your dad."

I wanted to say that I needed one on earth, too, but when my mouth opened nothing came out.

It was quiet in the store. Nate looked troubled.

"Did they forget your birthday again?"

I shrugged off the question, pretending I didn't care if they did or they didn't.

"Is it your twelfth?"

I nodded.

Nate's broad smile filled the room.

Nate wasn't handsome at first glance, but when you'd stared up at him as many times as I had, or had seen him smiling or singing softly to himself, you'd see his features rearranging into such symmetrical perfection that strangers would think someone else had walked in and taken over the grill.

"I remember twelve. Now, that's a great age. You suddenly feel all grown up, finally on the march to being a teenager." He smiled down at me. "Well, I haven't forgotten. I've got something for you."

He came around the counter and put his hands on my shoulders and led me to the back storeroom. From behind the door, he pulled out the most beautiful hand-carved kite I had ever seen. The wood looked light and flexible, and the thin, silky cloth was a pretty turquoise color. It was almost as tall as I was.

How did he know today was my birthday and that I had really wanted a kite? "How did you know?" I asked when I'd found my voice.

"Still think I'm an angel?" Nate was gently teasing. "Yes, just give me wings and a tutu and I'm right at home," he said, and he kept right on raveling up the kite's string. "I used river birch, the lightest and best kite wood around."

I touched the wood. "It's real nice. It's going to fly great. But I never mentioned it was my birthday to anyone," I persisted.

"Ella, believe me, everyone in Ricksville knows the day you were born, and as a matter of fact, I brought the midwife to your house to help with the birth. I think I was the third person in the world to see you. What a pretty baby you were."

I stared into his lying face.

"Yes, you were. Sure enough, you looked nothing like your ma, but those big eyes of yours lit up your whole face. Still do, and don't let anyone tell you different."

I forgave him the lie.

"As to what you want, I can read you like a book. You've just got one of those wide-open faces. Too much emotion."

Nate crouched down till he was at my level, the worried look back on his face. "Ella, let me give you a piece of advice. You feel too much, and everything you feel is right there on that face of yours. It's in your voice. You've got to close that face of yours or people will keep hurting you. Put on a skin of toughness and hide yourself. You know, like a crab."

His hand reached out and shook me a little, his eyes searching mine. I didn't know what he was looking for, but it seemed like he didn't find it, for he just shook his head, looked at me in exasperation, and handed me the kite.

"Go on, take it out for a run. I know there's nothing you like better than running, and you'll have to run like the wind to get that kite in the air. Put it in your mind that you're an African running away from slave hunters deep in West Africa and you will fly."

I reached for the kite slowly, wondering if it was really mine. The urge to fly it was too much. I was ready.

"Take it around the back, use Perry Lane," Nate said. I scarcely heard his voice. I stretched out my hand and held the kite. It felt so light, so delicate. How it would soar! At Perry Lane, I started running like there were a million devils chasing me, slave-hunter dogs nipping at my heels. Yet my mind was clear, and an age-old rhythm pounded in my blood as I ran, till I felt the tension in the cord and the reassuring noise of the kite rippling in the wind. And still I ran, not even stopping to watch the kite, because by then the joy of running had oiled my joints, and that bucket of water behind my eyes had finally dried up, and I couldn't stop running, and from there it was Perry to Woodlawn, Woodlawn to Grace, and Grace to Ricksville. It was there I finally stopped, close to home, and turned to watch. I saw the large turquoise kite rise to meet the blue sky, bucking like a wild bronco as it got caught in updrafts and then growing stronger and pulling, tussling with me and the wind till it was finally soaring straight and high above me, like a bird on a wire. As I watched, the kite and the sky knitted together and became one.

CHAPTER 6

Philadelphia, Mississippi, August 1954

She loved her father more than her ma, and certainly more than Randy. Her daddy was big and strong and was the boss of the farm. He had dark brown straight hair like hers and everyone said they were two peas in a pod. She tried to walk like him, talk like him, and by the time she was sent to the big school up the road, she refused to wear anything other than pants and a shirt, just like him. His laugh was as loud as the church bells on Sunday, and when he walked across the farm, everyone disappeared. All the farm-hands, who were always white, and all the nigger boys; they all ducked out of sight until he called them out. That they were scared of him made her realize that he was a king.

My daddy's a king, she would say to Bessie when they played.

"That's right, chile," Bessie would agree.

When he got angry at the nigger boys, his voice would thunder, like a vicious storm had come across the land, and Bessie would come running out of the house and gather her up and take her inside.

"Nothing for you to see," Bessie would whisper, even though she wanted to stay and watch what her father would do. While he thundered, she could hear, from inside, screams and shrills and all kinds of commotion, but Bessie wouldn't even allow her to look. Sometimes there was the swooshing sound of a slap or a whip, over and over again, and the screams then seemed to fill the sky.

"What's he doing?" she would ask Bessie.

"Just making sure everyone is working good," Bessie would say.

Mary would suck her teeth hard.

Sometimes her mother would come out, too, and scream along with her daddy at whoever was making them mad. It was a concert of screams, her mother's high-pitched excited shrieks, and her daddy's bellows. It was the only time Bessie seemed to get annoyed. "What's that woman doing out there?" she would mutter. "Slavery times been over. No need to treat 'em like that." Mary always had an answer. "Woman just adding her two cents. Lying on the couch all day, this is the only exercise she get. Wish she come in here to get some exercise cooking, and cleaning and pressing." Mary always seemed to find that funny, and she would laugh and slap her thigh and push on Bessie, who just pushed her away. "Stop it," Bessie would say, "the chile can hear you talking about her ma like that."

Mary would make a face and say, "Let her hear how lazy that woman is. And they say black people lazy." Mary would suck her teeth over and over again.

She didn't like Mary one bit, but oh, how she loved Bessie.

CHAPTER 7

On choir nights, it was my job to keep an eye on Kitty. Ma didn't say why, but I was smart enough to know that it was up to me to make sure that Kitty made it to evening choir practice on Wednesdays, the day Ma worked late at the diner. I was pretty sure that it had something to do with what Fats had said a week ago. He had come up to me as I walked along Ricksville Road to Mr. Macabe's and said that he had a secret about Kitty.

"What secret?" I had asked curiously.

"Kitty's wild," he replied with a smirk.

"What are you talking about?" I asked. He had gestured to me to stop walking, and when I did, he whispered in my ear that Kitty had to be watched because she was likely to be found going down on Luke in the alley behind Tucker Lane. I couldn't figure out what he said so I just stared at him, wondering what he meant.

"She completely melts everyone's hearts when she sings 'Amazing Grace' in that voice they all say is just like an angel. And then she does that."

"What's 'going down' mean?" I finally asked. Fats had just looked at me and laughed fit to burst his big ol' gut. I had pummeled his arm until he stopped laughing but he still hadn't told me.

"You're like a baby, Ella. You don't know anything."

"Am not. I know a lot of things, I just don't know what that is."

Fats just rolled his eyes and lumbered off. No doubt to tell someone else who knew what going down was.

I almost told him. Almost told him what I did know, just to watch his eyes open wide and see what color his face would turn, red-brown or pale brown. But I didn't.

Kept my secret buried deep down.

I looked in the dictionary to find out what "going down" meant but I couldn't find it.

It was Wednesday a week later when I waited on the front stoop for Kitty to come home from summer school so we could walk together to choir practice. It was five in the afternoon. The air was hot and sticky, and even though my T-shirt clung to me, the air was still cooler outside than indoors. I could've walked a few steps and stood under the shade of the magnolia tree, but I didn't want to sit on the ground, where the fire ants would have bitten me to shreds. So I sat on the cement stoop, enjoying the occasional sticky breeze and once in a while getting up to peer down Ricksville Road to see whether Kitty was coming. The street was deserted. All the kids were either having their baths or, like me, just about to set off for the Oh Precious Heavenly Voices Children's Choir. While I waited, I savored my most recently acquired new words. I had underlined them in the dictionary and all day long they danced around in my head. Now I took them out from where I kept them in my mind and played about with the sounds in my head as I clapped my hands to the beat of the new words. "Per-fi-dy, pres-ti-gi-ous, plu-ral-is-ti-cal-ly."

The next time I got up to peer down the street, I spotted Kitty in the distance by the sashaying motion of her hips.

She wasn't alone.

When they were two houses away, I recognized Luke, captain of Ricksville Senior High School's football team. He was tall and had a mop of curly hair. Kitty had mentioned how cute he was. I'd once seen him at school, but I couldn't figure out why she thought he was cute.

When they got a little closer to our house, I ran up to meet her.

"What do you want?" she said coldly.

"Ma's here."

"Don't be an idiot. I know she's not. Stop your stupid tricks." She pushed me out of her way and walked towards the front door.

I was close on her heels. "I tell you, Ma's here, and him over there"—I gestured at Luke, who was right behind us—"is going to get it."

Kitty looked at Luke. "She's lying, Ma is never here this time on Wednesdays."

I really didn't care, so I sat back on the stoop.

"Are you lying, Oreo?" she demanded.

I wasn't about to say another word.

"Luke, wait out here while I check. I swear I will hit her if she's lying."

Kitty disappeared inside. I looked at Luke. Wondered whether Kitty liked that crooked way he smiled or whether she liked him because his hair was curly, just like Leroy's. But the resemblance ended there. Luke was brown-skinned and brown-eyed and although his hair was curly, it was black. Leroy's hair was pale brown and his eyes a piercing green. I went back to looking at my words, but out of the corner of my eye, I saw a movement. I glanced up and saw Luke fidgeting, like he just couldn't keep still.

There were no voices from inside, and I could tell this made him anxious. He paced in front of me, then glanced at Ricksville Road, a few yards away. He took a step in the direction of the road. He was leaving.

He swiveled back, decision made, and climbed over me to get to the door. As he did so, his hand reached down towards my chest, and before I knew it, I had smacked his hand so hard I could tell it would smart right into next week. I ducked out of the way as his hand came down again, this time to hit me back, and ran to the middle of the yard.

From there I saw Luke raise his hand to knock on the door, one last-ditch effort to see where Kitty had disappeared to. I almost ran back to tell him that it was true, that Ma was home because she'd forgotten her change of clothes for the midweek church service, but what he had done made me mad enough not to care what happened to him. I saw him hesitate, then knock loudly.

Ma opened the door.

"It's just one of those good-for-nothing boys." Ma's voice was loud and annoyed. Then she shut the door right in his face.

Luke should have left right then, but he was still standing there when Ma opened the door again.

"You still here?" This time, she looked Luke up and down with obvious distaste. "Tell me something, boy. Do you think you can get into Morehouse College or Lincoln University?"

Luke stood there like he was made of stone.

"That's right," Ma said disdainfully. "I didn't think so. A piece of nothing, just like all the boys in this dusty town, sniffing around at something beautiful. Well, she's not within your reach. Just keep on walking right out of here and stay away from Kitty. She's marrying up, not down." She stood at the door, waiting for him to disappear.

I saw the tremble in Luke's legs as he slunk away, stumbling over the stoop. Saw by the contorted grimaces on his face that he was close to tears. Yet even with this, I could feel the anger rolling off him in waves. I watched in fear, knowing that shame and anger could crowd into one venomous wave of fury. As he stepped out onto Ricksville Road, he turned angrily to look back at our house. My heart raced a hundred miles an hour: Would he have the courage to yell out, "Who do you think you are, when your husband never even finished high school? How dare you look down on us when you are nothing but a whore."

"God, please keep his mouth sewn shut," I prayed. I didn't want to ever find out what such words would do to Ma, or what she in turn would do to him.

But he never called out. He was now on the street, his bowed head slowly straightening.

The hammering in my chest slowed down and finally steadied into its regular thump.

I am not sure what made me run after him. Perhaps it was because I knew just how he must feel on the inside, like a piece of garbage.

I ran as fast as I could, calling softly, "Hey, Luke."

He ignored me. Or perhaps he just didn't hear me. He was striding hard ahead. Almost running.

"Hey, Luke," I finally yelled.

He stopped. Turned around. Tried to hide the streaks on his cheeks with a quick brush of his hand. Now those hands were folded in front of him. Indian stance. Hostile.

"Sorry," I said. I tried to explain, finally catching up with him, a little breathless from running so fast. "It's just that Kitty's special to Ma." It wasn't much of an explanation, but it was all I had. I couldn't tell him that Kitty was our one-way ticket out of Ricks-ville and into a better life. I couldn't tell him about that trunk at the bottom of the stairs filled with linen and beautiful dresses for Kitty's married life to some Morehouse doctor.

I should have stayed away, because what Luke couldn't say to Ma he could say to me.

"What are you stupid people afraid of? That she'll turn out to be a slut just like your ma and give birth to little pieces of dark shits like you? Well, she is a slut, and no one from any Morehouse or Lincoln is going to marry some half-wit girl just because she happens to be pretty."

I picked up a rock and aimed it at his head, half wanting it to explode open like a ripe watermelon, and half afraid of that feeling. The rock fell short, just swiping his leg before it bounced off. He gave me the finger and took off down the road.

I walked slowly back to the house, feeling sick to my stomach. Why didn't you keep your big mouth shut? I said to myself. Why can't you just let things be?

CHAPTER 8

She had seen Edgar's thing at school. All the girls in first grade played *Show Me*: they would run to a boy, tag him, and say, "Show me." Then the boy would meet the girl behind the school fence and take out his thing and, after she took a look, she would pull down her pants and underwear. Sometimes they made a deal to pull down their underwear at the same time. She had seen seven so far, and they all looked like the baby grass snakes she was used to, only smaller and pink. Each time she had said yuck in real revulsion and then pulled down her underwear for them to see how much prettier and tidier she was. She had been disappointed by their reaction so far. They hadn't seemed impressed, and James had looked and looked and finally asked, "Where is it?"

Not more than two days later, she was out playing with Curly, Bessie's six-year-old nephew. Bessie, her brother, his wife, and their five kids all shared one room at the end of the farmyard. Curly was the youngest and her best friend on the farm. She and Curly had vied for Bessie's lap when they were toddlers, but invariably Bessie would push Curly off her lap and she would have Bessie all to herself.

Curly was sitting waiting for her to get back from school to play. He was small for his age. So small that he looked like one of the kindergartners at her school. He was wearing his play shorts and T-shirt, one of Randy's old shirts.

A thought came into her head that she hadn't thought of before. Curly was dark brown, but was he the same all over? She wasn't sure. Maybe all boys' things were pink.

"Want to play a new game?" she asked as she got closer. He nodded. That was Curly, always ready to play whatever she wanted. They had played dolls yesterday, then kick the can, and the day before they were splashing by the side of the pond before Bessie had pulled them out and put them to work feeding the chickens.

"Here's what you do. You tag someone and then say, 'Show me.' I'll do it first." She ran up to him and tagged him. "Show me," she said.

Curly looked at her in confusion. "Show me what?"

"Show me," and she pointed down at him.

Curly backed away. "No."

"You have to, I tagged you. It's a new game."

"I don't want to play."

She was annoyed now.

"You have to." She stamped her feet. She knew Curly had to do what she said.

Curly looked scared, and the more scared he looked, the more determined she grew.

"You have to," she said again.

"No."

"Well, then, I'll, I'll . . . I'll never ever play with you again."

Curly ran.

How dared he.

She chased him. He was fast, but he was smaller and much skinnier than she was. She caught up to him and pushed him to the ground. Sat on his stomach and pushed those shorts down. Curly didn't struggle, didn't make a sound. Just looked like he had given up, staring helplessly at her with those huge eyes in his tiny face. She pulled on the elastic of his underwear and stared.

She was disappointed. He wasn't two colors. His thing was just like a dark brown baby snake, like the rest of him.

She got off as he struggled to pull his shorts back up. "Now I have to show you mine, and it's much better than yours," she said, and she pulled her pants down, and just as she started to pull down her underwear, she felt herself yanked with such force off the ground that it felt like she was flying ten feet high in the air, and before she could say a word, her left eardrum went dead from the sound that her father emitted, like the sound of the world collapsing into itself at the end of time. This was followed by such a storm of whupping that for the first two seconds she was silent with shock. All she could hear was her father's cursing as he hit her. What are you doing with that nigger? I will kill you both. His bellows were said to be heard a mile down the road. Then her screams began, high and frantic, like a pig that was being castrated.

The whole household erupted into the grass, reaching them in seconds. Ma started crying, pulling at Daddy to stop, Bessie fell on her knees and begged, Mister, please stop, you will kill her. Bessie made such a racket that Daddy stopped what he was doing for a split second and hit her. The blow hit Bessie on the side of her head and she went quiet.

Perhaps it was seconds, or hours, but her screams finally stopped, her voice worn out, but her father still remained hitting, pummeling, cursing, cursing, and cursing, saying the most terrible words she had ever heard. Two of the farmhands were called by the nigger boys, and they managed to pull him off her and onto the ground. Finally, hands lifted her up, limp, bloodied, and half dead, and carried her into the house.

She learned her lesson well. She never asked what happened to Curly. She heard the whispers—that the very second her daddy had picked her up, one of the nigger boys had dashed twenty yards across the green lawn, and in seconds had stuffed Curly into his shirt and carried him off. Five minutes later, Bessie's brother, wife, and Curly and all the kids had disappeared.

Taken nothing, just the clothes on their back. Not a trace of them left, only Bessie stayed behind. She heard whispers that it was only God's intervention that made her daddy pick her up first. If it had been Curly, the whisperers said, there would have been a funeral that day.

Her father had nursed her back to health. He had dedicated the whole month to looking after her. No one else, not even her ma, was allowed to feed her or change her bandages. Each night he caressed her face and kissed her cheeks like she was the most precious thing in the world. He slept on the floor by her bed, never getting up except to use the bathroom. Day after day, he had talked to her about his farm, his father and grandfather before him, and why he had to do what he had to do. Damn near killed him to beat her like that but it was a lesson she should never forget. She should never believe that Bessie or Curly were her kind. He filled her head with talk of who she was and the order of things on earth. She couldn't take it all in, but she understood that the niggers were very bad, even though sometimes they seemed kind, and good, like Bessie. They couldn't help it, that was just the way they were. No, she was told when she asked, they couldn't change.

Daddy brought out his Bible and laid his big hand on it and swore on it that he would never hurt her again. She looked hard into his brown eyes and what she saw reflected in them made her realize just how much he loved her. It filled her up, puffed her up till she was so overcome that she could only fling herself at him and hold on, clasping her arms around his thick neck. He held her tight, stroking her hair, rocking her to his chest, like he would never let go.

It was then she knew without a doubt that he would never harm her again.

She could never look Bessie in the eye again after that. She would come into the kitchen and order food and drinks in the same sneering, demanding tone as Randy.

"Told you," Mary said loudly, two months later when she walked into the kitchen with a flounce to order some tea. "Didn't I tell you? They all turn. He done beat the very devil into her."

Bessie hadn't answered. Just kept on scrubbing the pots till they were sparkling clean.

CHAPTER 9

"Kitty, we're late for choir practice," I yelled.

"Shut up, you," Kitty hissed through the window, "I've got to change."

She came out ten minutes later, stood in front of me, and gave me a slow withering look from head to toe. Finally she said, "Stop yelling so loud."

"I had to, you weren't listening."

She reached over to slap me, and I ducked out of the way. When she was annoyed, Kitty could be as mean as a coyote caught in a trap. We headed off to the church and, as usual, she walked so fast ahead of me that I had to run to keep up.

The AME church at the corner of Ricksville and Pike had originally been a slave church, made mostly of wood and said to have been constructed by two hundred slaves. A former slave owner had donated the land in the hope that the church would have a calming effect on the Negroes in the plantations nearby. Ma's maternal great-great-grandfather, a free man, had given much of the funds to build it. Many slaves had learned to read there and had in turn taught others inside the walls of the church.

Now the church had enough broad wooden pews to seat about three hundred people. Every Wednesday and Sunday, it was fully packed, with standing room only. The altar was made of a large granite stone resting on two giant timbers. Behind the altar were about twenty wooden benches where the adult choir sat. Miss

Evangeline presided over both the children and adult choirs. She was a short woman with a huge bosom and, as Fats said, a gigantean posterior. Whenever she turned around and it waggled, I would see the boys next to me in the boys' section try to cover their mouths with their palms to keep the giggles in.

By the time Kitty and I arrived, children's choir practice had already started, and Miss Evangeline rapped our knuckles with the flat end of her ruler for being late before allowing us to stand in the choir formation to the right of the altar. We sang half-heartedly, knowing that we only really got to perform once a month, despite our weekly practice. After we were dismissed to sit in the front church pews, our famous adult choir, the choir that ensured that every seat was filled on Sunday mornings, rose triumphantly and headed to the right of the altar to stand in formation to begin their practice. How magnificent they looked in their robes, forty men and women strong!

Our Ricksville choir was so loud that I heard Miss Evangeline boast that you could hear the choir at Heaven's Gate. Miss Evangeline started the tempo and the choir began to sway, first to the left and then to the right, like the sway of a pendulum. The motion was mesmerizing, and I was soon moving to the rhythm. First with my hands, then my waist, and before I knew it, I was on my feet clapping in time to the beat.

The choir's singing was well warmed up and the beads of sweat on Miss Evangeline's forehead broke forth, like from a dam, and spread in miniature rivulets down her face. It was then that the Holy Ghost showed up out of nowhere, knocking choir folks flat on their backs and causing such a hollering and a screaming for so long that the remaining members who had not yet succumbed were also finally caught up in the spirit. Whipped into a frenzy by the organist and drummer, the choir produced such magnificent sounds that I was sure even the angels wept. After a few such exhausting songs, Miss Evangeline herself collapsed in a heap on the floor from the sheer emotion of the moment, and was out of commission. This new freedom propelled the adult section of the choir to even greater heights, and they burst into impromptu song after song: "God Is Standing By," "Go Down Moses," "Amen." I did feel that spirit come rocking through the church, and when it did, I reached out my hands and caught it coming over me in waves.

When the final notes had died down, we finally made a move to head to our regular seats in the pews. The oldest members of the church and the more prominent people had assigned seats in the front of the church. Our family seats were in the back, in the last pew. We'd lost our family's assigned seat up front because the pastor's wife didn't think we deserved it anymore, not after what Ma had done to get me.

I was walking down the aisle, and Kitty was ahead of me, but when she ducked into the third pew from the front and sat down, the happy feeling I had gotten from the music disappeared in an instant.

"You can't sit here," I said.

"Why not?" Kitty's tone was hostile. "We used to sit up here before you came along."

I looked around nervously. Nothing seemed amiss. People were busy chatting to each other and others were finding seats in the pew. No one seemed to have noticed.

"Are you sitting down or not?" asked Mr. Griffen, the town barber, and I scooted to the far end of the pew next to Kitty and sat down. We were saying the Lord's Prayer when I glanced back and saw Ma entering the church with Stevie and C.T. She slowly lowered herself into the last pew, and I crouched myself as far down on the bench as I could, for if Ma had seen us there, she would have fixed her glassy "I'm going to give you that bitch lick" glare on us, and we would have had to hightail it to the back pew.

Kitty looked at me in exasperation. "Stop thrashing your arms about, Oreo, or you'll get us kicked out of here."

The organ started and I looked back again. The church had filled up and I straightened back up, safe. When I saw Kitty making googly eyes at the boy in front of us, it all made sense why we were sitting in the front of the church.

The Very Reverend started his sermon, and I soon fell asleep.

"And who here is sick of sin, tired of their life, tired of the way things have been going? Who here wants a new life, wants to be born again, born in the Spirit, steeped in His Blood!" The Very Reverend's voice was thunderous, carrying with it both a threat and a promise. His words penetrated my dream and with it, the words themselves seemed to reach out to me and penetrate the innermost layer of my soul.

Before I knew it, I was on my feet.

"Sit down, idiot!" Kitty hissed, trying to pull me down. But I was in a daze and knocked her hand away. Everything looked very hazy. My feet felt heavy as I walked down the red-carpeted aisle towards the Very Reverend Bishop T. Walker, Jr.

There was absolute silence in the church. Not a cough, whisper, or rustle could be heard. Never before had a child taken to answering the altar call, and the whole church seemed stunned.

"A child, answering the call," Reverend Walker said, wiping the sweat off his brow as he came towards me and drew me to the front of the church. It was there that I woke up fully.

"A child, answering the call!" he yelled heavenward.

"A child," whispered the whole congregation.

"Ella, do you know what it is to be born again?" the Reverend crooned as he took hold of my hand.

"Yes, sir," I whispered. And suddenly I wanted that more than anything.

"Out of the mouths of babes!" he shouted, and then he said, "Now tell the whole church what it is to be born again."

"To get a new life. To become a new person. To wipe away all my sin," I whispered.

"And? And? And?" screamed Reverend Walker.

"Well, to give your life and self to God, to . . . to . . . to stop your old bad ways and be forgiven," I stammered out.

"Alleluia!!!" Reverend Walker thundered.

"Alleluia!!" the congregation shouted.

"Let this be an example to you, Church. Let this be an example to you! The Lord has called this little girl—what about you? This child that was conceived in Sin. I say, conceived in Sin, but is now Born Again. I say, *what about you?* Turn to your neighbor and say, 'What about you?' All those of you who are thirsty but instead of sipping at the Lord's Table find yourselves day and night in local bars! All of you who are alone and scared, who feel empty and un-fulfilled, who wonder what you are doing in this world! All of you who are sick and troubled! This little girl has led the way. I saaaaay led the way!" The Very Reverend was getting very worked up and I could smell the acrid sweat, rising like fresh dung, from the pits of his armpits. I tried to slide my fingers out of his moist grasp, but he clung on to the very tips of my fingers.

The organist slipped into his chair and started increasing the tempo, and soon the whole church was on its feet, rocking and swaying, and many more people had decided that this was the time to give their lives to the Lord. When I glanced at Kitty, the flirty look was gone, replaced by stunned embarrassment.

After church, I saw the Very Reverend speaking to Ma. I watched, hidden behind the last pew, and saw Ma, nodding her head, a smile lighting up her face, and then the Very Reverend hugging her. A few minutes later, the church elders walked to the back of the church and requested—no, ordered—that Ma should take her rightful place towards the front of the church.

I stood by Ma, watching in awe as lies dripped off her tongue.

"Oh, yes," she said earnestly, "I do read the Bible nightly to them. Make sure they know right from wrong." Ma said this softly, bowing her head, as though in penitence.

I couldn't help but rejoice in the lies she told. Once her deaconess position, a role that was almost her birthright up to three generations, was restored, I knew the life she had had before me would be hers again.

I could barely keep quiet on the road home. Stevie and I played tag as Ma walked alongside C.T. and Kitty straggling behind. I kept glancing at Ma, but she seemed deep in thought. She hadn't spoken a word to me, but I knew she was taking it all in. I had seen the excitement on her face.

It was only when I shut the front door that I saw her other face. The distant one she reserved for me. Yet in another instant that, too, changed, and I saw the angry, disgusted face I see only fleetingly, when she looks at me when she thinks I'm not looking. This time, though, her anger was unsheathed. My legs started to tremble all on their own. I backed up to the door, but when I turned around to open it and flee, it was locked.

"How dare you? How dare you, you piece of trash from the gutter?"

So disgusted was her tone that it evoked a response in me so automatic that I barely had time to turn and retch, my stomach responding in fear. She shoved me, hard, her face grimacing as she worked herself into a state such as I had never seen before.

"How dare you put my business in front of the whole church and shame me like I was a piece of nothing. My family gave the funds to raise that church. I have borne this shame for *years*. Finally, people were beginning to stop talking about me behind my back. Yes, they were! In a few years, I could have taken my rightful position in the church slowly but surely, with my head held high, but now everyone will be talking about what happened twelve years ago. I know you did it to hurt me. You are an ugly, wicked, evil child."

The waves of nausea had stopped, and I stepped to go around her, to get away from the punishing words, but her bulk had me pinned with my back to the door.

Stevie tried to pull me to his side, but Ma turned on him, pulling his ear, and told him to take C.T. upstairs. He didn't even glance at me as he picked up C.T., swung him onto his hip, and rushed out of the room. I saw Kitty's face peering over the banisters from upstairs; in a flash she, too, was gone.

"What kind of a monster do I have sitting in my home? I know He was punishing me for my sin, but did He have to strike me down when I was barely standing up?" Ma's voice was shaking now, and the rage that was just barely tethered suddenly broke through.

"But Ma . . . Ma?" In my confusion, I reached out to touch her hand. She quickly swiped it away, and what I had been about to say was stopped short by two punches across the face that hit me with such force that I didn't wake up till the next day.

I woke up in my bed with all my clothes still on and my face covered in dried blood. I crawled to the bathroom and gingerly pulled myself up to look at my face. My cheek was swollen, my lip was split, and I had a loose tooth. The house was completely quiet. I crawled back to bed. Yet what welled up in me was ferocious and ugly enough to fill the depths of hell.

"I hate you, I hate you, I hate you, I hate you," I screamed over and over again till it became a mantra. As drowsiness began to fog my brain and my eyes began to flutter shut, I had a sudden and bright flash of knowing, just like a lightning bolt had lit up some dark corner of my brain. I returned to the bathroom again.

I looked past the bloodied face I saw in the mirror, taking in my midnight-black skin that was shades darker than any person's I knew in Ricksville, my generous mouth, and my wide nose, so different from the rest of my family. How odd it felt to be looking at myself with someone else's eyes. For the first time in my life, I really saw what they saw. It was then I understood what Ma felt towards me. And it was there, in that bathroom, staring into my face, that I realized the only person I had ever really hated was me.

CHAPTER 10

Philadelphia, Mississippi, June or July 1960

She didn't have to go to church, not since the first grade, and she was now eleven and in the sixth grade. Ma didn't like this, but there was nothing she could do. What Daddy said was what went, so Ma would dress up, and Uncle Jeb, Ma's brother, would come and drive her off to the Methodist church two miles down the road. Daddy didn't believe in church. He said church and the ministers were the cause of all the problems in the South. Said he didn't know what the ministers were doing when they introduced God to the niggers. At first it seemed like a good idea, to tell them that the Bible talked about slaves and masters and this was the natural order of things. It would help them accept their place in the world. But what did the niggers do? They just jumped right on Exodus, and Moses, like they were the chosen people being led out of slavery by the Lord himself. They quoted scriptures that said all slaves should be released after seven years from their masters with compensation. That Bible gave them airs. Now that slavery had long ended, the niggers wanted more, more, and more. Daddy said mark his words, they would beg for more till they were sitting at his table, dipping their wooden spoons right into his bowl. Niggers were like that, stomachs that were never satisfied. Only yesterday some of them had gone to the farmhands to say that they didn't want to work on Sundays. That it was the Lord's Day. They didn't dare ask it to Daddy's face. The Lord's Day, indeed. Who had introduced them to the Lord? So Daddy sent the message right on down the chain—it was work on Sundays or pack up and go. They

shut up real quick after that. God couldn't compete with food on the table.
One thing about niggers, Daddy said, they sure know what's good for them.
They all knew that Daddy would have made sure no one hired them within
a twenty-mile radius.

She was just like Daddy—she hated those niggers so much she wanted
to spit when she saw one . . . and she couldn't go near a church without
getting angry.

In June, Leroy entered our lives again, a month after I turned twelve. Every time he went away, as the weeks stretched into months, I would make up my mind that he was never coming back. Perhaps he was dead, run down by a speeding black car, lying limp and spread-eagled across the road, so completely bloodied and flattened that there was nothing left to bring back to Ma. I so believed in his death this time that it was a shock to come home and find, on our doorstep, a basket of red roses and fruits, all tied up with a pretty pink bow. I carried the basket inside and placed it on the kitchen table. Leroy had been away for ten months and it was clear that he was returning. I knew this was just a first step in apologizing to Ma for being away so long.

When Ma got home, she took the basket, and from the dreamy look in her eyes, I could tell that Leroy didn't have much more begging to do.

On the day of his arrival, Ma was beside herself with preparations for Leroy's return. Her voice, normally loud and precise, was soft, like butter left out on the counter. It was hard to think that this was Ma, who could give me what she called "one bitch lick" with Ma O, the snakelike cane that hung innocently behind the kitchen door.

At seven o'clock sharp, we were all bathed, dressed, and fed, looking clean and fresh in new nightshirts. Leroy's meal, crispy fried chicken, greens, mac and cheese, and peach cobbler, was laid out, covered, on the kitchen counter. The sounds of Ray Parker, Jr., on the boom box filled the air. Then there was a knock on the door. Stevie and Kitty sped to open it and Kitty was swung up in the air by the tall, thin, handsome, high-yellow man who stood at the door smiling crookedly.

"How you've grown, still looking so pretty," he said. When he finally put her down, he enveloped Stevie in a hug and playfully punched him.

"How's your basketball game?"

Stevie looked bewildered for a second before saying, "Oh, I gave that up a long time ago."

"What you do that for? You were good."

Stevie shrugged. "Too much schoolwork, and I need to focus if I'm going to become an engineer." He looked so small and res- olute, standing next to Leroy. I saw Leroy smile, but the smile didn't quite reach his eyes.

"I'm not saying that you ain't, but we don't have money for a fancy degree. A basketball scholarship could take you places."

Stevie didn't answer, and I knew that Leroy's continued dis- pleasure would eventually have him back trying to win basketball trophies.

Leroy looked past Stevie, to Ma. I was still sitting next to her on the sofa. She was holding C.T., who looked like he didn't know what on earth was going on and was about to cry. As Ma stood, she handed C.T. to me, and we watched as she put her arms around Leroy, burying her face in his neck like a little girl. They stood sway- ing till C.T.'s crying broke them apart.

"See, your son don't know you anymore."

Leroy bent over C.T., ruffled his hair, and sat down. Stretching out on the worn brown sofa, he put one leg on the coffee table.

"Been working like a dog all this while, trying to get my business together. Put food on the table. First, I was in Alabama workin' as a hired hand on a farm. Put some money together and then moved to Tennessee, started my own business, selling encyclopedias and dictionaries door to door. Worked out pretty good."

He put his hand in his pocket as he spoke and brought out a wad of cash and licked the tip of his fingers before flipping through the bills, like a deck of cards. There was nothing but hundreds in there.

"See that?" Leroy said triumphantly. He was not as refined as Ma, and he didn't always use his tenses correctly. She'd married down, but he had partially made up for it with his dashing good looks.

"My, there must be five or six thousand dollars in there. You made that all from selling books?" I heard the anxious tone in Ma's voice and looked at Leroy again, but he didn't look like a man on the run. I knew that he could sell sand to a desert nomad if he put his mind to it. All I knew was that he still hadn't figured out how to hit the big one or how to keep what he had. Give him three months, and all that money in his hands would be gone on booze or gambling or both.

He hadn't said a word to me, and I wasn't holding my breath.

"Leroy hates me," I had once told Cammy. We had been sitting on her stoop, eating her ma's mini apple tarts.

"On account of you not being his?"

I didn't answer. I had already said too much so I shrugged, and after that we just ate our tarts.

I made my way to Cammy's rear porch. The front door was open and I could see Miss Claudia sitting in the kitchen, rollers in her hair, watching *Gimme a Break* on TV.

"Is Cammy back?" I asked from the doorway.

Miss Claudia barely glanced at me. "No. Her dad's decided to keep her longer. She'll be away the whole summer." Then she looked at me again closely, as though remembering something. "How's it going? I heard Leroy's back in town."

"Yes, ma'am."

There was a look of sympathy, and something else, in her eyes.

"Come on in, have a slice of my sweet potato pie."

"No, thank you, Miss Claudia," I said politely, and turned around to walk on back home.

As I walked, my eyes caught sight of the soaring blue sky. The clouds were dancing across the heavens, effortlessly. But even that couldn't lift my spirits as I trudged back up Ricksville Road, all the way back home.

That night, I could hear them through the thin walls. I covered my ears with my pillow, closed my eyes tightly, and tried to say my prayers. I had to say them quick so I could join the front of the queue of all those evening prayers going up to God.

Please send him away again quickly, I pleaded with God. Why hadn't God heard my prayers and kept him away? Perhaps it was because God expected us to have our sins forgiven first before we prayed. Was hating Leroy a sin even though I had good reason?

It was then that I had an idea so brilliant I knew it could only have come from Heaven. Cammy had told me how Catholic people confessed their sins in a box private enough to keep the priest from seeing you and embarrassing you. Perhaps confessing to a priest would unblock my prayers and make God put me at the top of the prayer line.

The next Friday afternoon, I looked up a Catholic church that was far enough from Ricksville but still on the bus route. It took me a few minutes to find one, but there it was, written in bold letters in the yellow book, Christ the King Church, St. Elmo Street, Lordsville, open from 8 a.m. to 7 p.m.

I took the number 42 bus barely two blocks from Nate's. The driver may have wondered about the small girl who boarded the bus all alone, but he didn't say a word. The bus was filled with older white people. I had that momentary shock of surprise when I realized that I was the only black person on the bus, and I wanted to get off. Now, why had I used up all my Saturday money to buy this expensive return fare? If I walked off, that would be it, there would be nowhere left to go. I was still of two minds when I felt a lurch and almost ended up on the floor. The bus had started moving. I clasped on to the backs of the seats, staggered to the back row, and sat down. We kept stopping to pick up people, but no one came to the back. I amused myself by pretending that this was my bus and we were picking up poor old white people just to be nice. I would nod to them as they stepped onto the bus, acknowledging their thank-yous, and magnanimously direct them to take a seat. I played this game for a while, stopping only after I tired of it. Then I gazed out the window, staring at the rolling green countryside and the large colonial-style mansions. How come white people had all this? I pondered. Nate had said it was just plain and simple, the early bird gets the worm. Those who came before had weapons and swept out everybody else and got all the best stuff, that's it, plain and simple. They had swept it all up and folded their arms and had everyone else do the work. All ours! Mine! Mine! Mine!

I looked at the best stuff out the window, large planted trees, beautiful tarred streets with not a single pothole, playgrounds and schools with every kind of swing and slide, hospitals, large buildings, and not one building with peeling paint. What a strange world it was.

All too soon, the bus stopped at St. Vernon's Peak, and it took me a few seconds to realize that this was my stop. I got out of the bus and trudged the last mile up the road to finally arrive at my destination.

Christ the King Church was a brick building with steeples and arches. It looked so magnificent that I stood for a moment, wondering whether whoever was in there would listen to me. He would have to be like a prince, in beautiful golden robes to match the splendor of this church. A notice hanging by the round iron knocker of the church door said Confession was from 2 to 4. It was now 3:15. I pulled open the heavy door and stepped inside.

On the bus, I had worried that there'd be a long line of people in a hurry to get rid of the sins they'd committed all week, but when I entered, the church was empty despite its many pews. I looked around for the big box Cammy had told me about but didn't see it. Finally, I called out cautiously, "Hello, is anyone here?"

A door opened at the corner of the church and a pink balding head peeked out.

"Come here, child," the pink head said.

I wasn't too happy. Hadn't I heard that the priest wasn't supposed to see you? And here he was, clearly observing every step I took. As I approached, a short man wearing a flowing white gown emerged. As I got close to him, he stretched out his hand and took mine in his. I felt my face grow warm as he looked straight into my eyes.

"What is it, my child?"

"I came for Confession," I said nervously.

"Oh, yes. It's about that time, isn't it?" He led me over to the front pew and motioned for me to sit. I climbed in and he sat beside me.

"Isn't there a box?" I said in bewilderment.

"What box? Oh, you mean the confessional? Well, it's back

there, where the curtain is. But since you are the only one here, there's no one to hear you."

He must have seen the look of panic in my eyes, for he added, "Would you feel more comfortable in the confessional?"

"Yes." My response was emphatic. I didn't want his shocked eyes staring at me as I told him my worst secrets.

He looked at me again. "Have you had your First Holy Communion?"

I had no idea what that was, but I thought I'd better say yes or he might not listen to me.

"Yes," I said firmly, making up for my initial hesitation with volume.

"Okay," he said. "You go around that side and I'll meet you."

I pulled back the curtain and went inside the dark space. I looked around. It was almost exactly what I'd expected. It wasn't a box, but they made it dark enough so you didn't have to feel embarrassed as the priest watched you confess your sins. There was a type of pew bench to kneel on, and the window dividing my space from his was made up of a wooden lattice. I let out all the breath I had been holding. This was what Cammy had told me about. The holes in the lattice were so small the priest could barely see me.

"Okay," he said, a deep voice in the dark, "you can start."

How to start? I wondered. Then I blurted out, "I hate my stepfather. I wish he would die. He keeps touching me."

There was silence from the other side. Then I heard him clearing his throat.

"Child, what is your name?"

"Ella."

"Ella, you may have forgotten, but you start by saying 'Bless me, Father, for I have sinned.' And then you tell me if it has been one week or two weeks, or however long it's been since your last confession."

I started again, stumbling a bit to get through the "Bless me, Father, for I have sinned, it's been . . ." and then I paused. It was one thing telling a lie out of the box, but quite another to tell a lie right there inside the box. Surely God would strike me down if I kept on lying. I mumbled past the part about how long it had been since my last confession and waited to see how this would go down.

"Carry on."

Carry on? Did he want me to say it all over again or was I supposed to continue? I was trying to decide what to do when the priest spoke again.

"You hate your mother's husband, he has touched you, and you want him dead."

"Yes, Father."

"Is there anything else?"

I pondered. Should I confess anything else? Wouldn't that distract him from the main problem? The priest was clearly waiting.

"That's it," I said.

"Are you sure?" came the response. "Have you told any lies this week? Hit anybody? Stolen anything?" His voice sounded disbelieving.

Clearly, I had to make it more authentic. So I started pulling things out like a rabbit from a hat, making up some sins and throwing in a few others that I thought I might have done. Eventually, I was sure he was as exhausted listening as I was talking.

"That is quite a list you have." This time he sounded satisfied, almost cheerful.

He made the sign of the cross—I could only just see his moving arm in the box and hear mutterings, talking to God.

Then he said to me, "Your sins are forgiven. Say eight Hail Marys and three Our Fathers."

How simple. But did I feel better? The answer was *no*, but the confession was done. So now would my prayers reach God? I wanted to ask what a Hail Mary was, but I didn't know if that was allowed. Did he expect me to leave? I peered through the lattice. Yes, he clearly did. He was already getting up.

"You can go now, my child."

"Is that all?"

"Is what all?"

"You didn't tell me what to do. What to do about Leroy. You didn't even tell me if God will now hear my prayers." I was indignant. "I know I didn't pay anything, but I did come all the way on the bus."

"Leroy, your father?"

"My *step*father," I corrected.

"I just forgive sins here in the name of the Father, and yours have been forgiven. If you want counseling, wait till four and you can see a priest for counseling."

I left and went to sit on a pew bench. At four, the same pink-headed bald priest came out of the same side door and started walking towards the altar. I ran to stop him. "Who is the counselor?" I asked.

"I am."

I looked at him, confused. "Where do you counsel?"

"Right here, if you want." He sat back on the nearest pew and again reached out his hand to me, but this time I kept my hands folded tightly together as I sat next to him.

"Okay, so you want to know what to do about . . . what's his name again, Leroy?"

"Yes."

"First question. Can you tell your mother about what he is doing?"

I wanted to tell him that my mother hated me, but I could see that this would probably shock him too much. I must have looked horrified, because suddenly his eyes looked grave. It was only then that I noticed he was quite young despite his bald, egglike head.

"Well, then can you tell God?"

"I have, but can I ask Him to kill Leroy?"

The priest looked disturbed. "You seem to have forgotten that you've just been forgiven for hating him. Asking for him to be killed is just as bad, Ella. But God can do everything and anything. Just pray and wait. An answer will come."

"But I need something done now," I said.

He looked at me. "Have some faith, little girl," he said. "You continue to pray to God for help and believe that He will send help, and He will. Until then, tell someone, an adult you trust. Then you need to stand up to this man. If he does anything like that again, hit his hand away and say you will tell. Sometimes not showing fear scares away a bully."

"I can't do that. He'll kill me." I was beginning to think that this priest was as useless at solving problems as I was.

"I would like to send somebody to help you if you tell me where you live?"

I kept my lips pressed together firmly.

The poor priest was running out of ideas. He was beginning to look red and flustered. I wanted to end his misery, so I quickly thanked him and reassured him that I would pray to God. With great relief, he took my hand in his, closed his eyes, and muttered a prayer. He walked me to the door of the church and opened it for me to leave. I was about to say goodbye when I saw that he was looking at me curiously.

"Do you live around here, Ella?"

"No, I live in Ricksville."

"That's a long way for a little girl to come on her own."

I nodded and gave a little wave but his voice stopped me again.

"Ella, God go with you. Try not to hate anybody, Ella, even if they do things that are deserving of hate." As he started to turn back, he paused. Then he turned around and looked straight at me.

"Isn't there anyone you can stay with, at least for a while?"

Suddenly it seemed to me that the white of his smock was brighter than before and the sun's glare reflecting off his gleaming head made it look like a halo. Could God really work that fast? I flashed him a smile and nodded, although I could have kissed that shiny head.

I took off, making it just in time to catch the 5:00 bus back to Ricksville.

As soon as I got off the bus I ran down to Cammy's house. I didn't even knock. Miss Claudia was sitting on the couch, rolling up her hair. I sat next to her and asked whether I could stay with her for a few weeks, just for a change. Her hands stopped rolling for a smidgen before she continued to wrap her hair.

"That bad, Ella?"

I didn't say anything.

"Well, as you know, Cammy and Laura have gone to their father's for the summer. So you're welcome to sleep in their room if your ma says it's okay. Just don't expect me to be fixing you any food. This is kind of a vacation from taking care of the girls, and I deserve to go and come as I please."

"Don't worry," I said. "I'll take care of myself. I can cook a little."

"Okay, just don't burn the house down. You can use what you see but don't expect me to be buying anything for you. I'm strapped as it is."

"Yes, ma'am."

I couldn't stop smiling all the way home. Things were wonderful, stupendous, swell, prodigious, incredible. I stopped to think of more words. Marvelous, awesome, amazing. I thought of ten more before I reached home.

When I told Ma that Miss Claudia had invited me over to stay a bit, Ma had seemed relieved and said she'd give me three dollars every week to buy food. It wasn't enough, but at least I wouldn't starve. I felt like my life was turning on a dime. As soon as I reached my room, I fell on my knees. "Thank you, God," I whispered.

CHAPTER 12

Philadelphia, Mississippi, Mid-December 1963

Every weekend she could remember for the last three years, her daddy and his friends would meet either in the house or in the barn to sit and drink while talking about what was happening up north. They would get real angry about all those nigger loving ideas that they were trying to bring down south. They were making the niggers uppity. Sometimes her daddy would let her join them because she was almost fifteen, so long as she sat quietly and didn't talk. She knew that life was unfair for white farmers like her dad, who worked their tails off to farm the land. They didn't have it easy because the price of nigger labor was going up. Now these niggers were trying to buy their own farms and some traitors had sold some of their land to niggers. Little patches of dry dirt they called their own. Where did they get the money from? That's what they all wanted to know. Those pennies they got from working on white farmers' farms sure weren't enough to buy a farm. It was probably those northerners, supporting those niggers, or it was stolen money. And now they were talking about the vote. The vote for the niggers. Daddy had ranted and shouted when he heard that. There was an emergency meeting in their barn one day and it was filled to the brim, a hundred strong with more out the door. Everyone was up in arms. She wondered why niggers wanted to vote. Vote for what when they could barely read? Hardly write? Why, they'd just be puppets, with someone telling them who to vote for and what to say. Someone up north telling them what to do. She couldn't stand the thought of those niggers trying to vote. Next, they'd be trying to put their own in the White House. She felt sick at the thought.

Bessie crept into the room to fill their glasses and then slowly and silently padded out, her bare feet heavy on the floor.

"That one is getting real old. Better put her out to pasture," Daddy's friend Benny said.

Her daddy laughed. "She came with my wife. Born here. Her grand-mother was a slave to my wife's family. When they decided to free those slaves, they had nowhere to go, so they continued working on the farm. She's been here her whole life. If it were up to me, I'd show her the door. But I can't. Seems my wife's mother made Bessie's mother a promise that Bessie could stay for as long as she wanted. You know what's odd about all this—my wife doesn't even like her." Daddy laughed. "Nope, thinks she's slow and dimwitted. Moves like a snail. But there it is. Goes to show, never make a pledge with a nigger."

Daddy turned. "Up to bed, kiddo. Real men have to talk business. Give your old daddy a kiss."

She giggled. "You're not old, Daddy." She kissed his cheek with a smack and threw her arms around him even though she felt almost grown. Then she followed Bessie out the door and as she passed her, she shoved her aside. Bessie stumbled but didn't say a word. That Bessie, she thought, always underfoot.

CHAPTER 13

I knew all about the civil rights movement. And, being within an hour's bus ride from where the murders of the civil rights workers Michael Schwerner, James Chaney, and Andrew Goodman happened, the treatment of blacks by whites had been a topic of conversation among grown-ups for as long as I remembered. But still, even though we knew we lived in separate neighborhoods, the civil rights movement wasn't something we kids thought too deeply about because all that happened before we were born. Then, one day, it seemed that all the problems of the civil rights times came walking right up to our front doors, jolting us awake and forcing us to remember that while time had marched on, some people were still the same.

One quiet Tuesday night there was a knock on the door, and Mr. Graves, who lived about a half-mile walk away, was standing at Miss Claudia's front door. He was a stout gentleman with a bushy, silvery mustache. He often visited Ma, too, and I'd always been fascinated with him because he had the most enormous feet I had ever seen. At home, it was often left to me to open the door when someone knocked. I would first peep through the window to see who it was; since the window was not at the right angle to see their faces, I had to judge whether I could open the door by looking at their shoes. Neat and polished men's shoes meant either a salesman or someone from the church. I would then crane my neck to see whether the person was carrying a briefcase or suitcase, and if they were, I didn't open the door, because they were definitely salesmen. If the shoes were delicate and high-heeled, I always let them in, because they were always welcome on account of what they would be carrying. Kitty and Ma would happily spend hours exclaiming over every item before sending the saleswoman on her way, sometimes without a single cent exchanged. Other times Ma would put the item on credit and the saleswoman would be back several more times before the item was lovingly packed away in Kitty's trunk.

But if the feet were about three and a half times the size of mine, I would immediately yell, "Ma, it's Mr. Graves." Mr. Graves stopped by about once a week on his evening constitutional. Ma said he only ever stopped by for whiskey, and she doubted that he ever made the walk back home sober. "Just one for the road, Thelma," he'd say to Ma. "One for the road."

This time, I yelled out the same warning to Miss Claudia, and she scuttled to put away her best whiskey before opening the door.

"Got something to tell you, Claudia," Mr. Graves said in that gravelly voice of his as soon as he had wedged his large foot into the crack in the opening. "I'll only sit for a moment and then be off."

Miss Claudia slowly drew open the door. Mr. Graves came in, sat down, and she waited for the news, but clearly Mr. Graves's mouth would open only if it was wetted. He licked his dry lips a bit before looking her full in the eye. "Mighty dry out there tonight."

She pursed her lips for a moment before yelling for me to give Mr. Graves a drop of whiskey. "Only a drop," she said, and turned to Mr. Graves, "on account of it having to last till Christmas."

"Oh yes, oh yes." Mr. Graves's voice had become very jovial and very loud.

I brought the little glass of amber liquid to Mr. Graves, and he reached for it with a big smile.

He swallowed his whiskey in one gulp; let out a long, satisfied sigh; and then leaned over to Miss Claudia and whispered, as loud as a normal person talking, "That old white lady, Ms. Catchedy, she's done gone up to the Lord is what I heard."

He looked suitably reverent and shook his head sadly.

"Oh yes, we surely remember when she was working with Joe at the grocery store, kept an eye on everything, she did. Wouldn't be the first to say she was a little stingy with the sugar and the flour but probably she had to be when Joe was laid-back about everything."

He paused, waiting for Miss Claudia to fill in the silence, per-haps with an anecdote or two, but she just sighed and said quietly that she wondered how Nate was taking it. I noticed Mr. Graves's eyes narrow, waiting for some good gossip about Nate and Mrs. Catchedy, but Miss Claudia, quick to see his sudden interest, just thanked him for the news, firmly said good night, and all but pushed him out the door.

I had known Mrs. Catchedy was dying, because over the last two weeks, Nate had become unusually quiet and moody and had handed over the store to Ma once or twice so he could take a trip up the hill to visit her on the white side of town.

The next couple of days, all was quiet till the Friday of that week. Miss Claudia came home full of stories of long black limousines gliding smoothly up the road that led in front of Nate's, past the town center, and out to Mrs. Catchedy's mansion for the viewing. I listened, spellbound, imagining tuxedoed gentlemen and elegant ladies, all dabbing their eyes with black lace handkerchiefs as they entered Mrs. Catchedy's home for the viewing. I could never imag-ine them weeping and hollering and fainting, because I knew only black folk did that. Surely we were the only ones to feel the pain deep down in our marrow so that it had to come forth, spewing up in moans and groans and chants, till we felt better. I wondered how they kept their pain all twisted and knotted up inside, like a corked bottle.

"Will Nate go?" I asked Miss Claudia, only to be given a piercing look from her that said I should know better. The only black people there would be Lucille, who would be wearing her maid's uniform and opening the front door, and perhaps one or two others to serve all the hors d'oeuvres on dainty black napkins.

I was helping to clean the diner on the day of Mrs. Catchedy's funeral service. It was Saturday morning, and Ma was on the grill when Nate walked in, dressed in a new black suit, complete with a black hat. I thought he looked very handsome. Ma stared at him because she couldn't believe he was going to the funeral service. But his very next words confirmed that he was. Ma didn't say anything at first. Then she reached up to him and straightened his tie.

"Is Lucille going?" was all she asked.

"She'll probably be there, sitting at the back of the church," Nate answered.

"Well," Ma said calmly, "you just go right on up and sit next to her at the back. They'll probably think you're her son."

But that very afternoon, after the funeral was over, the gossip was all over town. The drivers, who during the funeral had been waiting patiently for their employers, could barely keep their eyes on the road, trying to listen to what was being said in the back seats. What they heard made them want to drive off the nearest cliff. Scandalous, was the consensus. "Who did that big black man think he was, walking right up to the front and sitting down, just like he was family?" By evening time, all the black folks in Ricksville were abuzz with rumor, talking about what a stir Nate had created. He had not walked to the back of the church and sat down quietly next to Lucille. No, he had walked straight up the aisle, looking neither left nor right, and sat down just one pew behind the Catchedy family relatives. We heard that the church had become as quiet as a tomb as he walked up the aisle. Most of Mrs. Catchedy's surviving family didn't live in Ricksville and so not one of them, not even her only son, who lived a two-hour flight away in Baltimore, had ever heard of Nate. He was unceremoniously picked up by five burly men and thrown out the door. It was thanks to Lucille, who started to beg and cry, saying that Nate was a simple, retarded man, that nothing worse had happened. For his part, Nate was very quiet when he came back that evening. He didn't show any surprise that the diner was packed full of customers, those who were just curious, those who wanted a bit of gossip, and those who felt they had to be there to support Nate, just in case something happened.

Nate just took off his hat and his jacket, put on his apron, and went back to the grill, heedless to the noise and chatter around him. The diner was supposed to close at nine o'clock in the evening, but by midnight it was still crawling with customers, and Nate finally held out his hands.

"Folks, I really appreciate your coming tonight. Tomorrow is the Lord's Day and we've got to close up shop. I'll be happy to take one last order of drinks." Despite that, a few people hung on till we finished washing and drying every dish, and then they walked Nate on home. It was 2 a.m. by the time Ma and I finally got to the junction and started down Ricksville Road.

"Ma, think they'll do anything to Nate?" I asked, scared from all the talk I'd heard.

It seemed like suddenly our carefully separate worlds were colliding, all because Nate had crossed that invisible line.

Ma didn't respond to me. I was scared of the pitch dark, so I reached out and grabbed her hand. She didn't pull away this time. I held on to that limp hand and imagined that it was just me and my ma alone in the world. Just us. It was a wonderful dream that lasted all the way till we reached Cammy's house, a few houses down from ours. She didn't say a word as I turned into Cammy's yard and made my way up to the front porch. I turned and waved, but Ma just kept right on walking.

When I later asked Mr. Macabe about what would happen to Nate a few days later, he just pulled my braids and said, "Nothing, Ella. Nothing happens in a little place like this. We're all civilized to each other. What happened to those civil rights workers isn't going to happen here."

I was relieved. And I was overjoyed—especially Ma—when we heard that Nate had been called to the office of Mr. D. Thompson, Esquire, because his name was mentioned in Mrs. Catchedy's will. It felt like Nate's good fortune was ours. He would at least get five hundred dollars, Ma said, perhaps even as much as eight hundred dollars. Hadn't Lucille been left the hefty sum of a thousand dollars for her twenty years of service? She had picked that money up and got on the first train back to Arkansas, where, by all accounts, she had left her family to come to work in Ricksville all those years ago. She never said goodbye to anybody, just dusted that Ricksville dirt off her feet and disappeared without looking back.

I just happened to be at the diner when Nate came back from his meeting with Ms. Catchedy's lawyer. He walked back in like he always did, removing his jacket and putting on his apron. But I knew something was wrong. His eyes, normally bright and alert, had skimmed us unseeingly, and he hadn't uttered his normal "Morning, Thelma. Morning, Ella." There was a strange smile flittering around his face, but when he looked up and finally saw us, his eyes looked scared.

"What's the matter, Nate?" were the first words out of Ma's mouth. "Didn't you get anything?"

The strange smile was still there, so we waited. It sure seemed like Nate was taking a long time to answer. When he finally did, his voice was a deep, croaky rumble.

"I sure did get something," he said quietly. "She left the whole damn thing to me. The house, a hundred thousand dollars in cash, and all her stock options."

Our jaws flew open and held. I started to laugh and joyfully rushed to hug Nate, happiness flooding over me. But then I felt, rather than saw, the stillness in the room. When I looked up, I saw the pain on Ma's face. The one she normally reserved for funerals.

"What is it?" I cried out, but no one answered. Instead, Ma enveloped Nate in a sorrowful hug while he wept like a little boy.

"Said I was like a son to her," Nate said, withdrawing from Ma's hug. "She knew I was her husband's child the minute I mentioned my ma's name, but we never discussed it again. All these years I've marveled at how she could accept her husband's by-blow the way she did. But she did. Bless her, she meant well, but she's surely hammered the first nail in my coffin."

I was confused. How could Nate be old Mr. Catchedy's son? I couldn't make sense of what they were saying and no one seemed ready to tell me anything, so I went outside to sit on the diner's front stoop. While I was doodling in the dirt with a stick, Ma came out and motioned for me to get along.

The next three days felt like the Angel of Death was passing over the black community. Everyone spoke in hushed tones. Streams of visitors came from all over the town, whispering with the neighbors up and down Ricksville Road all the way to Perry, where

Nate lived in a small one-story house. They had all heard about Nate. How I don't know, but in a small town like Ricksville, bad news travels faster than the beat of a jungle drum. All of them were cautious and alert, as though someone was lurking around the corner, listening. For the next few days, I wasn't allowed near the diner. All I knew was that a group of men walked Nate to work in the morning, and they walked him back home in the evening.

Then the news was all over town; someone, in the dead of night, had placed a burning cross on the diner's front yard. Flames lit up the night sky, drawing crowds from every direction of South Ricksville. The message spoke volumes, so clear and direct that it had the grown-ups climbing in their skins with fear. Taking our cue from the adults, we kids fell silent and the neighborhoods became like tombs. Throngs of adults crowded around Mr. Graves's barber shop to talk, in half whispers, about what was happening. The front page of the *Ricksville News* showed a picture of Nate standing beside the burning cross, looking worried. It was "a schoolboy's prank," the paper suggested.

A few days later, Miss Claudia and I pored over the newspaper, which said that Mrs. Catchedy's son, Mr. Joseph Catchedy, Jr., was contesting the will, which in his estimation had been drawn up by his fragile, sick, and deluded mother, who undoubtedly was manipulated into leaving all her possessions to the town drunk. The next day, another editorial screamed the headline "Nate's Diner Fraudulently Acquired." The story read that Mrs. Catchedy had been forced to give over her old grocery store, a property that had been in the family for generations.

Nate's problems were clearly just beginning, and we were hounded by the fear that we would be swept along with it. We felt certain that the burning cross had simply been the calm before the storm. Ma still went to work at the diner every day, and I resumed my Saturdays there. Business was booming, even with all the tension, for as Miss Claudia said, misery loves company. Each day the store was filled with customers eager to discuss the latest problem that had befallen Nate.

"All lawyers, the whole lot of them," Miss Claudia would say sarcastically. "Never stepped a foot in college and suddenly they know how Nate should respond to the charges in the newspaper."

"Sue the paper," some cried. "Write a letter to the paper saying the store was sold to you," others had said, even after Nate had patiently explained that it wasn't the money he had paid that they were questioning, but whether he'd coerced Mrs. Catchedy to sell her store.

There were no more horrific acts in Ricksville, but Joseph Catchedy, Jr.'s use of the *Ricksville News* to berate Nate finally began to take a toll on business. Even though customers were always there and willing to buy, Nate depended on regular deliveries of meat, bread, and other supplies from the white butchers and farms in the surrounding northern counties who also read the paper. Deliveries began to arrive late, and finally, goods were just not delivered. In the month that followed, when I saw Nate becoming gaunt and lean, I was tortured with the idea that he might return to his old drinking days. I missed that grin of his and the way he used to move around the store, so strong and proud. Now there was a slight stoop to his walk, eyes downcast to avoid the probing, sympathetic looks of onlookers. I'd grab his arm when I saw him in the street, but he never looked me in the eye.

One bright summer morning we walked into the diner and saw that the storeroom was full again. Rather than face financial ruin, Nate had made a deal with Joseph Catchedy, Jr., and put his signature on a document that relinquished all claim to any money or property of Mrs. Catchedy in return for keeping the diner and

Joseph stopping the newspaper smear campaign. The paper moved on to bigger and better stories. On one hand, we were relieved; finally, it seemed like a chapter in our lives had come full circle and closed, and over the next few weeks as normality resumed in Ricksville, Nate's tall shoulders gradually unbent and straightened. But Nate had lost a part of himself when he signed that document, and he never again seemed the same to me.

Maybe the grown-ups should have known. That's what Miss Claudia said. Maybe they should have felt the stirring of trouble like a distant slow wind sweeping over the land, silent but relentless. They could have noticed when they felt goose bumps in the height of summer, instead of just thinking someone was walking over their graves. Maybe all of us could have taken to wearing ginger and garlic like Mr. Macabe does when he feels an evil wind brewing, a slight chill in the air in an otherwise scorching day. The grown-ups felt they had let their guard down, and it worried them.

One night, not long after signing over his inheritance, Nate said something to a customer that I overheard and would never forget. He said that he'd finally realized that he had never been the puppeteer, controlling his own destiny. Instead, he now realized that black people were just puppets on strings. The strings were so long that they reached far above them—so far out of their vision that they never saw or knew who the puppet masters were. He only knew that when they yanked at the strings and said to dance, he had no choice but to dance.

CHAPTER 14

Philadelphia, Mississippi, April or May 1964

She was too close to her daddy not to know he was excited about something. She knew it had to do with the almost daily meetings in the barn. Men came in droves, lining up out the door to hear what was going on inside. There were all kinds of interesting sounds coming from the barn: raised voices, cussing, and clinks of glass, which she knew were the many bottles of whiskey and beer that she saw Bessie deliver to the barn. Her daddy had told her not to come near the barn anymore and she was mad. Being mad made her sneaky. She didn't think it was fair because Randy was allowed into the barn to listen in. He wouldn't tell her anything, though—it's men's business, he would say with a smirk.

Her mother, lying on the couch as usual, would sigh and say, Those men are like a dog with a bone. Why don't they leave well enough alone?

As the days crept by, the voices around the barn grew quieter, and the line of men out the door disappeared, until there were only fifteen men or so in the barn. She would stand outside the now closed barn door, hidden from sight, and try to listen in. It wasn't easy. They now spoke almost in whispers. Sometimes on a quiet, windless day, she could hear a snatch or two. Something about the vote for niggers. Something about nigger lovers, who she knew were just white folk who loved those niggers so much that they had turned black on the inside.

After they all left, she would go through the papers they left behind: lists of names of niggers from everyone's farms, someone's name, Mickey, circled in red, a map of the area and the surrounding roads. There was a large map with towns including Ricksville, Meridian, Silversted, and her town, Philadelphia. The map had pen marks and scribbles with red circles around roads. Roads she noted that left each city. There was also a list of how many guns each man had. She saw that Daddy had six, including two rifles. There was also a list of bullets to buy.

They were plotting something. She was sure it was a war. A war against the niggers? She knew how to shoot. She would get hold of a gun, but where was the war going to be?

She hated it when Daddy kept secrets from her.

◈

In June, she had gone over to Carmen's house and they had talked about boys all afternoon. The lunch Mrs. Maldoon had given them was delicious, and Carmen had finally revealed the secret she had been holding on to—that Bobby Palmer had told her to tell Kate that he liked her. She had almost swooned right there and then. They had gotten off the bed, clasped hands, and jumped up and down like jumping jacks. Then Mrs. Maldoon had come over and interrupted their fun. She'd had an odd look on her face, and for a second, Kate had thought that something was wrong at home. But Mrs. Maldoon just told her to run along home quickly as it was getting dark. She was surprised because it was only five and it was just an odd thing to say when she often stayed over as late as nine in the evening. She had thought of Bobby Palmer all the way home.

When she got in the yard, she saw that Daddy's pickup was gone, but she didn't bother to check on her mother. Instead, she went to the kitchen to get herself some water, but on entering, she stopped, because there, sitting on a kitchen stool next to Bessie, was a strange man she hadn't seen before. He had long legs, was very dark, and his body was thick with muscles. She hadn't liked the look of him. For one, he hadn't stood up and taken off his cap and wished her a good evening, and for another, they never had the nigger boys in the house.

She immediately went for Bessie, because she should have known better. "What's he doing here? Don't you know that the nigger boys are not allowed in the house? Get him out of here."

Bessie hadn't replied, but it was the nigger boy's look that shook her. He had stood up, looked right at her, through her, and she had felt something in his hard look—animosity? Insolence? Something she did not like, staring down at her.

"Get out," she ordered. He hadn't moved an inch.

"Get out," she said again, throwing her arms out to shoo him.

Again, that look. Distaste? Dislike? Pity? She couldn't put her finger on it, but it scared her. The fear was like a flame that started in her chest, tiny at first, like the mini spark of a struck match before it flared, causing her breath to come in gasps and her heart to race.

"Go on," Bessie said to the man, and, after a moment, he turned and left out the back door.

She had taken that fear out on Bessie, calling her stupid, a cow, an idiot, and all the foul names she could think of that fell from her father's mouth. She was so shaken, she had quite forgotten why she had gone to the kitchen in the first place. All thought of Bobby had vanished as she lay on her bed, thinking about the audacity of that man. If she was a man, she would have shot him dead. Oh, yes, she would have.

She must have fallen asleep, because she woke to the sound of Daddy's engine revving up the driveway. She ran downstairs to meet him, and it was only then that she realized how long she had slept, for the clock on the hallway wall said it was fifteen minutes past midnight.

Daddy barreled into the house, leaving the front door wide open behind him, and as she rushed to shut it, she saw him stumble and sway. It took her seconds to realize that her daddy was so drunk that he could barely put

*one step in front of the other. By the time she shut the door and came back
to him he was swaying, like a big oak about to topple. She grabbed his shirt
to steady him but he was already falling. He went down hard, first to his
knees, then keeling over onto the floor. He fell with a thud, and for a second
she thought that he had knocked himself unconscious.*

"Daddy! Daddy!"

She was relieved when he moved and muttered her name, "Kate."

*"Yes, Daddy," she said softly, patting his back, as though she were talking
to an infant, "what is it? Are you okay?" He didn't answer, and it was then
that she noticed how badly he smelled. His shirt was muddy and wet with
sweat, beer, and something else, mildly acrid, almost like vinegar.*

*Then he started to snore. Oh, Daddy, she thought, why did you go hunting
without me? He got drunk only when he went hunting with the boys, but never
drank enough to be this drunk. Almost as though he'd heard her, his eyes
opened. Then he turned his head to face her and said, very clearly:*

"We did it, Kate. We did it."

His eyes slid shut and he was back to snoring loudly.

*We did what? she wondered briefly. She put his head in her lap, and was
in this position an hour later, with her feet cramping in pain from being
curled up enough to cushion his head, when her mother came downstairs.*

"Is he dead?" Her mother looked fearful.

*"No," she answered disdainfully. Men like her daddy didn't just die. "He's
just drunk."*

"Has he said anything to you?"

She had looked at her mother. Why was everyone acting so odd today?

"Go to bed and don't leave the bedroom till I tell you to."

*She couldn't figure what had come over her mother. She didn't even let
her move Daddy's head gently off her legs; instead, her mother shoved her
legs aside, pulled his head roughly off her lap, and said, "I'll take care of
him, just go to bed." That was the beginning of everything that followed.*

She remembers that everything was odd after that. It started with Mary the very next day. That cow. She still had that snide way about her. She was serving breakfast when she said, ever so casually, "Good morning, Miss Kate."

Kate had been startled because Mary never spoke to any of them unless she was spoken to.

"Did you see Curly? He came to visit Bessie yesterday. I remember how the two of you were best of friends when you were little. How you used to play with those dollies together."

She was aghast. That was Curly? The memories came flooding back, along with a side of anger, causing her to flush so strongly that her ears throbbed with pain. How dared he look at her like that? How dared Mary speak to her in that tone?

She turned to lash out at Mary, but Mary, her evil deed done, had slipped quietly away.

CHAPTER 15

One early July afternoon, I raced into the house, hot, sweaty, and damp from a day at the river with Fats, ready to make a sandwich, when I saw Miss Claudia standing over by the kitchen window. She turned and walked to the table with a pie in her hands. It was my favorite, peach cobbler. I sat down while she brought out two plates and forks, and I started to eat hungrily.

"Ella?"

"Yes, ma'am," I responded, my mouth full of buttery crust. I hadn't seen her look this serious before.

"You know I've loved having you around for company and you've kept everything neat and clean." She paused. "I'm sorry to have to tell you this, but Cammy is coming back early this summer. Her father took ill and he's going to be in the hospital for a while."

It took me a second to realize what this meant. I slowly stopped chewing. The soft peaches started to taste like cardboard.

"Do I have to go?"

"I'm afraid so, Ella."

"Can't I stay in Laura's bed? I'll be real good."

"It's not the space, Ella. It's just that I can't feed Cammy and not feed you. It will be awkward for Cammy and for me and I don't have enough to feed you both and save some money. While the girls were away, it was my time to try to save some money for the school supplies that will be needed when school starts back up."

"When do I have to leave?" Holding my breath, I hoped it wouldn't be soon.

"Tomorrow, honey. I really am sorry. I just got the news this morning. Cammy called, all in tears."

"Is he going to be all right? Her father?"

"I think so. It's appendicitis and it looks like they got it in time."

I took a deep breath. "Thanks so much for having me," I managed to say.

The next day, I was standing in front of my doorstep. Through the door I heard Leroy's booming voice and Ma's lighthearted response. I was about to intrude on their happy home. I knocked and the door swung open. Leroy loomed above me.

"Look what the cat's dragged home," he said as I pushed past him.

Five pairs of eyes looked at me, and then C.T. ran and hurled himself into my arms. I picked him up and swung him around, taking in his sweet smell.

By the end of my first week home, Leroy had started up again and I felt the old panicky feeling come roaring back. It was a Friday that he caught me. I'd taken two steps inside the house before I noticed him standing motionless by the door. Before I could back out, his long fingers had snapped around my wrist, and I was dragged to the stairs. In the moment of indecision as he glanced at the door, realizing that it was unlocked, I twisted loose and ran for the back door, flying like the devil himself was after me, feeling my bowels turn to water and empty, a stinky, sodden mess, into my underwear and pants, even as I reached for the back door key. The place where it usually dangled to the right of the sink: empty. By the time I turned around, Leroy was at the kitchen entrance wrinkling his nose.

"You stink," he said in disgust. "Go and change."

I twisted past him and ran upstairs, my mouth still open in

terror and my eyes overflowing with tears. I stayed under the shower for as long as I could, till I could hear him calling.

"Oreo, get down here."

I would have given anything to stay up there, but I knew he was waiting, and the longer I made him wait, the worse it would be for me. But I also knew Ma would be home soon, for today was her early day back, so I dragged it out as long as I could, folding and unfolding my clothes. Then he called again, and I knew in a moment he would be climbing those stairs angrily, so I called out, "I'm coming, Mr. Johnson," and took mincing steps to get down, waiting with each step for the sound of Ma's key in the lock.

When I reached the bottom, Leroy laughed. "Fresh and clean, you silly child. What did you think I would do to you?" He started singing a silly song, "Now I got you where I want you, now I'm going to eat you up." Then he laughed, as though we were playing a game.

But it didn't feel like a game to me. I wasn't sure what he was thinking about doing, but I knew it wouldn't be good. When he came at me, the world slowed down. Slowly, he wrapped his hands around my waist and lifted me high into the air, twirling me around faster, and for a few seconds it felt like we really were playing a game, then he dropped me and I landed hard against the living room floor, my breath wiped out of me and my head reeling. I hadn't said a word, but the minute he lay on top of me, I went mad. I bit him and screamed and tried to roll him off me, but he grabbed my throat and squeezed till I started to choke and gasp.

The door suddenly clicked open, and Leroy jackknifed up. Ma was standing there, looking confused.

Leroy was standing over me, with a bundle of bills in his hand.

"You know what this daughter of yours just did?" His voice filled the room, shaking with anger.

"She just stole from me. She had the money hidden in her pocket. I had to wrestle her down. This isn't all of it, so I don't know where she's put the other half. Just what type of daughter are you raising?" He shot a disgusted look at me.

Ma's look of confusion disappeared in an instant, and in a flash, she was towering over me. She took me by my T-shirt and pulled me up, right off the floor, till I was standing next to her.

"You stupid girl. Now you're stealing, too, and from the very hand that feeds you?"

I used my elbow to shield my face and braced myself for her fist, but suddenly Ma seemed to lose interest. She pulled my ear and headed upstairs.

Leroy stormed off after her.

No doubt to fill her ears with more lies.

I was still shaking. It seemed that the shakes would never stop.

It was right after this that my heart started acting funny. I would get winded just climbing the stairs and would have to take deep gulps of air while my heart hammered hard against my chest till I got dizzy and would have to go lie down. When I lay in my bed, I would count the paint patches that curled off the ceiling, and watch as they fluttered to the floor. Yesterday, I counted forty-eight. Today, twenty-six. My pulse slowed to normal as I lay counting in my bed, but the moment I got up to go downstairs, my heart would flip-flop in my chest and the pulse in my neck throbbed to a crashing crescendo. A few days after that, the twitching in my face started up again, and the thoughts in my head dashed around crazily throughout the day and night, not making any sense, leaving me exhausted. *I am going crazy*, I thought. *I am going to go stark mad and run around the streets naked, just like naked crazy Sammy.*

"God, I need an answer fast," I yelled up at the ceiling. And then felt guilty for yelling. How could I, a speck of dirt on the ground, yell at the great God, who had already saved me so many times?

"What's up with you, Ella?" Fats said one day. He had stopped by my house unexpectedly.

I shrugged.

"Cammy says you don't even play with her anymore."

"Cammy's changed." And in my mind, she had. She had arrived from her trip to California with a glossy blow-out hairstyle that made her hair flow down to her hips. She had started wearing makeup and lipstick and every sentence now started with, "My daddy this" and "My daddy that." *So what if her daddy has money,* I'd thought meanly.

"I think you've changed, Ella."

I didn't care. Let him think what he wanted.

"Mr. Macabe's asking for you. Told me to tell you to go on and visit him."

"Is that why you came here?" I had no intention of going over there for Mr. Macabe to ask me a million questions.

"Yes."

"Okay, now you've told me, you can go."

Fats stood there, looking miserable.

"You look sick, Ella. You need to see someone. Your whole face is kind of twitching."

I couldn't take it any longer.

"Get out of here, Fats, get your fat ass back home."

I could tell that I'd hurt him bad. As surely as if I'd taken an arrow and shot it right into his heart. He knew I was being deliberately mean. He looked at me for a long moment, and I looked away; my eyes could not meet his. He turned away, walking slowly back to his house.

Go ahead with your fat ass, I thought meanly. What did I care.

◆

It was Nate who finally told Ma that she should take me to Dr. Shepardson down on Meadow Lane, just because something was "clearly bothering the child." Ma was reluctant, but when Nate said he'd let her off one Friday and pay her the wages, she agreed. Dr. Shepardson wasn't a real doctor, but he'd gone and done all those courses up north, and people said that he was two exams shy of becoming a doctor when he received the news that his old mother was dying. He'd grabbed his coat straight off the back of his classroom chair and rushed right out of there, making it all the way down to Mississippi in fifteen hours. He had spent the next six months nursing his mother back to health. Pity, people used to say, because he never returned to the North to finish his medical degree, on account of his mother falling in and out of sickness but never letting go enough to die. Even now, she was still clinging on to life, living with her son and looking pretty spritely for ninety eight.

Dr. Shepardson charged only what his patients could afford. For Nate, he charged money, or a week of food at the diner. For Ma, he charged a small token or asked her to do a basin full of his laundry. The richer you were, the more you paid, but no matter the price, rich black folk still drove down from as far north as Vermont and drove up from as far south as Louisiana and southern Texas and lined up in his waiting room right along with everyone else. For one thing, no one could beat Dr. Shepardson's advice on how to get rid of a hex that's been put on you, or how to take the root of a mulberry tree and boil it down and add an oak leaf and mushrooms to cure a cold. His cures were a mixture of old and new medicine and whatever his old mother whispered after the initial diagnosis, for she was at every consultation, propped up on pillows on the chaise lounge behind him.

On the Friday that Ma took off from work, she dragged me into Dr. Shepardson's office, which was really just part of his living room, cornered off with a large curtain of brown matted rattan. Old Mrs. Shepardson was lying in her usual place on the tattered lounge, covered with a bright red-and-blue blanket. I stared because the top of her head was bald, but from the sides of her face, white hairs, thin and wispy, stuck out at every angle. Her face wasn't very wrinkled for someone that old, but her hands were a grayish spiderweb of thickening veins and wrinkled skin. We sat on the couch in the middle of the room, and Dr. Shepard-son ambled in.

"Heard all about you from Nate," he said, looking at me. "Clever little miss, you are. So, what's bothering you?" When I didn't respond, he asked me to remove my shirt, which had me burning in shame, and proceeded to tap and prod me until I was finally told I could sit back down. He asked Ma about what vaccinations I had taken and whether I'd ever had breathing difficulties before. Then he turned around and scribbled on a pad.

"Can't find a thing wrong with you. Healthy as an ox. No asthma. Perhaps it's anxiety—are you worried about school starting up again, making friends, Ella?"

"No," I mumbled.

"Well, okay. Thelma, I think we can call it a day. I won't charge you anything, nothing wrong with her."

As we stood up to leave, we heard a fit of coughing coming

from the chaise lounge and we turned to see old Mrs. Shepardson pointing at me. Dr. Shepardson hurried over, soothed his mother, all the while saying, "Yes, yes," while she was saying something to him that we couldn't hear. Then he came over and told us to take a seat again.

"Old Ma there says she can see that something's troubling the girl, making her right sick. She says make her some peppermint tea and put in some St. John's wort and a drop of crushed pepper juice, and while that won't cure her, it'll ease her mind, calm it down, and after about a week of this, she'll be ready to tell you what is bothering her."

Ma nodded and thanked the doctor for his time.

As Dr. Shepardson led us to the door and shook hands with Ma, he said, "You know what, Thelma, my old ma has never been wrong. Don't know where I'd be without her helping me out."

Ma shook her head in disgust as we walked up the path.

"All that mumbo jumbo African voodoo stuff, and to think that a grown man, almost a doctor, listens to all that rubbish."

She pushed me towards the road to head home.

"Don't know where all this is coming from, but you need to pull yourself together. There isn't a thing wrong with you."

CHAPTER 16

Philadelphia, Mississippi, Early August 1964

It was dark when the men came, first one or two, filing past the front door, silent and almost reverent. It was her mother who let them in. Her daddy was in his study, receiving the visitors. They came one by one, all informants with tales to tell. She could hear them because they didn't whisper when they were inside the house. They grew agitated, angry, their eyes wide-eyed. They told her daddy strange things, that the FBI was here, in their town, searching. Looking for evidence, marking spots on the road, taking samples. Looking at deep truck marks in the dirt, carrying shovels of mud away with tracks running through them. People were saying that three men had up and disappeared. Men turning out the vote. There was one nigger boy and two nigger lovers, riding all over the towns in that car of theirs, like they owned the world. The nigger should have known better. He was from Mississippi and knew how things were, but the others were from up New York.

The informants said not to worry: the sheriff, Uncle Billy, who was Daddy's cousin, and his boys were not saying anything, keeping their mouths shut. No one was talking. Pictures of the nigger boy and those nigger lovers, all over the town, taken down as soon as they were put up, but they kept putting them up, all over the town, on trees, doors, and windows. Where were those boys, they asked, the ones registering the black vote? What happened to them? Now people up north were asking a lot of questions about the white ones. Her daddy came to the door of the study when they took their leave. They shook his hand and he clasped his hand on their shoulders, patted them, reassured them. It was going to be all right.

Then Uncle Billy came the next day. He said there was talk of a cash reward. He was anxious, people may talk when cash is waved about. He asked about the niggers in the house—Bessie and Mary—could they have heard anything? She listened by the door, heard Daddy murmur that everything that was said was outside, never in his house.

Was Daddy in some kind of trouble?

She went to her mother, asked her whether everything was okay. She was lying on the couch staring at the ceiling, doing nothing, just staring. Ask your father, was all she said, I've given up asking questions.

Uncle Billy was about to leave. She saw her daddy patting him on the shoulder and shaking his hand up and down. They were both grinning, then they pummeled each other on the back.

Just seeing that made her feel better.

That was the calm before the calamity. They left under cover of darkness two days later. Her blanket was tugged off her sleeping body. Someone had shaken her violently—Daddy. Then the hand to her mouth, telling her to shush, not to say a word. The hushed tones, they didn't want to wake the servants. The whispered instructions. Take only two changes of anything warm. Nothing else. No to everything else she held up—her toothbrush, her journal, all her makeup, her beautiful debutante ball dress. No, no, and no, till she gave up. It must look as though they just were away for a short time. Less than a day. Come. She was pushed, prodded, and hurried. Her mother looked afraid, her father more anxious than she had ever seen him. She was in shock. Could they wait till morning, till she could say a few quick goodbyes? Her ma snarled at her, No. It was then she began to panic. She looked over at Randy, but he was silent. Fury written all over his face. She knew what he was thinking about—the girlfriend he loved, the local college he was to attend in the fall. Maybe they would be back soon. She had left her toothbrush.

She could only think that it might have to do with Uncle Billy's second visit that evening. He had come late, just as she was going to bed. She hadn't stayed up to eavesdrop, but he hadn't been there for long. She had heard the front door slam shut just as she was about to doze off. They drove and drove, and finally, after about five hours on the highway, Daddy stopped at a gas station. It was where she heard him ask directions to Boston. That was how she found out where she was going. Boston. Up north. Boston. Why Boston? They might as well have been going to Alaska. It was only then that the terrifying thought came—that they might not be back anytime soon.

CHAPTER 17

I had a burning question for Mr. Macabe. I walked up to his front door and pulled the knob to let myself in. To my surprise it was locked. I peered through the frosted glass but I couldn't see anything. I knocked but no one answered.

"You there, Mr. Macabe?" I called.

Still no answer.

I knocked harder.

It was as quiet as a church in there.

I sat on the porch, waiting for Mr. Macabe to come back. The question I had wasn't a good one, and I wasn't sure who to ask, but I figured that at least with Mr. Macabe, since he was blind, I wouldn't see his eyes to see how shocked he'd be when I asked the question. I could have asked Fats, but he'd probably die laughing that I didn't already know.

I was still waiting when I heard heavy steps on the porch, and the high black beehive hairstyle of Mrs. Robertson came into view, followed by her broad bosom and thick arms, carrying a large pie. She sure was surprised to see me sitting at Mr. Macabe's patio table.

"Now, what you doing here, Ella?" She sounded all flustered. The short six steps had her breathing heavily.

"Just waiting for Mr. Macabe," I said.

"Well, Ella, it isn't seemly to have you here on his porch while he is not here. Why don't you run on home, leave him a note or something?"

I looked at her, taking in that purple eye shadow, which matched her purple skirt, lilac blouse, and purple and blue shoes. Her lipstick was bright red.

I suddenly knew why she was here. She was a widow, and I'd been telling Mr. Macabe for a long time to be careful or he'd be netted, just like that old goose that used to come around, pecking holes in all our laundry.

"Mr. Macabe can't see," I said slowly, as though talking to C.T. "He can't see any note I write him." Then I added for good measure, "Pity he can't see your purple outfit either."

Mrs. Robertson's eyes sprang open, like a baby doll does when you stand it up after it's been lying down. Her eyes had that annoyed look adults get when kids say something they haven't thought of themselves. She carefully put the pie on the patio table.

"Ella. You need to mind how you talk to grown-ups. Come on, git, or I'll be telling your ma how you're bothering Mr. Macabe."

I could tell that I'd just made another enemy. I slowly got out of Mr. Macabe's chair and wound my way past her and down the stairs. As I got to the bottom step, I turned and looked at her large frame and billowing bosom and stuck out my tongue. Her back was to me, so I added for good measure, "Mr. Macabe always wants me to visit and to stay as long as I want, not like *some* people." I drew out the "some" as long as I could to make my statement as offensive as could be. Then I turned and ran before she could clamber down the stairs to give me a whupping.

It was about three days later that I got to ask Mr. Macabe the question. We were sitting on the front porch, and I had just gone in to get us a glass of the lemonade that Mrs. Robertson had left him.

"She doesn't like me. She'll have a fit that I'm drinking all her lemonade," I warned him as I sipped.

Mr. Macabe smiled. He was "taking the sun," as he liked to call it. He waited till that ol' sun was high in the sky, which was just about two o'clock, and then he pushed the long deck chair right in its path. Then, with the cane he used sometimes, he maneuvered into the deck chair and pushed the headrest back, so he was lounging.

"Why you doing all that, Mr. Macabe?" I asked. "You'll only get blacker and blacker, till you're like me."

"And?"

Mr. Macabe was laid out as far back as his head would go. He was so relaxed, his voice sounded like it was coming from his toes all the way up through his legs and chest before bubbling out.

"Well, you wouldn't want that," I explained patiently.

"And why not, Ella? You and me, as Africans, we are built for the sun. We have to take it in, embrace it. It warms these old bones." He stretched out his arms as though to give the sun a warm embrace back. I scooted away and back into the shade; I didn't want to get any darker.

"Think like an African, Ella," Mr. Macabe said. "They don't love or hate their skin. They don't even have to think about its color. It's just a part of who they are. Their notion of beauty has nothing to do with the color of any part of their body. They sit in the sun all day long and never think about what it does to their color. What freedom!"

"You'll catch a sunstroke," I warned.

"Never!" was his enigmatic response.

Since he was relaxed, and he wasn't at all facing me, I decided to ask.

"So, Mr. Macabe," I started cautiously. I wasn't sure how to ask or what to say.

"Yes?" Now he sounded sleepy to me.

"Are S and F ever good for you? Like a pill or something? Why do people like to do it? Or is it always bad?"

"What are S and F, Ella?"

My mouth trembled, and the words stuck in my throat. I couldn't say the words out loud, and if he didn't know what they were, I didn't want to shock him.

"S and F are what, Ella?"

"S rhymes with *lex* and F with *buck*," I barely managed.

Mr. Macabe sat up so fast that I thought he'd keep moving and keel right over till his head touched his feet.

It took him a minute to start talking, and I was glad he couldn't see me. He turned to try to face me with those milky-white eyes, and his hand reached out to me but missed. His mouth started to move, but no words came out.

"What brought this on, Ella?" he finally said when he got caught up on his words. "You don't seem yourself today."

"Nothing, just wondering."

"Seems like there is a lot going on in that pretty little head of yours, Ella. How do you know about these adult words? Well, what am I saying," he added, almost to himself, "look at where we're living."

I waited.

When Mr. Macabe had finished talking to himself he just sat there for a while. I felt sorry for him. Here he was relaxing and taking in his sun, and I'd come to worry him.

"It's okay, Mr. Macabe. I'll ask Fats."

"You'll not do that." It was the loudest I'd ever heard him speak. "That boy will probably tell you that it's very good for you."

"It's not, right?" I said to be sure.

"No, it's not. It's never good for you till you're old and married. Got that, Ella?"

I nodded and said, "Mm-hmm," but then a thought came into my head. "But sometimes it's done when people hate you, right?"

Mr. Macabe beckoned me over with his hand, and when I came right up beside him, I could tell that he was troubled.

"Well, that's a different thing, Ella. When it's hate, then that's a very bad thing indeed." He looked as though he wanted to say more, but he stopped.

"So when is it good?"

"When you're married," Mr. Macabe said promptly.

"Well, what about all the people on Ricksville Road who are *not* married and have babies?" I didn't add anything about people like Ma, who were married but had done it anyway with someone else. I didn't know anyone who was like me. "Doesn't it mean that they done it anyway, without marriage?"

Mr. Macabe's face was the angriest I'd ever seen it. I should never have asked, now he was getting all worked up and muttering about all these men, having babies and leaving their kids for someone else to raise. "Littering the whole earth," he kept saying. "Women with no sense of their value. May as well be back in slavery times when the men were sold off and women and babies left behind. This time, they're doing the leaving all on their own, no one selling them off. Those that don't like black people must be laughing and laughing."

It seemed like Mr. Macabe had gone on into his own world, so I left him and went and filled my glass with some more lemonade. When I got back, he was sitting in the shade.

"Had enough of that ol' sun, Mr. Macabe?" I asked.

"Had enough of enough," he said grumpily.

Now, Ella, look at what you did, I said to myself. *You should have just asked Fats.*

When I finally got home that evening, it was to find that God had been working overtime on my behalf. Not only did Ma give me an extra helping of chicken and chips, but best of all, Leroy was gone.

"Where's he gone? Is it for long?" I whispered to Stevie at the dinner table.

"He said he had to make some money. That you'd stolen half his money. Not sure when he's coming back." Stevie gave a shrug and went back to eating.

"You believe that I stole his money?" I whispered urgently to Stevie.

Again, that shrug.

Why couldn't I just be happy that he was gone?

CHAPTER 18

Boston had been bad. Her mother became a secretary at a law firm and was always tired. They couldn't afford house help, and, for the next two summers, she and Randy had to scramble to find jobs, just so they could help pay the household bills. They were poor in Boston. Not dirt poor like the very poor in Mississippi, but blue-collar poor. Her father worked in an auto-mechanic shop those early years, his tinkering and fixing tractors and engines on the farm helping to earn a small living. They all hated Boston. It was too cold, too Irish, and too liberal. Her father had to mind the names he called people, because whenever he slipped up, they always looked shocked and disapproving, as though they, with their own biases, were somehow better than the ones that called a spade a spade. Despite all this, her father had hope then. In those early years, always social, he wasted no time finding friends in the network. They had chapters everywhere, and they were the ones that had found him the job, dropped off clothes, and put food on their table. Everyone told them that things would die down back home in Mississippi and they could head back. They were still rounding up people in the Klan. If the feds arrested one or two suspects, they would rest, and she could go back. Yet year after year her father got word that it was still too dangerous. She saw the hope die in his eyes, saw how much angrier he got, how much more he drank. The atmosphere in the house, once alive with hope, became crushing in its despair. It reverberated around them. Randy never made it to college and finally took off down south to Texas, never bothering to contact them again. She made only two friends— Carl, the boy next door, and Alison, the friend she sat with sometimes at lunch table during school. Her southern accent and her ill-fitting clothes had isolated her from the rest of her Bostonian classmates.

CHAPTER 19

Boston, Massachusetts, July 1969

This was her last entry. She could feel her excitement building as she skimmed the pages of her therapy journal and saw the memories she had written of her childhood laid out before her, snapshots of her life at five, six, eleven, and fifteen. She glanced around her room. She has been here for two and a half years. Living in this place that looked like a beautiful old mansion on the outside but was really a place for people that had lost their minds. Yet she was one of the lucky ones. She had recovered and she was getting out! She glanced over all the entries and skipped over the three pages she had written when she was quite mad. She had scribbled over those crazy pages, things that had happened when she was fourteen and fifteen, blacking them out with her pen. But she was proud of the rest of her journal entries. They had been as candid as the counselors encouraged and described everything about her Mississippi childhood that she could remember, as well as the move to Boston almost five years ago. She can't believe that she has been in this Boston mental hospital for this long. She has learned so much about herself and her father in these years, and it has finally paid off. They told her that it was rare that someone recovered from a total mental breakdown, but she has done it.

She thinks back to the event that brought her here. The counselors had brought her the section of The Boston Globe *when they felt she could handle it. One article was dated January 13, 1967, and the headline read "Father Kills Daughter's Fiancé After Argument." Another read "Judge Hands Down*

Ten Years in Prison for Killing All-American Boy Carl Stevens." There was a picture of her dad, tall and broad, with his head bowed and his arms shackled. Next to him was a bigger picture of Carl, smiling and handsome, his hair framing his angular face and strong chin. It was a black-and-white photo, so she couldn't see his blond hair or blue eyes, nor could she see his features, as much as she tried to peer into the picture. His features were blurred, just as they were in her mind.

They didn't need to remind her why she was here. She had been there when the two men she had loved most in the world had died. Carl had died a real death, and her father, a different type of death. People used to say they were joined at the hip, she and her father, two peas in a pod. The counselors said that the shock of the killing, at her beloved father's hand, was what caused her to spiral into madness. The counselors had dissected her father's behavior, showing her at every turn how much anger he had stored up. An anger that had been building, so intensified by his failures in Boston, that it was at the point of erupting. The drinking and the argument had set him off, they said, and Carl, unfortunately, was in the wrong place at the wrong time. She hadn't said anything in response to their inaccurate assessment, but something in the therapy sessions had finally gotten through. She could now see how violent and manipulative her father was. They had talked about her father's character—his Klan membership, his disregard for her mother's opinion about anything, his raging anger that had finally driven Randy away. But even so, it was hard to completely hate him, even as she acknowledged the truth about him. He had been a loving and devoted father, and they had been so close that she often felt that she knew his every thought, almost as though she were an intrinsic part of him, like a limb. But she could let him go. She had to, if she was to live her life free of him. She could pretend that he didn't exist, and that was made easier by his long prison sentence.

The door to her room opened finally. The counselors came in, all three of them. They were smiling.

"Do you think you are ready to leave, Kate?"

"Yes." Her response was vehement. She couldn't wait.

"You are still young, just twenty-one. You have the world ahead of you.
Your mother says she will send you to her cousin's farm in Canada, and then
when you are ready, you can apply to colleges. What do you think of that?"

She had said it sounded like a wonderful plan, and it did.

The counselors asked her to do something bold to signify her new freedom,
and freedom from her father. They had asked her if she wanted to change her
name. She had agreed. She chose a new one, Katherine. She could tell they
were a bit disappointed. It wasn't too far from Kate. However, she had easily
shed her father's name, Summerville, and decided to use her mother's maiden
name, St. James.

Just before she left, she wrote a final sentence in her journal.

I am no longer Kate Summerville, no longer part of Daddy.

I am now Katherine St. James.

PART TWO

CHAPTER 20

Princeton, New Jersey, April 1982

After getting over her initial surprise that Dr. Livenworth was black, his class had challenged her every bit as much as she had expected, and more. What was a class called The Rise of the Black Working Class if it didn't examine slavery, racism, the American civil war, and the rise of black consciousness, black migration, and civil rights. The class had questioned her every assumption, her every notion, and she had enjoyed the debates, arguing with Dr. Livenworth about the plight of the white farmer, the rising costs of labor after the civil war, the brunt of the North's oppression, and more. She had written brilliant essays using farm economics before and after the civil war, not arguing for slavery or oppression, but always maintaining the balanced view that after the Civil War white farmers were indeed in a tough spot, and it was important to understand their motives. How could she not argue that point? It was a fact, and she was probably the only one in class who had grown up on a farm in the South. One day Dr. Livenworth had asked the class to role-play. She was to play the role of a black sharecropper, and they were to keep their roles all week. At the end of the week, their assignment was to write a paper, twenty pages, from the perspective of whoever they were playing—landowner or sharecropper. As part of the paper, she was to assess how much income the sharecropper had at the end of each month after he had paid the landowner either rent or crops, as well as other necessities.

She had turned in the work and her paper had been returned with a D, with red comments all over the page. It was only then that she remembered that lank-haired freshman's assessment of Dr. Livenworth's grading. She couldn't continue to a thesis with a D grade, so she had panicked and asked to meet with him. Dr. Livenworth had been calm but clear. She hadn't followed instructions and kept to the identity she was given. Half of her paper focused on the role of a landowner. She had explained that she had grown up on a farm in the South and that her father had been a landowner in Mississippi. She said that if he assigned her the other role, the one of landowner, she could write a brilliant essay.

He was elderly, probably in his sixties. He had listened to her quietly, and when she was done, he said sorry, he didn't allow do-overs. Then he had asked a strange question: "Where is your father today?" She had replied that he had died in jail of a massive heart attack back in 1971, while serving a prison sentence. She hadn't said why he was in prison, and he hadn't asked. Instead, he just asked, "How did that make you feel?"

It was a strange, intimate question, and she wondered if the way she had responded had given away more than she thought. She'd felt nothing for her father since her release all those years ago. In a way, it was as though he had died that day along with Carl. Her father had lived only two more years after she had been released from the hospital, and she had never gone to visit him. At first, she had been in Canada and still recovering, so that was an easy ex-cuse. Then she had applied to NYU and started there the following year. She had never made it to the Boston State Penitentiary that year either, not because she was too busy, but rather because she was not ready. Not ready to be sucked into his orbit again. And then he had died suddenly.

She remembered when she got the news about her father's death. It was just a phone call. The voice at the other end had spoken quietly, sadly. She could choose to bury him, or the prison would do so. Her mother, by this time, was too sick to be called upon to make any decisions. She had just asked them to go ahead and do what they needed to do. Then she had sat down, had her evening meal, watched some TV, and gone to bed.

She was silent, not answering, while her paper lay on his desk between them. She was not sure why she started talking. Maybe to fill the awkward silence. Maybe because she would not be allowed to start her thesis research with a D. She told him about Carl's death, shot by her father. Then she added that her father was one of those angry, embittered people. It was her way of explaining why she felt nothing for her father. She was calm as she talked, factual and distant. She was also calculating. She made sure to distance herself from her father. He was the KKK member. She was the victim, the one with the fiancé, Carl, who had been killed. So she felt nothing, she said.

"Where was he laid to rest? Your Carl?" Dr. Livenworth asked suddenly.

The question surprised her.

She stared mutely at him. She had no idea.

She had gone plain mad right afterwards, and after that, she had closed that chapter of her life.

"You've shut the door on a cupboard full of hate, with such a father," he said finally. "But, tell you something, unless you open that door and do real cleaning, some of that hate's going to come crawling out, even if you think you've locked the door." He waved the paper in his hand at her.

Later she couldn't explain why she burst into tears. Why she had sobbed for so long. Perhaps it was the look of distaste on his face as he shook that paper in her face, after she had laid herself bare in front of him.

And he had just stood there, watching her. He hadn't comforted her or tried to calm her down. Instead, after she had finally gotten ahold of herself, he had handed her his handkerchief to wipe her face. Then he just said, "Redo the assignment. I'll grade it again, but you need to take your assigned role seriously." As she was leaving, she tried to give him back his handkerchief, but he ignored her outstretched hand. Instead, he said, "Go home, wherever that is, and try to unlearn what you have learned."

She can never forget the way he looked at her. It angered her as much as it haunted her. He thought he knew her when he did not. He knew nothing about who she had become, and what it had cost her to emerge on this side of sanity.

Perhaps it was that look, and the challenge of proving him wrong, that got her thinking about actually doing her research in Mississippi instead of New Jersey. Back home. She didn't know why she hadn't thought of it before.

She redid the assignment to the best of her ability, and to his credit, he had given her a B. She had a spark of an idea, did her research, and picked two towns she could potentially work in. One was a small southern town called Ricksville, and the other was her own town of Philadelphia. It seemed like fate smiled upon her because she had then won the prestigious Thurston Thesis Award, which would pay a small stipend for her research and accommodation. After that, there wasn't really any excuse not to go. She would spend the first few months in Ricksville, and then a couple of months in Philadelphia before returning to New Jersey.

She got on a bus and went home. Home to Mississippi.

CHAPTER 21

The day the white lady crossed the invisible line and walked down our dusty road and right into number 15 Ricksville Road, I was sitting by the side of the road in front of the walkway to our house with Cammy, who I was sort of talking to again. My face had stopped its twitching the day after Leroy left, and I was feeling calmer. My legs were crisscross apple sauce, and I was wearing a faded gray-and-blue pinafore dress. I doodled in the dirt, drawing great round circles with a stick while listening to Cammy go on and on about how to get Ron, Fat's best friend, to like her.

The lady's appearance stopped up Cammy's mouth, almost as though someone had shoved a cork in her open mouth. We stared at the apparition. We couldn't see her face from that far away, just a smattering of yellow, like a yellow jacket. As she drew closer, we took in the yellow pencil skirt, the matching checked yellow-and-white blouse, the white belt that cinched her waist into a tiny band, and the off-white pumps that were now partly covered in reddish dust.

I focused on her skin color to be sure, because there were some black folk who looked mighty white to me, but no, she was white, all right, as pale as the picket fence around Fats's house.

"What she doing here?" I mouthed to Cammy. No white person, other than the police driving around, had ever wandered down our street before, never so much as stepping even a toe into our part of Ricksville except when they put flaming torches on Nate's lawn in the dead of night.

In a few minutes, the lady was right across the street from us, her heels crunching in the stones and dust, her eyes fixed dead ahead, glancing neither to the left nor right. Her hair was dark brown and it swept to her shoulders, straight but curving slightly inwards to her neck. Her nose was tidy and pinched, and while we couldn't exactly see the shape of her lips, they were painted a bright crimson red.

She looked real enough, but oddly enough, she didn't look lost. If she was lost, she might have called over to us, perhaps a bit nervously, wondering whether she'd taken a wrong turn, but no, her stride was determined, purposeful. She passed us as though we weren't there, and as she did, my eyes scanned the black suitcase in her right hand, the old worn brown leather briefcase in her left hand, and the brown leather purse slung low over her left shoulder. She walked all the way to the end of the street, where it dead-ended, about three houses past mine but on the other side of the street, and turned up the path of number 15. Just marched up to the front door, opened it with a key she produced from her bag, and disappeared inside.

And just like that, Miss Katherine St. James came to live among us.

Cammy never did remember that she had a crush on Ron or that she had half of an elaborate plan to make him fall in love with her. Something far more interesting had come into our lives, igniting a boring summer with endless possibilities. Without saying a word, we walked the three houses down until we were opposite number 15 and sat at the side of the road. We sat gawking at her through her window as she moved back and forth, from the dining room, disappearing for a second behind the closed doors, and then into the living room before walking back again, carrying and arranging things. We sat there long after dusk had fallen and the fireflies had come out. Long after the bag of chips I had with me had emptied, filling our eyes with the endless movement of the lady, just like we were watching the first showing of a movie.

CHAPTER 22

The best thing about being in Mississippi was that as soon as the bus came off the highway, she knew she was close to home. She could almost smell a difference in the air when the bus stopped at that first small town and swung back its doors, letting in the still, warm, sticky air. She was shocked by how close to tears she was as the bus weaved in and out of narrow roads, stopping at small town after small town. It was home, and she felt embraced even though she had not been back since she was fifteen. The trees were like old friends, and as she gazed out, she saw, from her high vantage point, her father in the men walking on the streets below, doing everyday things such as loading their trucks or coming out of stores, their arms full of what should have been tools of some kind, or sometimes a baby or two.

The bus stopped in Philadelphia. She gazed, transfixed, through the window, at a main street that she still recognized after all this time, almost expecting her mother and father to walk by. In Princeton she had not spared a thought for her father, but suddenly her thoughts were full of him. She was shocked by the overwhelming sense of longing for what was. She retreated back into her seat, her heart pounding.

She was actually here.

Then, moments later, they were off again.

An hour and thirteen minutes later, the bus pulled into Ricksville. It didn't look like much at first glance. She got off the bus and glanced up and down at what had to be the main street. Tired-looking mom-and-pop stores, about fifteen, all in a row, and that was about it. A little ahead she saw what must be the post office, and some other official-looking buildings.

She dragged her suitcase from under the bus, and then asked the driver for directions to South Ricksville Street. He had shrugged, but then a fellow passenger, also getting off, had looked at her oddly, before pointing her in the right direction.

Now she moved through the scarcely furnished house, putting her things away. She arranged her notebooks and pens on the dining room table. Then she folded her clothes and put them away upstairs in the wardrobe. She could tell that she was on edge. Calm down, she said to herself. She counted to ten in English, then in French, and finally in Russian, all the while breathing in and out deeply after each word. It was something the counselors had taught her. It was a technique that had worked for her and still did, all these years later.

She picked up each item of clothing, inspecting them for signs of wear. Unfortunately, even her garage-sale clothes were picked with exacting care, and she despaired finding something that allowed her to fit in better. She was coming up short. She was so excited to be back in Mississippi that she hadn't thought too much about her first stop. Now, why hadn't she thought about the reality of being in a poor, black part of the town? That reality had dawned on her as she walked from the bus station to the house, and had seen the potholed roads, filled with red dirt, the worn-out buildings, and, most jarring of all, the people. Except for a few who looked like they were dressed in their Sunday best, many wore faded clothing, held together with a dignity that belied their impoverished condition, and served only to highlight her bright and well-fitted clothing. It was on Ricksville Road that she finally woke up from the bubble that had been her life at Princeton. Princeton, with its manicured lawns and majestic period buildings, was indeed an island, or an oasis, where real life stopped, and your mind could quite literally just feast on the buffet of intellectual discourse around you.

There was something that had been bothering her the last couple of days. She couldn't figure out what it was but finally it dawned on her: She knew she would be living in an all-black part of town. The owner of the house had made that clear and asked at least a couple of times if she knew that and still wanted to rent. But what she hadn't expected was that she would recognize them. Not in any specific way, but rather in the slow gait of black people used to walking in the sun, in the way they looked down as she walked by, and by their loud laughter. As a child, she had seen these types of people almost every day of her life, on their farm and walking about in the town.

It was then the fear came, hitting her like a bucket of cold water thrown in her face.

She was loath to admit it, but perhaps it was something about living in their neighborhood that set her on edge.

She told herself to stop being stupid. Why on earth would she be afraid of them? In college her friends were from all over the world and were many different shades.

She told herself again to stop being stupid. This was not the turbulent '60s, these were the '80s, and these were not the same black people that lived in Philadelphia in the '60s, when she was growing up. She herself had grown up, moved on, and now was a graduate student at Princeton. She wasn't Kate, she was Katherine, someone with a completely different history. She repeated this till she felt herself relax.

She could do this.

CHAPTER 23

Ma shook her head in irritation when I told her that there was a white woman staying on Ricksville Road, and she said bitterly that she guessed these folks could just go and live wherever they pleased, and kick hardworking black renters out of their homes by offering double the rent, but I didn't pay her much attention. I didn't even listen as Ma muttered about what would happen if one of us went to live in their neighborhoods. Instead, I set about sharing the astonishing news, first with Fats, as a bribe for forgiveness for how rude I had been to him. Rumors have legs—fast ones. By three o'clock, the entire neighborhood of kids was buzzing with gossip. Later that afternoon, at least half a dozen of us stood on the dusty road at the end of the white lady's driveway, staring at her house as though we could miraculously see through its walls. It was curiosity that brought us to that spot, that and the lack of something better to do, but it was something else that kept us there, even after an hour had passed and then two. I didn't know exactly what it was, but without anyone saying so, I knew it had to do with the fact that no white person had ever come to live in South Ricksville before.

Number 15 was almost identical to our house in size, but it had a few touches that made it much better. For one, it had six high steps which widened into a large raised front porch, making it look much bigger than ours. Our house had one small step, followed by a slab of concrete and then the door. Her house was painted a bright white with blue trim, whereas the paint on our yellow house had all but peeled off. Tati and Sonny, twins who were Stevie's age, used to live there with their ma and dad. They had left, suddenly, a month before Miss St. James arrived and the landlord had painted it and made it look brand-new again.

It was Fats who took the first bold step. He walked right up to the house, zigzagging across the front yard to avoid the planted shrubs, and headed straight to the living room window. He reached out and, using the window trim as leverage, hoisted himself up and remained there for about five seconds with his face smushed against the glass before crashing to the ground. He did this twice more before coming back a hero.

"So what you see? You see her?" A dozen competing voices filled the air.

Fats's smile was broad. He knew how to milk a crowd.

"Yep, sure did." He paused. Sat down right on the ground and folded his arms. About ten kids sat down around him, as close as they could get.

"I tell you, she's in there. Gave me a little wave and all."

His voice was drowned in hoots of disbelief and exclamations and questions. Ron, just to show he could be as brave as Fats, jumped up and headed to the house, causing a trail of boys to quickly follow. Soon, they were all on one another's backs, peering in. We could barely see the window, what with three rows of kids taking turns on the bigger boys' backs. Cammy and I were the last to join them. We couldn't see through the throng that pressed their faces against the window, but we heard enough from the boys babbling to know that she had no curtains, no tables, a couple of chairs, no rugs, and a bare wooden floor. There seemed to be no light shades, just a single bulb hanging from the ceiling and lighting up her pantyhose, hanging on a line that stretched clear across her living room. As for the lady, she was nowhere to be seen.

Observing Miss St. James soon became a morning ritual. Since Fats was the tallest, he would hoist himself up to the window and call out whatever she was doing. Sometimes it was "She's having breakfast" or "She's sweeping the floor." Once he called out that she was taking off her underwear, and there was such a stampede that ten boys literally climbed up Fats to see what was going on. Turned out that Fats was just being Fats. After that, we enlisted little Ty to get on Gerard's shoulders and look, as insurance to keep Fats honest.

I couldn't believe that Miss St. James didn't see or hear us, but the minute she started making for the door, Fats would shout, "She's coming," and we'd all scatter. Then she would emerge, looking neither to the left nor right. She would just slam the front door, lock it, check that lock twice, and be on her way, walking through the red dust that covered parts of Ricksville Road. Sometimes she had on her black boots and other times just plain brown pumps, but her hair was always in a ponytail. We watched it bouncing to and fro as she strode all the way up the street, till she was a small dot that eventually disappeared. Where to, we had no idea.

We had our theories of why she had come and what she did. Simon, who lived on Perry but who spent many of his days on Ricksville, said she was a secret agent from the government, leastways that is what his father said, and he had marched with the great Dr. King. We looked at Simon with growing respect till Ron interrupted to say he'd heard that she was just an old hooker who had customers up on Monrose, two streets north of Perry.

"No, she's not." Cammy got all het up because she was convinced that Miss St. James looked like a model she had seen on TV. "She can't be anyway, no men ever come to her house, and hookers are hookers even when they get home after work."

As the theories swirled around, and our voices got louder and louder as the arguments heated up, it seemed like the only thing we could agree on was that the white lady was in the wrong place—we all knew that she shouldn't be here, in the black part of town.

"She must be poor," I said. I wasn't firm on this notion because she had nice clothes when I saw her, but she had no furniture when even the poorest of us had a table and some chairs, even if they were secondhand, mismatched, or beaten up.

"I'm sure someone would give you a place for free if you were white and said you had no place to stay except with the niggers," Ron chimed in.

"You watch your mouth, Ron," I called out, "or I'll march on down to your ma and just say, 'Mrs. Rivers, do you know what word your Ron just said out there in front of all the kids in Ricksville?'"

"Shuddup, you."

"You shut your stupid face."

"Piehole."

"Turd."

And before we knew it, Ron and I were up in each other's face, shouting our heads off.

"Stop it," a voice called from far away, but I didn't pay it any mind. I was too busy looking at Ron's face. The one that always taunted and teased. My anger, never bottled deep enough, came bubbling up. Then I heard someone scream "Fight!" and when I looked down at my balled-up fists, they were smarting.

The next few moments were a blur. Ron was on top of me and pummeling and I was hitting back as fast and furious as I could when I heard a strange voice shouting. The voice was so strange that it stopped Ron, and even though I kept punching, the stillness in his body made me twist out from under him and look up. It was her, Miss St. James, right up close and on the ground beside us. Eyes brown, skin so close to mine that I could see the tiny creases around her eyes and on either side of her mouth. She looked older than from far off. Her mouth was open, and her thin lips, painted their usual bright red, started yelling like you never thought a lady could yell.

"Get off her. How can you hit a girl? Is this what happens in my front yard when I go to work? You two, come with me." Her hands grabbed the neckline of our T-shirts and, with surprising strength, she yanked us up. We were too shocked to say a word. The crowd of kids around us parted and melted into the bushes, till seconds later it was only Fats still watching us, standing safely away on the other side of the street. Before we knew it, Miss St. James had grabbed our wrists and marched us straight to the front door of her house.

Now, if she'd been black, we wouldn't have been terrified. We would have hung our heads and walked in shame, as meekly as lambs to the slaughter, but with this lady holding our hands, we glanced at each other, bound by mutual terror. It was a terror born of the in-bred knowledge that she could be a racist that made us start twisting and pulling our hands, trying to escape, but her bony fingers pressed down and tightened, stopping our efforts. My heart was thumping so loudly it was coming through my ears, and then I made the mistake of glancing at Ron. His lips were pressed together, hard and trembling, and his eyes were tightly shut to stop the tears. His terror flew right over to me, and I bit my lower lip so hard that it bled. The tinny taste filled my mouth.

Her mistake was in letting go of our hands to reach for her keys to open the front door. No black woman would have done that; she'd have tucked our hands firmly under each armpit with such a hold you would've thought your hand was in the jaws of a lion, before digging into her purse for keys. As Miss St. James fumbled in her bag for her key, our hands were free; for a few seconds, we stood in a daze till Fats shrieked, "Run!" from across the street, jump-starting our brains into flight mode. Ron shot over the stairs with me stumbling along behind, until he swiftly steadied me and pulled me along and finally pushed me forward, ahead of him. Once we were on the street, we didn't stop, we pushed our chests out and ran like our feet were on fire. I did not stop till I came up on Mr. Macabe's house. Ron bolted up the stairs after me and we fell onto the porch with a clatter, heaving. In minutes, there were at least ten kids all swarming around Mr. Macabe's patio table, talking loudly and over one another.

"She would've called the *pooleece*," Fats said, panting and out of breath from all that running he wasn't used to.

"No, she looked nice. She was probably going to give you milk and cookies." This was ever-optimistic Cammy.

"No way. She probably has a husband who'll hand you over to the Klan."

It was during this heated discussion that Mr. Macabe came out to see what all the ruckus was about. We quickly moved from the table and cleared a path for him.

"Now, what's all this excitement?" he asked, after a moment. "You all sound like a swarm of angry bees. How many of you are on my porch anyway?"

"About twelve," I said.

"My, my, what's got all of you stirred up this much?"

"The white lady, down on the other end of Ricksville Road. She almost kidnapped Ella and Ron," Fats answered, still a little winded.

"Kidnapped?" Mr. Macabe's head jerked up. "Now, that's a serious accusation."

"Well, Ella and Ron were fighting and she came along and yanked them and was taking them inside her house."

Mr. Macabe seemed stuck on the word *fighting*, and try as we could to move him past that to the bigger picture, he wasn't seeing it.

"Fighting, Ella? That's not like you. Ron, you know it's not seemly to fight a girl." Mr. Macabe shook his head disapprovingly. "Fighting? In the street? Now, what was that all about?"

"Ron used the word *nigger*, and that started the fight." This was from the idiot Mark. A Ricksville Road boy who always spoke first and thought later.

And there it was. Like a bomb had been put in the middle of the porch and someone had lit its fuse, for it sure lit up Mr. Macabe. And we had thought the word *fighting* was a problem.

"*Nigger*? Do you know what that word really means, what it signifies? You'd better go ask your parents! Think you can use that word any way you want? That's a dirty word you don't need to use."

We knew he was just getting warmed up. The kids who were standing on the lower steps were just barely able to turn around and tiptoe away, but the rest of us stood frozen on the porch like we were trapped between an alligator and a hornet's nest, unable to move, because Mr. Macabe could hear a whisper from as far as a block away.

Mr. Macabe's words took on a buzzing sound that drowned out our individual thoughts, making us fall half asleep, but in between we caught snatches that made us think. Made us wonder why Europeans had visited Mali, Great Zimbabwe, and other places long before slavery and written about their experiences, marveling at the learning, wealth, and civilizations, yet slavery could happen just a few hundred years later. We knew slavery existed before it ever showed up in Europe and America, but the thought that it had no color dimensions was new to us. Mr. Macabe said that in the Bible, slavery happened between Hebrew people and that it was often voluntary, or to pay off a debt, and sometimes it was through war. Even then, God had told Jewish people that they had to release their Hebrew slaves after seven years, no exception, unless a slave wanted to stay. That part we got. The part that just had us staring at each other and making faces was when Mr. Macabe started in about all the marketing stuff, about black folks being on the wrong side of a business deal.

When can we leave? I wondered. I was going to kill that Mark boy. When Mr. Macabe asked us how we thought slave sellers and the government convinced an entire population that black slaves for white people was justifiable, we kept silent, our tongues held back because it was too complicated for us.

"Marketing!" Mr. Macabe answered for us. He started thumping his hand on the table. "Convince the ignorant populace that these slaves and all of their type were subhuman, unintelligent, and so on. A slight edge over your horse and donkey. It was a smear campaign that the population bought hook, line, and sinker. Rushed to buy. Didn't want to think it was wrong because of the economic incentive. The government said here were these people, not even above retard grade, ready to work for free, and everyone rushed out to buy or expand their farms, make more money. Then they sealed it all by forbidding people to teach the slaves to read and write English, and made us forget our own languages."

Our shoulders slumped as we tried to keep still and stifle the urge to move our arms and legs, jostle one another, or even make one another snicker behind Mr. Macabe's back. On the other hand, we knew that this was serious, that slavery was a serious business, and that he was sure getting worked up over it. So we stood as straight as we could. We got it now. It was marketing that sold the slave as a "beast of burden," and the government that forbade people to allow the slave to learn to read or write, on the "pretext that he couldn't or that he could merely imitate." Could we go now?

But Mr. Macabe hadn't finished. "Now, how many people do you think taught their slaves mathematics and reading? Hardly anyone. Why didn't they at least try, as a scientific experiment? Why?"

We stared again blankly, even when he asked us, "Have you ever given a book to a horse to read?" He knew better than to wait for an answer. "No? Exactly. You wouldn't even think of giving a book to a horse or ask it to do a math problem, because you wouldn't expect that a horse would be able to read or do math. And likewise, if you were a slave owner, you wouldn't think of giving a book to a black person to read. Now, when they did find out that a few slaves were hiding and reading and could do math, they had to think of something different very quickly. So then they said, well, they can do a little math and read, but not as well as white people. Now, if they had set up a good system of schools that was truly equal, well, it would have brought down their whole deck of cards, would've made their whole system come tumbling down. Greatest marketing ploy ever. Still working its magic today. And that word *nigger* sums up what they thought of us, all wrapped up in that little itty-bitty word. So don't use it."

We looked at one another, thoroughly ashamed and chastened. In our shame, we pretended he couldn't hear as we started to slip silently from the porch, but Mr. Macabe said, "Now, about that woman."

His words stopped our mass exit. Made us turn right back on our heels and scurry back.

"I heard . . ."

We all held our breaths.

". . . that her name is Miss Katherine St. James. Don't rightly know what she does or what she wants, but she needed a place to do some writing for a few months and I think everything else farther north is too expensive."

We exhaled. Disappointed. That was it?

"Bet she really is a spy," Ron said.

"She's a pros—" Fats stopped himself and looked at Mr. Macabe. He didn't want to set him off again.

"Why don't you just ask her when you see her?" Mr. Macabe said calmly. "If it means that much to you all."

We mulled over this novel idea.

"You mean we should talk to her?" I asked, still feeling a little shook up by all the talk on slavery.

Mr. Macabe shook his head impatiently. "What I just told you has nothing to do with Miss St. James. For all we know, she's a very nice person. She came to live here of her own accord—far as we know, no one's forcing her to, right? So she must want to live in this part of town. Person who wants to do that must be a bit of okay, in my book. As to the kidnapping—you know as well as I do that she was fixing to give you an earful of what-for. Wouldn't any ma on this street do the same thing? They'd probably give you a good whupping first, though."

As we took in his words, his quiet logic sunk in. Fats was the first to speak it. "She must be okay. She came here, right?" We all nodded and then said our goodbyes to Mr. Macabe, who waved us off, telling us to stay out of trouble.

And that was the day that Katherine St. James became accepted by us kids.

◈

For a while, the boys followed Miss St. James around like little puppies, but the sight of her walking to and fro on Ricksville Road became familiar, and eventually they lost interest. Soon it was "Good morning, Miss St. James," as they ran past her on their way to the river. The first boy would yell it, followed by a chorus of five or so other boys. When even this greeting became too much for them, they belted right by her, smiling if their eyes caught hers, but too intent on the fun that lay ahead to utter even a quick greeting. She never replied, but the boys never seemed to notice.

Cammy and I, having nothing much to do, still sat for hours wondering what she did. Every morning we came out of our houses at exactly eight thirty, to look at the outfit she had put together for that day. We stood on Ricksville Road and stared as she walked past, noting each article of clothing. It was often that yellow skirt from the first day, but she had such a bevy of belts and tops that she gave us something to talk about during the hour that followed, and we learned much about how to stretch out your clothes and look like you had so much more than the three skirts and eight tops that we saw her mix and match from one day to the next.

"She's not that pretty," I said finally, after a week of watching her.

Cammy didn't say a word. It was better for her to remain quiet than to acknowledge she was wrong.

"Kitty's much more beautiful," I continued.

"Well, everyone knows that Kitty's from outer space or something," Cammy retorted. "That's not normal pretty. I think Miss St. James is . . . well, good-looking."

"She's old," I said, "much older than even Ma."

"White ladies can look old if they spend too much time in the sun, but not Miss St. James," Cammy said finally.

"Give it up, Cammy," I said. "She's nothing like a model. She's about forty and real everyday-looking."

Even Cammy had nothing to say about that, so I turned on my heel and went inside the house, but not before hearing her taunt, "You only jealous, Ella, that you can't look half as good as that."

I slammed the door with a loud thud. I could tell that I was going to get plenty sick of that old white woman.

CHAPTER 24

Mid-July arrived like a slow mule dragging a river of heat and mugginess behind it. There were only a few kids out on the street now, because it was just too hot. Most were inside their houses sucking on ice cubes or staring glumly at the fan, as it buzzed, as close to their faces as could be. I thought for a moment about stopping by the diner, because it was the only place with anything close to air-conditioning. Nate had installed a rickety, noisy air conditioner unit in the restaurant window that worked on and off, sometimes blowing frigid air, cold as the North Pole, and other times, warm, steamy air, but that, too, would be better than sweltering on the stoop of our house. It was only the thought of walking all the way there in the heat that kept me rooted. I was still making up my mind when I saw Fats, looking like chocolate melting in the sun. His shirt was off, and he was using it as a towel as he came along, dripping and heaving, past my house. He put up his hand in a lazy hello as he trudged on. I returned the wave and wondered what he was doing at my end of Ricksville. Maybe he'd been to see Miss St. James. That in turn had me wondering how she was surviving the heat, but my mind turned to an even bigger problem: Miss St. James was causing a real ruckus in Ricksville without even knowing anything about it. When Mr. Graves had stopped by during the week to fortify himself with some of Ma's whiskey, he had gone on about how she was just a spy looking for another way to bring down black folk.

"She's going to stop by Washington, DC, on her way back to the North and report what we like to eat and drink, and how we make our money. Then they'll try to find some way to take that money back again by raising the prices on the very things that black folk like to eat and drink. They can't rest now that we are no longer slaves. Want us back just like before. Those were their good ol' days."

"Come on," Ma had said, and I could tell she was getting fed up, but whether it was because of what he said or because he had reached out, on his own, and taken another tipple of the bottle, I didn't know. "Think the government all the way in Washington, DC, is worried about what we think in this heap of nothing of a town?"

But Mr. Graves was mighty stubborn about it. "You watch my words," he said. "The price of chitlins, collard greens, and baby-backs going to soar."

"Go on, you," Ma said, shooing him out. She made it seem like a joke but I knew that if she could, she would have taken her broom and swept him out.

And Ty's grandmother had been talking all up and down the street, to anyone who would listen. She was one of those bent-over kindly grandmothers who somehow always ended up taking in her grandchildren, with her children nowhere to be seen. Ty and Ray were her grandchildren and lived with her for as long as I could remember. Four years ago, another two grandkids had shown up, and it looked like they, too, were here for good. When I was working at the diner last Saturday, Ty's grandma told Nate and Ma that she was clean out of her mind with worry. Real worried about her seventeen-year-old grandson, Ray, because he was in and out of the house like a yo-yo, and she couldn't keep tabs on him right because of her age. "What if," she had said, "that white

lady said that Ray or one of the men on Ricksville Road had done
something to her?"

"Now, hush now," Nate had scolded her. "That Ray boy, well,
he has enough sense to stay so far away from that woman that you
wouldn't catch him two miles downstream of her."

She had ignored him and went on fussing. "We don't even know
how she rented that place. It belongs to that racist Mr. Collins up
past Main Street. How she know him?"

Nate just shook his head. "For all you know he put an ad in the
paper, is all."

Ty's grandma just shook her head. "I'm afraid for Ray. These
young ones aren't afraid of anything. They know about what happened during the height of the movement, but they can't feel it.
Knowing it and living it are two different things. It's history to
them. They don't know what we've seen. Can you imagine what
would happen if that lady got it in her head to call the police on
some pretext or other? Why, they would sweep through this place,
arresting all our boys and men over the age of thirteen. Remember
the killing of those three boys turning out the vote? Remember
Emmett Till?"

Nate said quietly, "Ain't nothing no one's ever going to forget."

Why Ty's grandma was bringing up the lynchings again, I didn't
know. Made me feel all unsettled inside and gave me the shivers.
How could Miss St. James cause all this fuss and worry just by
being here? When Ma and Ty's grandma were out of earshot, I'd
asked Nate why everyone was so fixed on Miss St. James.

"Ella, you haven't been through what we have. It's hard to forget.
Wasn't but eighteen years ago when those election workers were
killed by the Klan, and this whole state was burning up. Black folk
couldn't even walk around freely without fear of being killed."

I was sure Miss St. James didn't know she was the center of all gossip. Funny how it seemed like we had nothing to talk about before she moved into number 15. You'd think with all that talking, folks would find an excuse to go up to her and plain ask her what she was doing here, but no, no adult wanted to be seen talking to her. Not with Mississippi's history resting on their shoulders. Not with reminders about what happened with Nate's Diner. She had to notice that when she was walking up Ricksville Road, heading to Main Street, anyone walking down it would quickly step to the side and seem to walk fast in the other direction, or if they were going the same direction, they would step from the side of the road right into the middle of the road, giving her a side-eyed look, as they lengthened their stride and went on by, all the while noting exactly what she was carrying and where she'd be heading. But Miss St. James always nodded to the ladies in a friendly kind of manner, and a few would feel ashamed enough to nod back, just barely, and keep on walking. Maybe she thought that was how black folks were, mighty unfriendly. Well, it certainly seemed that apart from Mr. Macabe and us kids in the neighborhood, no one else would be talking to her.

⸻◈⸻

The summer heat of Mississippi was so bad that grown-ups always walked slowly, stopping to mop their heads or to catch a breath and sigh about how hot it was, or how humid. Mr. Macabe always said that the rhythm of Ricksville was the slow shuffle of the women and the slow, cool jaunt of the men. Miss St. James didn't fit in at all in that way, too. She walked as though she had somewhere important to get to in a hurry. Her eyes always looked dead ahead of her, never even glancing to the left or right.

One day I happened to be twenty steps behind her, playing a game of stepping in her shoe prints and fixing my toe at the exact dot her heel made in the dust. She likely heard me stomping behind her but she never turned. She kept a brisk pace towards Main Street and I wondered if all the people walked like this from wherever it was she came from. How odd, I thought, walking like a robot without taking any time to gaze at the trees or holler at that sun for how badly it was treating you.

Mr. Graves walked by heading the same direction and gave her a wide berth just as she also stepped aside and shied away, causing me to have to jump almost twice the distance to stay in her shoe print. I stifled a giggle. Seemed to me that they were both staying mighty clear of each other. She carried on walking fast till Nathaniel came down our side of the road whistling. He was seventeen and had graduated school last year but not well enough to make it to college. He didn't have a job, so he lived with his ma on Perry, and occasionally came onto Ricksville Road to find out if there were any odd jobs to be done. The minute Miss St. James saw Nathaniel, she stopped in her tracks and moved clear off the road into the bushes, causing me to groan when I lost her footprint. Nathaniel didn't seem to notice; he raised his hand and waved at me as he walked by. This time I didn't giggle. The next and last time a man walked by us, Miss St. James stopped, standing so still you'd have thought she had turned to stone. This time, I was close enough to see the shudder that shook her body and the fear in her face, making it even paler than usual.

I left her at the Ricksville Library on Main Street, ran up to Nate's, and, at the counter, threw my words down triumphantly. "Miss St. James doesn't like black people. Or maybe just black men," I amended. "She looks scared when they are around."

Nate didn't even raise an eyebrow. "Aren't they all, baby?" he said, and went right back to frying.

"She does nod to the women a little," I added, thinking, *but never the men*. "Why is she so scared and if she's so scared, why is she here?"

Nate shrugged, then said, "Ella, you beat a dog till it's so afraid all you have to do is to say boo and it will run into a corner. You get used to that. Then one day you're walking into the yard without a care in the world and that ol' dog slips in behind you and bites you. Makes you want to whip it all the more but now you're afraid. That ol' dog is not as afraid as you thought, or perhaps it's afraid but now it hates you more than it fears you. You don't know which is true but all you know is you got to be careful lest it come up again from behind and bite you. So you lock it up, good and tight. But you wonder if it might just slip out."

I knew Nate just told me that dog story to mess with me, so I didn't mind him none. I just had one question. "What about that ol' dog? How's it feeling after the man locks it up?"

"Well, being locked up all the time he's feeling hate and fear. The minute that hate grows bigger than the fear, well, you better watch out for that ol' dog."

I thought for a bit, and said, "I feel sorry for that dog. I'd treat him nice, give him some bones, stroke his fur."

Nate laughed and laughed. "You do that, Ella," he said finally, wiping his eyes.

The way Nate was talking, I figured he could have talked about dogs all day long. Made me wonder why he didn't just go get himself one. I did notice though that he still never answered my question about why Miss St. James would move to Ricksville if she didn't like black people.

Leaving Nate's an hour later, I spotted her just coming out of the Ricksville Library, her right arm clutching about six heavy books. Mr. Wilkinson's hardware store was just a few doors away, and as usual, he was standing in the doorway, giving black folk that dirty look that kept them stepping right past his store and to the bus stop that would take them ten minutes away to the other hardware store, the one that didn't mind who came in, so long as the money they were holding was green.

I watched him tripping over himself to get at Miss St. James. I didn't think she was that pretty, but you would have thought she was the most beautiful woman on earth the way he carried on. He pulled those books out of her hands before she even had time to say hello, and before I could wonder what he was doing, he had turned back into his store and within seconds he was out again, her library books now sticking out of a nice white carrier bag. Miss St. James put out her hand and touched his shoulder, and then he was a-talking, smiling and laughing—we'd never seen him so much as show his teeth before. He was all ready to walk her home, too. I could tell by the way he took out his keys from his pocket and locked the store door. But then she stopped him and pointed south, past Main Street. He shook his head and pointed north, as though she was confused. I know he was thinking, *This is just another lady with no sense of direction*. But she shook her head slowly and pointed south again. Mr. Wilkinson sure stopped smiling then. He now took her arm, almost twisting it, and unlocked that store door, opened it, and pulled her inside and shut the door. I waited to see what would happen; after fifteen or so minutes, she was out again. And she looked mad. I could tell because she just stepped right onto Main Street without looking left or right to check for cars, and she crossed the street real fast. She'd already been walking fast on her way to the library, and now she was almost running.

I had to run to keep up. On Ricksville Road, four men passed by on the other side of the street. If she was black, they would have crossed over and quickly said, "Let me get that bag for you," even if it meant them walking ten minutes back in the other direction, or they might have said, "Whoa, girl, slow down, whatcha walking so fast for? These aint slavery days." They didn't so much as glance at her, but I knew they saw her. Watched her as the pupils of their eyes slid all the way to the side, stopping right at the corners, all the while thinking the same thing everybody was: *What is that woman doing here? Just isn't right.*

Seemed to me that Miss St. James's arrival was just stirring the pot, unsticking all those things we wanted to leave stuck at the bottom of the pot.

That night, after I said my prayers and prayed for Mr. Macabe, and Nate, and everybody in our house, I added Miss St. James to the list. I wasn't so sure why I did it, but I thought of her all alone in that house, the only white woman for miles, surrounded by a sea of black people. Nice people for the most part, but she wouldn't know that. And I now knew that she was scared of us. Just as scared of us as we were of her.

CHAPTER 25

*She had been watching the one girl for a while. The midnight-black child
who fought like a tiger and lived across the street. She saw her daily because
she would sooner or later sit across the street and stare at her window. Sometimes the girl was alone, and other times she was with her friend, the one
with the long hair. Occasionally she was with a group of noisy friends. It
had made her uncomfortable to be watched so closely, and she had thought
of investing in some curtains. She had ultimately decided against it—she
would miss the morning sun shining through the windows.*

    *She had been to the library several times already and met the librarian,
Ms. Perty. She was in her early fifties, with a short bob and thin, nervy
hands that had shaken a little when she told her about the type of books she
would be looking for, if not in their small library, then ordered from other
libraries in the state. She had also met Mr. Wilkinson. He had been kind,
till he found out where she was living. Didn't the landlord know she was
white, he had demanded, and would be alone, surrounded by nothing but
niggers? And when she had responded yes, he had immediately demanded
to know her landlord's name. He had cursed Mr. Collins out, calling him a
Jew and a few other choice words, for putting her in such a dangerous situ-
ation. She had told him that she knew how to take care of herself and that
Mr. Collins had treated her like the adult that she was, someone who knew
what she was doing and was able to take care of herself. She had walked out
irritated, but now she was even more conscious of how alone she was. What
did she look like to those black men walking by? She could be a target. A
well-dressed white woman walking alone up that dusty road. She tried to*

dampen down her rising fear, but it was always lurking there. So instead she walked with determination, without drawing attention to herself, striding, not walking, head high, eyes facing dead ahead, glancing neither to the left nor to the right.

If she was like this now, how on earth was she going to have enough courage to knock on their doors and interview them about black southern society during the migration, and what civil rights had done for them in the twenty years that followed? Her carefully researched topic, which seemed so right in the lauded halls of Princeton, seemed so silly here, absurd even, in the reality of this black town. She thought of her topic again. She was beginning to think she was mad to have chosen it. Yet there was no going back—she had already signed a six-month lease.

She looked out her window again. The same group of ten or twelve kids were walking by, this time not paying much attention to her house. She saw the girl again, the same one who had been fighting that boy in her front yard, and who was always staring at her window. She was walking behind the group, this time with the fat boy.

It was then, suddenly, that she had her brilliant idea.

CHAPTER 26

If anyone had told me that ten days after meeting her I would be sitting on a wooden chair, leaning on Miss St. James's table, I would have told them to shut up, that they were a bunch of lying juggernauts. That was my current favorite word. But there I was, sitting at her table, staring down into a plate heaving with a slice of Ma's apple pie. The way it had happened was not even that complicated; Miss St. James had simply walked to our house and introduced herself. I wasn't there when it happened, but from what Stevie said, Ma had just about slammed the door in her face before remembering that she was too genteelly bred for that, and for certain, her poor white father would be rocking in his grave. So she had plastered a smile on her face and opened the front door a smidgeon. But Miss St. James had pressed so close, Ma was forced to open up the door a little more, and before she knew what had happened, Miss St. James was sitting on the couch. Genteel manners surely demanded that Ma return the visit, only she wouldn't be seen dead walking over to Miss St. James's house, so there I was, the very next day, standing in the doorway with a pie in my hand. Ma's voice still rang ominously in my head: "Now, you give it to her and you come straight back. She came all the way here, and we have to try to be neighborly, but you come straight back. I heard about how you kids have been harassing her, hanging all over her front lawn. Never let it be said that my children are making fools of themselves over that lady. Hear me?"

I had nodded sharply. "Yes, ma'am."

"Get right back here or there'll be a whupping for you."

I had nodded again.

I heard the clip, clip of Miss St. James's shoes on the wood floors. The door opened, just a little at first, and then wider, and then Miss St. James appeared in the doorway smiling at me. She was wearing a straight black skirt with black pumps and the red polka dot shirt Cammy liked so much. I handed the pie to her. She made a great show of unwrapping it and oohing and aahing before saying, "I must have a slice while you're here, so you can tell your ma how much I liked it. Come on in and have a seat, Ella."

I was so pleased that she knew my real name, I just started talking without thinking.

"You could have looked through the window to see who it was first," I said, pointing to the living room window, "if you weren't sure." Then I fell silent. I couldn't believe that I hadn't even said good morning first. Those words had popped into my head and come flying out. But she didn't seem perturbed.

"Thank you for that bit of advice. I will remember it next time. Save me from opening the door and finding no one there."

"They still do that?" I asked, surprised.

"Now and then. Not every day now. But boys will be boys."

I stepped slowly over the threshold and closed the door behind me, noticing that she now had a dining table and six chairs. In the living room were a three-seater sofa and a small coffee table, but nothing else. No pictures on the walls, no rugs, and nothing matched. The laundry line for drying her underwear still ran right across her living room.

It was only when the pie was on the plate in front of me and I'd taken my first bite that it dawned on me that Ma was probably already grabbing hold of her switch to use on me for staying too long. I couldn't gobble it up, could I? I couldn't ask to take it home with me. I was stuck. I stabbed my fork in the pie and tried to break off as big a piece as I could without being rude. As soon as it was in my mouth, I saw her looking expectantly at me. Had she said something?

"I was asking, did you go to church today?"

I nodded. My mouth was too full to speak.

"Did you?" I asked politely back, after a gulping swallow.

"Oh no," she said lightly. "I'm not really one for going to church, don't really believe." An instant later she had covered her mouth with her hand. "I guess I shouldn't have said that. What I mean, Ella, is that church is not for me."

"Close your ears, God," I muttered under my breath.

"What did you say?"

She was looking hard at me. Had she heard me?

"I was just wondering why you don't believe in God when all you have to do is to go outside and look up, and all around you."

She laughed, a tiny tinkle of a laugh, as though I had said something funny when I hadn't at all.

I quickly swallowed the last of the pie and got up, just as she was asking if I wanted some milk.

"No thanks, got to go or Ma will have my hide."

Now, why did I have to go and say all that? Why couldn't I have just stopped at 'no thanks'? I could see from her smile that I had amused her yet again. Before she could say a word, I was at the door, yanking it open, and halfway down the porch stairs before I remembered my manners and turned and said, like the lady Ma wanted me to be, "Thank you, Miss St. James, for inviting me in."

She's nice, I thought as I ran home. Nicer than I imagined her to be. But in that instant another voice crept into my head, silent but insistent, sounding an alarm bell that struck a stubborn thought. I pictured myself eating the pie and Miss St. James talking and then going in and out of the kitchen. All that while, had she taken a bite of her slice of Ma's pie? No. Miss St. James had not even touched a morsel. Not even one little crumb.

Even though I ran like the wind, Ma was already waiting by the door. With every swish of the cane she called Ma O, I had to remind myself that having pie at Miss St. James's was every bit worth it.

I was sitting on the stoop with a book in my hand three days later when Ma called out, "Oreo, get in here."

When Ma called, you had three seconds flat to either respond verbally or to physically appear, and if you didn't do either, you'd get a wallop from Ma O that would cause you to remember everything you'd forgotten from a year ago. My legs were still all scratched up from taking too long at Miss St. James's, so I shot off the stoop and ran to the kitchen.

Ma was standing there with her lips pursed. I could tell that she was in a temper, because she wasn't standing still. She was pacing the floor like a great big lion ready to pounce.

"That lady, Miss St. James."

I nodded.

"You are to go to her house after church on Sundays between eleven and twelve noon for writing lessons."

I nodded a little more slowly, being careful to keep my face blank. I wasn't sure what to think except I was sure I did not want to spend my summer having lessons, but I was intrigued with the idea of seeing Miss St. James again.

"You'd better not disgrace me. You wear your Sunday dress, and don't you ever ask for anything up in that house, hear me? Not a book, not clothes, not anything you see up there." Ma's voice was twice as harsh as usual, and I wondered whether she was doing this against her will. She must be, I thought. For I had heard Ma say, "That Miss St. James, well, she has nice manners and is friendly but there is something that just doesn't add up."

Ma's instruction did not let up. "Don't talk out of turn, don't ask for anything to eat or drink. If she presses, politely refuse the first time and the second time. If she asks a third time, you can politely accept, but don't you ever accept a second helping. Hear me? And you come straight back here on the dot of twelve, understand?"

I nodded again. This time in confusion. If she didn't want me to go, then why was I going?

The answer came from Stevie, who had been there when Miss St. James stopped by again the day before. While she and Ma were doing their talking, he just stood still and practiced his listening. He told me that Miss St. James had said, "The Reverend tells me that your daughter loves words. He called it a gift, and I think every gift should be encouraged. There's about a month and a half left of summer, and, if Ella wants to, I can help her to improve. My first degree was in English. If that would be a help, that is."

I had to burst out laughing, because Stevie trying to imitate Miss St. James's voice and accent was just too funny. Apparently, Ma had quickly replied, "Oh no, that would be too much of a bother; besides, Ella is already good at language and writing," but Miss St. James had pressed, saying it wouldn't cost a dime, and it would give her something useful to do. Ma had quickly said no, that Ella babysits C.T. sometimes and she doesn't have the time. Miss St. James countered that this would only be on Sundays, right after church, not the weekdays when people had to work, and back and forth the exchange went. Stevie said it was like watching a tennis match. But in the end, Ma had finally given in. Stevie said, "I'll say this much for Miss St. James, she doesn't give up easily. With all the excuses Ma was giving, most people would have long given up." Stevie looked at me curiously. "I wonder what she wants with you. You'd think they were bargaining over the price of gold. Or a slave," he added wickedly.

I didn't mind him one bit. I filed all of Ma's instructions in my head, found a notebook and pen, and the very next Sunday after church, I was off to number 15, walking calmly and sedately, for I knew Ma would somehow make it her business to know how I was conducting myself.

CHAPTER 27

The first thing Miss St. James did after I arrived was to make up a jug of cold iced tea. Then, to my relief, she never asked me what I wanted to eat or drink. Instead, she laid out two slices of warm vanilla cake that she pulled out of the oven just minutes after I arrived. We sat at the rectangular dining room table, which was covered by a navy-blue tablecloth. She handed me a matching blue napkin, and I laid my napkin in my lap just so I could respond to Ma's questioning, that yes, my napkin had lain in my lap, and yes, I had used its edges to dab my mouth.

She wanted to know all about the killing of "those poor Freedom Summer civil rights workers in 1964. The ones working on the black vote." I told her she'd best talk to Ty's grandma about that, because she was living right in Longdale in 1964, only I didn't tell her that Ty's grandma would never let her in the house. When Miss St. James left to get our tea, I thought about whether she reminded me of anyone I knew. She fidgeted a lot, tying the ends of the tablecloth around her finger in loops, releasing them and then doing it all again. Her gaze was piercing. She looked at me the way Mr. Macabe would if he had working eyes, like she wanted to see inside me. I couldn't figure out why I would be that interesting to a grown-up. When she came back, she poured the tea and sat down, and then there was silence. I couldn't think of anything to say. Not so much as a single sentence. Miss St. James didn't seem to mind. Then she asked, "What kind of books do you like, Ella?"

I mentioned every adventure book I could think of, as well as some grown-up mysteries that I liked. When I stopped for a second to think of what other kinds of books I liked best, Miss St. James smiled. "Seems like you like books a lot, Ella. Do you use the library here in town?"

I nodded.

"I have some books on a shelf upstairs, and when we're done, you can take a look and see whether there are any you'd like to borrow."

I said a quick thank-you. Then she took out a piece of paper and handed it to me and quizzed me with a list of vocabulary words that I was to write on the paper, along with their meanings. We did about twenty, and then she looked over them. At the end of that she said, "Well, Ella, I can see your ma is right, you're very good at vocabulary. I have to think of something harder to teach you." I wanted to tell her I was good at math and most other subjects, too, but I kept my mouth shut so she wouldn't think I was bragging. Since Ma said I wasn't to stay more than an hour, I kept my eyes peeled on the clock that was in her dining room. Three minutes later I saw my time was up, so I picked up my notebook, thanked her for the cake and tea and for her time, and left.

All the way home, I kept thinking, *Should I like her, or not?* I thought I did but now I wasn't so sure. Miss St. James sure wasn't like anyone I'd ever met.

Ma asked me a million questions when I got home but I guess I must have got the answers right because I was to go again the next Sunday.

—◆—

That next Sunday came slowly, bringing with it summer showers that caught me by surprise as I ran to Miss St. James's house. By the time I rang her doorbell, I was sopping wet and stood dripping on the welcome mat. My braids were drenched, and my white cotton church dress clung to me.

Miss St. James came to the door, took one look at me, and said, "Oh my," and dashed off to get a large gray towel that she spread on the floor by the entrance. Then she made me take off my socks and shoes and stand on the towel while she went to get two large white towels, so white they looked like no one had ever used them before. The first she held like a shield in front of me and made me take off all my clothes behind it, right down to my underwear. Then she wrapped it around me, and the second one she wrapped around my hair. "Start rubbing the water out, Ella," she said, and then she left the room and came back with a blue towel. She sat in a chair watching me try to dry my hair as best I could. Even with the towel the water from my hair splashed onto the floor in little fat droplets. Before I knew it, Miss St. James was on the floor, mopping up. When she finished, she stood up and took over rubbing the water out of my hair.

"You're not getting all the water out, Ella" was all she said as she led me to a dining room chair and continued to rub briskly.

I felt myself grow warm, and a flush came down in a sweep, first spreading from my face, then down to my neck. Meanwhile my brain was saying, *This is terrible, Ella, Ma would kill you if she saw you near naked in this white lady's house. She would scream in embarrassment and you would be dead, dead, dead. All tore up from Ma O.*

But as Miss St. James rubbed, the feeling of embarrassment

went away, and I grew so languid and drowsy that when she finally stopped, I suddenly felt bereft. She left and returned with a long cotton nightdress.

"Now, put this on while I try to dry your clothes in the oven. We don't want you catching cold on account of me."

Dressed in the cotton nightdress, which piled up in a bundle at my feet, was about the coziest I'd ever felt. Miss St. James went out with the wet towels and brought back a box.

"This is a game, Scrabble. Have you ever played it?"

I shook my head no.

She went through the rules and added, "One more rule of my own: I don't want you to use everyday words but instead some of the bigger and more complicated words you know. Also, we will each take ten letters. instead of seven. That's not normally how you play Scrabble, but that will be our special way of playing it. And we have to give the definition of each word we put down."

We started. First, Miss St. James put down *quantum* and gave its definition. I mentally flipped through the pages of the dictionary in my bedroom: *abbreviation, abomination, abstract* . . . but enough of that. I needed Q words. I mentally flipped forward through the pages of the dictionary till I found what I was looking for: *quality, quantum, quiche, quintessential, quixotic, quite.* I had the letters to make *quite.* Thirty points. It wasn't as complex as I had wanted, but those were the letters I had.

"Good job," Miss St. James said encouragingly.

She used her T to spell *topical.* I took my O to spell *oxymoron,* which landed me sixty points. She raised an eyebrow and sat up in her seat. By my third word, she had gotten up and taken a stretch and then sat back down and grinned at me, her eyes curious yet excited. I knew then that she would have no mercy. She won the next two games, and I won the last one when I put down the letters to spell my final word, *isostasy*—which means the equilibrium that exists in the earth's crust—on the board. When I said that, Miss St. James pulled out her dictionary, and when she saw it was right, all she said was "My word." Then we were both grinning at each other.

"That was fun," I said.

Miss St. James laughed. "I don't think I've ever enjoyed a game more."

It was only then I looked at the clock and saw that two and a half hours had flown by. I rushed to the door.

"Come back, Ella. You still have my nightdress on." Miss St. James looked at me for a second before adding, "Do you want me to write a note to your ma since you are a little late?"

"Yes, ma'am."

After she handed me my now dry clothes, I went into the bathroom and quickly changed and rushed to the door.

"Hold on, Ella." Miss St. James came back minutes later with a note and a small plastic bag.

The note did nothing to help. If anything, it only made Ma madder, because according to her, Miss St. James would only have written a note if I had told her I would get into trouble for being late.

"I told you, don't be talking our business to nobody," she said with each swipe of the switch.

I limped on up the stairs and lay down for a second. Then I got up, got my dictionary, and I couldn't help smiling as I looked over all the words that we had put on the Scrabble board, remembering all that fun we had. Then I looked up new words and their definitions. I did that all evening, well into the night. Sometimes I would stop and think, Well, I guess this Miss St. James and I are friends, sort of, because everyone knows kids and grown-ups can't really be friends.

Also, there was something odd about Miss St. James. I had peeked
in the bag she gave me and there was the nightdress she had given
me to wear, all wrapped up. Did she not want it back? I stuffed it at
the back of my drawer, so Ma wouldn't think that Miss St. James
thought we needed her charity. I remembered her looking at my hair
as she dried it; she certainly hadn't seen anything like it before. The
way she'd pick a part of it up and rub it together like she was washing
laundry. Made me wonder why she was doing things she didn't seem
like she knew how to, when it wasn't like she was being forced to or
anything. Yet despite her oddness, there was something about Miss
St. James that I was drawn to. Something about the way she looked
square into my eyes as she talked to me. I did like her. I really did.

CHAPTER 28

She hadn't thought about whether she would like the girl, Ella, because she was so focused on getting her work started, but surprisingly she does. The razor-sharp mind behind the curious but wary big black eyes had been surprising. She had felt out of her comfort zone with the child in the beginning, but then she had thought of Scrabble. Playing Scrabble transported her to the few blissful periods in her life in Boston when she and Carl would play it for hours on end on the living room floor of the tiny apartment where he lived with his parents, each of them intent on winning, never sparing the other's feelings. It had been just the thing to break the ice with Ella.

She had asked Ella about her neighbors on Ricksville Road, trying to figure out who would be most willing to be interviewed, but Ella had seemed shy, or reticent, batting away her questions, one after the other, with the practiced skill of someone used to avoiding questions that were uncomfortable. She had finally retreated; after all, she would be here for a while. All she needed was a little patience.

CHAPTER 29

Leroy returned one Tuesday in late July. He'd only been gone three weeks, the shortest stretch he'd been away, but it had seemed so much longer, what with the excitement of Miss St. James's arrival. Ma told him all about Miss St. James, but to my surprise, he didn't ask anything other than what she was doing in Ricksville, and when Ma said no one was really sure, he just shrugged and went on to talk about how hard he'd looked for work to replace the money I had stolen. He said that this time he couldn't find any work. Set me wondering how he'd come back with four brand-new shirts and a pair of wing-tip shoes. I heard him asking Ma for money a day after he returned, and at the end of that week, she had wordlessly handed him her weekly paycheck. I knew then that we'd be eating Nate's leftovers all the next week.

I couldn't stand to be near him, and the stoop was still too close, so I was once again like those desert nomads, searching for a place to land. I often ended up at Cammy's. Today she was sitting between her ma's legs, having her hair braided. She looked so snug and relaxed in between Miss Claudia's thighs that I found myself wishing we could trade places. I'd had to unknot my own hair and comb it through for as long as I could remember, till I eventually learned how to braid it. Even then, it always came out with frizzy ends because I never had the patience to braid all the way. Cammy's hair was the smooth and silky doll-like hair I wished I had, and as I watched her ma glide that comb through it, give it a light touch with the curling rod, and quickly braid it down, I thought that she was so lucky to have Miss Claudia as her ma. I sat down on the sloping couch, next to Miss Claudia.

"Heard you've been hanging out with that white lady," Miss Claudia said, as she parted Cammy's hair to make another braid.

"Yep," I said.

Cammy twisted her head to turn to me. "You never say what she's like."

"She's nice," I said.

I could tell they wanted me to say more, but I wasn't sure I wanted to gossip about Miss St. James. I kind of wanted to keep her to myself.

"You'd better be careful, Ella. Just because she seems nice doesn't mean you should be talking to her, telling her everything about what we do here in Ricksville. You just never know. White folks is white folks."

"Yes, ma'am."

Cammy couldn't resist saying, "Oh, Ma, I don't know why you're telling Ella all that. I don't think there's anything harmful about Miss St. James at all."

Miss Claudia pursed her lips together and shook her head. "You girls just better stay away. Now, I know I don't have any say over what Ella does, but you, Cammy, should know better, you being half Indian and half black, yes you should know better."

Cammy bent her head over as her ma pushed down and twisted her hair into a braid, but a second later she'd swiveled around to look at me and smiled. The smile that told me she hadn't taken any notice of one word her mother had just said.

When she was done with Cammy's hair, Miss Claudia said, "Come here, Ella, let me tidy that up for you a bit."

A moment later, I was squished tight between Miss Claudia's thick thighs; out came the afro comb and a whole tub of grease. For the next hour I squirmed and squealed as she tugged and did battle with my hair using that hot comb, and all the while Cammy was having a good old laugh at my expense. But when Miss Claudia was done, I went and looked at myself in the mirror and was thrilled to see the neat, smooth braids and carefully placed ribbons. Why, my hair looked like it came right out of those *Jet* magazine ads.

"Thank you, Miss Claudia," I said, wanting to bury my face in the folds of her ample waist and feel her thick arms around me. But Miss Claudia was the doing type, not the hugging type, so I settled for linking my arm through Cammy's.

"Don't mention it," Miss Claudia said as she set about cleaning the combs and putting everything back into a basket.

"Can I come home with you?" Cammy asked.

I pulled away and looked at Cammy like she had two heads. She never came to my house. She was too scared of Leroy. She said his smile was too perfect, with all those straight white teeth that smiled at her even when she wasn't smiling back.

"Is Stevie home?" she asked innocently.

I looked at Cammy again, my eyes widening. "Don't tell me you now have a crush on Stevie?"

"He is cute."

"No, he's not." I didn't know what she saw in him. He'd grown five inches taller this year, but he still had those same buck teeth. And he seemed more skinny and gangly than ever. To make matters worse, he walked about like he wore clown shoes, not quite knowing where to put his long, size-14 feet.

"Stevie isn't interested in girls," I added quickly.

"Then what's he interested in?"

"Books. Engineering books. Anything with an engine that you have to build to make work. If you're not a book or know what's in a book, you can forget it."

Cammy gave me a cheeky grin. I could see she thought that books were no competition at all.

"You're wasting your time," I warned.

"Come on, Ella. I just want to say hello, not marry your brother."

I was hoping that Miss Claudia would tell Cammy to sit her butt at home and not go chasing boys, but she didn't even stir. If that had been Kitty talking about some Ricksville boy, Ma would've hauled her upstairs and locked her in her bedroom till she came to her senses.

Since Miss Claudia wasn't jumping in to save the day, I told Cammy she could come home with me and wait outside. I'd go in to see if Stevie would come out.

We strolled down Ricksville Road, and as we got near to my house, Cammy said so casually I knew she had planned it, "Can we stop by Miss St. James's first? You're the only one I know of who's been in there. I went by and knocked but no one answered."

"What do you want to see?" I had gone from surprise to irritation in seconds.

"Well, whatever she's got up in there."

"She's got nothing, Cammy Locklear. She's poor and she's busy most of the time, writing her thesis for her degree."

"What's a thesis?"

"It's like a big research paper. You need one before you can graduate."

"Then why didn't you just say a paper, why do you have to be all fancy? You are just a show-off, Ella."

I didn't mind her. Miss St. James had told me she was writing her thesis, but she never told me what it was about, even though

I'd asked several times. All I knew was that it was like a paper she had to write for school to get her degree, and it had something to do with all those books she was getting from the library.

"Anyway, didn't you say you wanted to see Stevie?"

"Well, I want to see Miss St. James, too." Cammy gave me her prettiest smile, like she was trying to turn my head the way she did boys at school. The odd thing about Cammy was that she never liked those boys. She always wanted the ones that didn't like her.

Her smile just made me mad. "You know that won't work with me, Cammy. I'm not one of your stupid boys, so you can stop that smiling. And I'm not taking you to Miss St. James's house, because once she sees it's you, she won't open the door."

I knew I was telling an untruth, but I didn't care. I didn't want Cammy anywhere near my Miss St. James. It didn't seem odd that she'd become mine so quickly.

Cammy was quiet then. Quieter than she normally ever gets. Her smile had melted away, and I could tell she was thinking how to cut me down to size.

"You can be so mean, *Oreo*," she finally said.

"I'm already doing you one favor with Stevie and that's a big favor," I hissed into her face.

Cammy drew in an offended breath. Seconds passed before she spoke, but even though Cammy was not book smart, she had other smarts and knew me all too well to keep pressing.

I left her outside our front door and went on in and up to Stevie's room. It was always closed now. I knocked and opened it. He was lying on his bed, holding a magazine in his hand, looking at me looking at him.

"What you want?"

I stared at him, wondering what Cammy saw. I narrowed my eyes, trying to work out if that was a tuft of a hair sprouting from his chin. I was just about to tease him when I saw he was still staring at me in irritation, and the words died in my throat.

"What do you want?"

I shrugged. "I see Leroy's back," I said lamely.

"Yes." Stevie looked like he was going to say something else about that, but he didn't.

"If you can't say what you want, leave. I'm busy."

"Cammy wanted me to ask if you would hang out with us," I said, in one swoosh of breath before I inhaled, and then held it, waiting.

Silence. Nothing. Then he went back to looking at his magazine and without looking up from it said, "Shut the door on your way out."

"Come on, Stevie."

"What?"

"Please."

He looked up and fixed his eyes on me. "When have we ever hung out, Ella? I'm barely allowed to talk to you, let alone hang out with you."

I suddenly felt like all the air in my body whooshed out like a ball that's been deflated. I was now as flat as a pancake. I didn't speak. Took that pain like the blow it was and swallowed it down, when what I really wanted to do was scream at Stevie, lash out at him for listening to Leroy.

Stevie went back to reading his magazine.

I hated him so much I felt my eyes burning, and before I could stop it, a tear seeped out and then it was too late and I was sobbing.

"Ella, I'm sorry. I shouldn't have said that. I'm sorry. Stop crying, will you? Just stop, okay? I'll give you anything if you stop."

After about twenty seconds, the tears stopped on their own and, try as I could to keep Stevie looking so worried, nothing more came out. Stevie's face was pale.

"I'm sorry, okay, Ella. Man, I hate this stupid house. If you want, I'll go see Cammy."

I held myself still and quiet, ignoring his feeble attempts to make me feel better. I didn't care about what he did with Cammy anymore because I was still hurt, but Stevie misread my silence and left the room.

I looked around at the pictures, notebooks, and textbooks, all on engineering and physics, filling up the whole room, enough to wrap him up whole like a cocoon, safe from everything. No wonder he stayed in here all the time, except when there was food being served. I wondered whether the words I loved so much could ever be enough to make me feel safe. I tried some of my favorites, *tattered*, *enigma*, *reassuring*, *emanated*, *unsheathed*. Each word brought me comfort, but I still didn't feel safe. Not the way Stevie was all wrapped up in his world.

The minutes dragged on. What on earth was Stevie saying to Cammy?

Then he was back.

"Okay, I talked to Cammy. She left, said she'd see you tomorrow. Happy now? I even told her that her hair looked nice—that was extra, for you. I'd even kiss her if it'd stop you looking so miserable."

I had to smile at that. He didn't have to look quite so disgusted.

I wanted to ask Stevie whether he hated it here. Living in this house. But all that came out of me was "I hate it here." He just sighed. Then I heard Leroy's footsteps on the stairs. Stevie opened his bedroom door quickly, and I just managed to squeeze out and into my bedroom before Leroy reached the landing.

CHAPTER 30

August arrived, and the sun's heat, like a flame that's been turned up on a stove, was hot enough to fry a side of bacon. Miss Claudia, fanning herself at church, said she didn't think hell could be much hotter.

I ran across Miss St. James's lawn, up her front steps, and swung open the front door, just as though it were my house. Miss St. James stopped writing for the barest second before her eyes went back to her page and she waved distractedly, before saying, "Fix yourself something to eat, Ella."

If Ma knew the way I ran around in her kitchen, I'd be as done as burnt toast.

I sat opposite her with a plate of bread and jelly, quiet as a mouse because by now I knew not to say a word as that pen flew across the page. I was used to her. Now the slight crow's feet at the sides of her face seemed to melt into the overall texture of her face, and I saw neither the stark paleness nor her sharp features, just the general form of what was Miss St. James, almost as though I now saw what was inside, what was really her.

I had asked her last week, "Don't you ever want to get married and have children?"

She had looked up from her writing, surprised, and asked, "Why do you ask? Think I'm getting too old, over the hill?"

I didn't want to say anything to hurt her, but I wanted to say she'd better hurry. Didn't look like she was getting any younger.

"I almost married, a lifetime ago," she had said, and went straight back to her writing. But when I looked again, she wasn't writing at all—just staring ahead, her face all scrunched up like a crumpled piece of paper.

I reached out and looked at the books she'd borrowed this week from the library. There was one on Martin Luther King, another on slavery, and the last one on the civil rights movement. I thumbed through them, waiting for her to do something other than stare. She had promised that we would play Scrabble today. Finally, she sighed, placed the cap on the pen, and started to put away her papers.

"Why are you reading all this?" I asked Miss St. James.

She stopped what she was doing for a second.

"Well, I don't know enough about the civil rights movement or slavery. The movement was happening when I was in my teens, but of course, I only heard snippets on the television. Now I can actually read about it, and it's good material for my thesis. I'm going to turn it into a book, I hope, when it's all done."

"Can I read it?"

"I haven't finished writing it." Miss St. James brought out the Scrabble and put it on the table between us.

"What's it about?"

"Ella, you keep asking me that question. I'm not sure you'd understand what it's about."

She handed me seven pieces for regular Scrabble and I placed them carefully on their wood holder but I wasn't giving up.

"Try me, Miss St. James. I read all kinds of books, adult books, even. I can understand most of them."

"You start, Ella." Miss St. James put the dictionary to the right of the board and pushed her chair in closer. I focused on my words. They were horrible. I had a Q, but no U in sight, an X, two Ls, an

O and a P and a D. I mulled over words in my head, trying to do something with that Q. Miss St. James had bought a timer because she said I was now almost as good as she was. "Ella, would you stop reading the dictionary as though it were a novel," she had complained just before buying the timer. "You can't be beating me as much as you do. Some of these words I've never even heard of." She hadn't meant to compliment me, but that was the best compliment I had ever gotten, and my head had swelled to twice its size.

"You've got about five seconds to make up your mind," Miss St. James warned.

I quickly formed the word *plod* and placed it slowly on the board.

Miss St. James smiled. One of her I've-got-you type of smiles. I knew she would have no mercy. Now all we both wanted was to win.

After she had thoroughly won and I had cleared the game away, I tried once again. "Can you tell me what your thesis is about?"

She sighed. "Well, I am looking at how the black migration of the '40s and civil rights in the '60s shaped and changed southern society."

"Is that white or black society?" I asked sharply.

Miss St. James didn't answer for a second.

"Does it matter, Ella? Society is society."

"I can see that civil rights must have changed black people's lives, but how did it change white people's lives? Other than them hating to give up rights to black people, their lives didn't change, did they?" I asked curiously.

"Ella, the black migrations and the civil rights movement did affect everyone, black and white, and not in the same way."

I thought about it a bit.

"I don't understand," I said finally.

Miss St. James didn't say anything for a while. She was biting her mouth as she does sometimes.

Then she said, "I meant, why do you think those white people were against civil rights? One has to look at their motives to see what made them think and behave the way they did. To do that, you have to look at what was going on around them."

I thought about the murders of the three civil rights workers during the Freedom Summer. They were part of a group that was helping to register black voters. They were stopped by the deputy sheriff and his boys. They were later found murdered. Killed for trying to get black people some voting rights.

"It's easy to see why they didn't want civil rights, they were racist! It was racists that killed those election workers, Chaney, Goodman, and Schwerner."

Miss St. James pursed her lips again and sighed.

"It's not that simple. It's too easy to just call them racists. The real question is why were they racist? Who were the winners and losers when the migrations and civil rights laws happened? I am looking at those events and their impact from all different angles."

I stared at her.

"You going to interview people in North Ricksville, too?" I asked.

Her brow was furrowed as her hand moved and picked up her papers and set them before her. Then she reached for her pen. I knew it was time to leave. I scooted off the chair and was out the door before I wore out my welcome.

In my bed that night I kept thinking about the civil rights movement. We all knew what it had done for black society— given us all a leg up, a chance at the dream. But what had it done for white society? Would she also interview white folk and ask them about that? All I knew was that the civil rights laws would not be looked at kindly by everyone. How was she going to write that civil rights were the best thing that happened to America, or that the Freedom Summer murders were bad, terrible, horrific, hideous, if she also interviewed people like Mr. Wilkinson? That Mr. Wilkinson, well, he would have a good ol' time with that question, and there she would be, writing it all down.

Well, if she thought she could hop from one side of Ricksville to the other, asking questions about civil rights and who it was good for, she would soon see that she couldn't. People in Ricksville, north and south, wouldn't stand for that. For her going between us like a yo-yo. The lines were already drawn in the sand. I didn't know a lot of things, but I knew that in Ricksville, white people and black people were civil, but deep down, they didn't trust each other, and so no one would stand for that.

Why would someone move to a black town and write something that was bound to make them mad? *A racist, you mean*, a little devil voice in my head said.

She can't be a racist, I argued to myself. *Or maybe only a little on account of her fear of men.*

Black men, the voice in my head whispered.

The voice wouldn't shut up, because then it said, *Are you so messed up, Ella, that you're friends with a racist?*

She's not a racist!

C.T. shifted in the bed; it was only then I realized I was talking out loud.

"It's okay, C.T.," I said as I soothed him. "Sorry, go back to sleep." When he lay back down, I put my fingers in my ears to try to tune out the stubborn voice in my head. All I knew was that Miss St. James had better be careful. People in Mississippi were still jumpy.

CHAPTER 31

She knew that Ella didn't understand her thesis topic, but then, she was just a child. Didn't really understand that she had chosen the topic because it was of interest to her and, of course, a thesis had to have a balanced view. She would be looking at all society, both black and white. In any case, she didn't have to interview many people for the white side of the story. She already knew what they would say, so the interview would just be a formality. She knew that many would say that all the violence of the civil rights era and before was a way to fight for their rights, their livelihoods. They would talk about their loss of real societal wealth, first after slavery, then after the migration of blacks, their source of cheap labor, to the North. Then came the civil rights movement, which they saw as the last straw. The economic impact of these losses over a few generations was immense. She would write about that in economic terms, the loss of cash and assets over time. In some families, it had taken them back economically by several generations. Her father's generation was poorer than his father's, and so on. Of course, many people she would interview in Philadelphia would be angry. That anger would come across in the pages of her thesis, in sharp contrast to the likely optimism Ricksville blacks felt, ushered in by the civil rights movement. The optimism that perhaps they still felt more than two decades later. It would make for an interesting thesis, and of course it would be balanced. One in which the real impact of civil rights on all society in terms of costs and benefits would be laid bare, exposed, for everyone to see. To date, most of the papers and discussions she had read on the topic were so one-sided, focusing only on black southerners. Her thesis would be a masterpiece of analysis. She could already hear the accolades in her mind.

But that was not what kept her up all night. It was, rather, Ella's question about whether she wanted to get married. That had brought it all back, an old wound, scabbed over. She had become friends with Carl when she was sixteen. Their apartment doors were across from each other. The door to his had a welcome mat and a hanging basket of bright yellow fake flowers. She had wondered who lived there before he emerged one sunny day. He was beautiful, with striking chiseled features, blond hair, and the clearest sky-blue eyes she had ever seen. She was immediately shy because she was nothing much to look at, not by comparison. Golden boy, she teased him, but he was unaware how beautiful he was. His personality was as sunny as the flowers at his door.

They had bonded over books, school, over both being poor and having to work, and finally over Scrabble. Soon they were inseparable. He was the only friend she had. He teased her about her accent and said that his father's family was from somewhere way down south—Louisiana. She teased him back about the way girls used to hang on his every word. He had no time for them. He only had eyes for her. He was what made Boston livable. His parents were barely around, always working, and with hers also gone, they were in and out of each other's house, cooking, watching TV, playing board games, doing homework, and growing up.

She had told him about growing up in the South, the farm, the farm boys, the black laborers who were always annoying her father, and the sudden way they'd left that night. She hadn't shared everything with him, but just enough so he knew what type of life she had lived. She was too smart for that, but she had told him her father had been in the KKK. He hadn't said much. Just stroked her back as he listened. He was unusually quiet after that night, and she had asked him if he minded that she was a redneck, that they came from farm country. His response was a kiss. That was the first time he had kissed her, and although he hadn't answered, she had been too distracted by the kiss to care. He loved her, that was all that mattered.

He had asked her to marry him a year later. She was eighteen and he was nineteen, heading for college, Dartmouth, in the fall. Sorry about the order of things, he had said, laughingly, caressing her hair. I should have finished university and then asked you but I just couldn't wait because someone else is bound to snap you up. She would have traveled to the ends of the earth to be with him, given up anything. She had simply said, I'll marry you, but you have to ask my father. She had first gone to her mother, and her mother was more excited than she had seen in a long time but she said, you know he'll have to ask. The ask was a formal affair, and Carl had gone to see her father and her father had given his permission. Then her father had invited Carl's family to dinner. He had worn a suit. Carl's father, medium height, with dark hair and a mustache, had worn one, too. He had spoken about his son, his intelligence, and the future in medicine they hoped for him. Carl's mother had not said much, just smiled a lot. Carl had inherited his fair looks from her. Kate had sat quietly, holding Carl's hand, hoping that her father would not drink too much or get too loud, or talk about what the niggers had done to his farm. It felt like she had held her breath the whole night. It had to be perfect. She didn't want Carl's parents to think that they were rednecks. That she wasn't good enough for their son.

The two sets of parents had gotten on well, even more so when they found out that Carl's father was from Louisiana. Her father had laughed and said, I know some people in Louisiana. She had crossed her fingers, hoping that he wouldn't say anything about his network of brotherhood in Louisiana and across the South, but he hadn't.

They started wedding planning.

She doesn't remember much after the wedding planning began. The drugs they gave her wiped out pockets of her memory. The only thing that stands out is the wedding dress. A hand-stitched crocheted long white dress that she had seen in the window of Neiman Marcus. It was an original. They knew they could never afford it. It was a thousand dollars. Carl had signed up for a credit card and handed it to her. It had a limit of a thousand dollars. Don't worry, he had said. We will pay it back slowly over time, but you only get married once.

She tried to remember Carl's face, which she knows was beautiful, but as usual, his face had blurred into the faces of others that still haunted her dreams.

CHAPTER 32

The sky was crying, big fat dollops of wet that clung to my braids, my nose, and everywhere else they could. I moved under the sycamore tree and it provided the umbrella, of sorts, that I needed, although I didn't care if I got wet or not. Fats came by in a hurry, the hood on his sweatshirt up. I knew he didn't see me because if he had, rain or not, he would have come over just to tell me how dumb I was to be standing outside in the rain. Miss St. James walked briskly by, and she must have seen me, because she glanced at me, long and hard and then again, a few yards past me, she turned to look before moving slowly on. I knew she was wondering whether she should stop. Something stronger pulled at her, and with one last look she was gone. Looking out from between the leaves, I knew that the thing that kept her going was the aura I felt going up around me, thick and hard, swallowing me whole, sending out a clear warning in every direction. I had put that up fast, like an expert bricklayer, building a wall so tall and thick around me that I am sure it stood out from a mile away. Maybe only Fats and Mr. Macabe knew how to climb walls.

Laugh, I said to myself. Laugh and laugh till you feel better. So I tried, but the only sound that came out was a groan. I tried again, and this time the sound was high, like a wail, and so I tried to pull it back inside me to where it had come from, deep down in my very marrow, but it had a life of its own. It tussled with me and came screeching out, a long wail that would not stop, shushed only slightly by the sound of the beating rain.

I tried to quiet my mind but still the flashes came. Leroy and Kitty and Stevie playing cards when I came in. My refusing to play and heading upstairs to my room. Reading *Peter Pan* with C.T., then the quiet downstairs. The slow, heavy thud of footsteps. Quiet as they paused outside the room. The door cracking open, then wider. Then the order for C.T. to go downstairs and stay till he was called. My querying look, unafraid. Ma was almost home, the others were downstairs. Then the look, and my answering, stumbling, querulous voice, panicked now. Where are the others? I had heard my voice speaking as though it were no longer part of me. Out, gone to buy beer. The sneer it was said with was like a slap across my face, uttered with pleasure, with malice. A bolt for the door to squeeze past him, but then: Caught. Trapped. My wrist. My other wrist. Thrown to the floor. Arms stretched out over my head. The heavy weight upon me, crushing me. And my screams. Hands released and his hand over my mouth and nose. Trying to breathe, gasping for air. Couldn't take in air. Would do anything to breathe. Squirm, struggle. Let me breathe. Hands fall off. Too weak to scream. Felt something try to get inside me. Kicked. Something trying to ram inside but it would not go. Leroy pushing and pushing and swearing. Then a cry. Not me. No breath to cry. C.T. crying outside the door, shouting something. The stillness on top of me. "I want to come in, Daddy, let me in. Let me in." Leroy gets up. Kicks me hard where the sun don't shine. The pain shoots up my core through my belly and lands in my mouth and blood shoots out. I have bitten my tongue.

"You're so ugly, nothing's working. Shit, you're worthless. Nothing but a drain on my pocket." Face contorted with disgust. I cringe. Happy I am so ugly and yet sad also. I try to get up, legs trembling. Stretch my hands to the bed like a blind man and pull myself up. See that look in his face that means he hasn't given up yet. The door slamming shut. Lie in the bed, not looking at anything. C.T. stands next to the bed, peering over me, his book in his hand.

"Ella, read me the story again, read me the Peter Pan story again. Read me the story again. I want you to read the story. Why don't you get up? Why are you so still? Ella, please read me the story."

I closed my eyes. Blotted him out. Blotted them all out.

The sun came out, and I moved from the tree to the curve of Ricksville Road. My mind was clearer, and within the safety of my wall I could still think. All I knew was that the way Leroy hated me was too much to come from just Ma cheating on him. It was my darkness that was a perpetual slap in his face. Yet living with Ma, he had to take it, like someone trying to stuff a hair ball down his throat, causing him to retch and fight to get it out. I shut my eyes and pretended to be lighter than I was, five times lighter. I was walking with my brothers and sister, four pale kids lined up in a row. That way, Leroy could pretend I was his. No one would laugh at him behind his back. He could have lived with that. The minute I was born, Leroy became an outsider in Ricksville even though he had spent most of his life here. He couldn't bear being close to men that would ridicule him behind his back or women that questioned the manhood of a man whose churchgoing wife would succumb to a stranger.

It was around the fourth hour that my brain had finally formulated

this story that made sense. It was that very day that I partly understood Leroy. Understood the fury that whipped within him, because
he had been brought low. Only when I became nothing would he feel
like a conqueror. If so, why hadn't he left Ma? But the answer was
obvious now. Who was he if not for Ma? He had no education, and
it was also Ma's low but steady income that kept food on the table.
Then there was me, the thorn that would not fall off, a constant reminder that he wasn't even man of his house.

But knowing all this didn't make me hate him any bit less.

The sun went down and I was still sitting at the curve of Ricksville
Road, not daring to go back inside till Ma came home. Dusk settled in, bringing with it a coolness from the aftermath of the rain. I
was still there when Kitty came walking up to the house with Luke
in tow. Apparently, he had clean forgotten what happened the last
time he was here, but he didn't look scared. If anything, he looked
twice as confident. They walked past me without a word and went
into the house. It was only then that I got up and walked to the
house. I peeked in the kitchen window to see if Leroy was home,
but it was only Kitty, preparing a sandwich for Luke. Clearly Leroy
was out, or Luke would have still been outside the front door. The
window was open and I could hear everything they were saying.

"Come on, Kitty, we've done just about everything we can do,
let's go all the way. You must want it just as badly. Ain't nobody
here. Your ma's still at the diner and your daddy's at the Still Water
Bar. Come on, you know you want it."

I saw Kitty shake her head, but by the coy smile about her lips, I
wondered how long she would hold off.

I went back around and sat on the porch stoop, and as I did, a thought came into my head like a lightning bolt.

As Luke came out of the house, I was sitting deliberately in his path. He stepped over me as I knew he would. This time when he reached over to touch my chest, I didn't stop him, and when his eyes drew close to mine in wonder, I whispered brazenly to him, "I'll give you some if Kitty won't."

Luke looked a little scared, rather than delighted.

"Okay," he said reluctantly, "where?"

"In the green outhouse by Nate's house. No one goes in there."

"When?" I could tell that he didn't quite believe me.

"Now if you want."

"Why?"

"Because I want to," I said, trying to stop the high-pitched nervous squeak in my voice.

"Well, if I do, it doesn't mean I'm going with you, you know that." Luke's voice was resolute.

"I know that you love Kitty."

Luke laughed. "I don't love Kitty, I just want her. She's beautiful." He seemed amused by it all. "Okay, if you want to give it a try, I can teach you how to do it."

"Okay," I said, miserably.

"Have you done it before?"

"No."

"Okay, I'll be gentle because you haven't."

I heard the door slam as Kitty shut the front door and then she looked at us suspiciously.

"Are you guys talking? What on earth can you possibly be talking about?"

"Just asking her how on earth she managed to have a beautiful sister like you," came Luke's easy response.

He put his hand out and they walked away hand in hand.

But then he turned around, and as he looked back, he gave me a wink.

I didn't change my mind. Didn't even ponder the decision. Later that night I snuck out of the house. Went down to Nate's and into the old outhouse. Ten minutes later, it was done. Luke had kissed me and it was pretty horrible. Then he put his hand up my underwear and took them down and then he got me on the floor and lay on top of me and rocked back and forth, and after a while, he got up and though I wasn't sure what exactly had happened, he said, okay, that was it.

"How come you didn't take it out properly?" I asked.

"I thought you said you'd never done it before?"

"I haven't. That's just what I thought."

Luke pulled my hair. "You're such a silly girl," he said.

When I walked home I owned the road. I brazenly walked right down the middle of it, daring any passing vehicle to knock me down. My head surged with a power I never knew I had, and with every step a voice in my head chanted, you defeated him, you defeated him.

I would like to say I wrestled with my decision like Jacob did with the Angel. But I didn't. I closed the door on God when my conscience tried to speak. Shut that door and locked it up. Forgot the words of the Very Reverend when he said God loves a virgin. Loves her obedience. She shall be blessed. The Very Reverend had screamed this part and all the girls in the youth group had jumped in terror, before dissolving into giggles.

A day later when Leroy put his hands on me, I slapped them away hard. When his shocked eyes met mine, my black-brown eyes stared brazenly back. He grabbed the back of my braids and yanked my head back till I thought it was about to break, but then I kicked out at him. He slapped me and put me in a headlock, bending me half over.

"You can't get past me."

Then abruptly he looked at me.

"You have had sex."

It was a question and a statement.

I smiled, then laughed, not knowing how he knew but I didn't care. He thrust me away from him. "You sicken me."

How I rejoiced at his words. I kept my eyes locked on his, utterly fearless. "You can't take that part of me away, it's already gone," my emboldened twelve-year-old eyes told him. I had taken away the one thing Leroy wanted to use to bring me low. It was the only way I could think to stop him. Let him know it meant nothing to me.

He spat at me, and the glob landed in a wet splat at my feet.

A power like none other I have since experienced surged in my head, and energized my body, leaving me dizzy and almost drunk with power. I wanted to open my mouth, beat my chest, and yell at the heavens and throughout the earth, "I have conquered Goliath. I have won the battle!"

Nate was always asking me to develop that hard shell, and I could feel it already growing and hardening, causing my back to hunch over under its weight, sharpening my voice and tongue into razor-sharp weapons that could devour in an instant.

CHAPTER 33

Hours later, I walked slowly to Nate's to see when Ma was coming home. While Nate was behind the counter, she wasn't there. She'd left early to see a visiting choir at church.

"What's up, Ella?"

"Nate?"

"Hmm?" Nate was washing up some plates now.

"You just come to say hi, Ella?"

I nodded.

"Nothing on your mind the way it sometimes is?"

I was quiet.

"Lord, you would try a saint. Sometimes you talk nonstop and other times nothing at all. I can't read your mind. What's bothering you? Now, I can tell something ain't right with you."

"Why did God make some people beautiful and others ugly?"

Nate didn't blink and he didn't ask me why. He just took off that apron of his and folded it very carefully and put it on the counter. We sat at a table, already covered with vinyl, with red place mats already set in front of each of the four chairs. Nate drew a picture of what I thought was a bubble.

"Nothing to do with God, Ella. This is the world, Ella. God made us all beautiful, but it was the slave owner who messed it all up by having all those coffee, cookie crumble, caramel, milky, yellow, and tan babies and then treating those lighter ones better than the deep dark ones. What's your color remind you of, Ella?"

"Coal, tar, midnight," I said.

"I would say dark chocolate without milk, I would say molasses. Use nice words to describe your color, Ella. Now, how would you describe me?"

"Toffee, caramel, coffee with cream."

"And your ma?"

"Vanilla, buttercream."

"And your Mr. Macabe?"

"A piece of brown oak furniture."

"We could go through almost everyone you know and they are all a different shade of brown. The range is so large. No one talks of that."

Then he went up and took a box of watercolor paints from the storeroom, and when he got back he drew more people on his paper. He colored them different shades of brown, sometimes mixing and matching to get the right shade. He should have stopped coloring but for some reason he didn't. He kept right on, the colors on the paper grew till the paper was now sopping wet, shades of brown weeping into each other. I looked at Nate, but he was intent, swirling his paintbrush in the brown, putting it in the yellow and the white, and mashing it onto the paper.

"The slave owner changed our eyes. But we let him."

Nate worked for another fifteen minutes without looking at me. The paper was a wet mess. He took that sopping paper and rolled it into a tight little ball in his hands. He squeezed so tight that the water dripped out. Brown drops that plopped onto the table. I wasn't sure he knew he was wringing out that paper so hard that the brown water was now dripping onto his arms, rolling down like lazy tears.

Perhaps he was thinking about Mr. Joe Catchedy, about how his father had him on the quiet. I wondered whether Nate had ever

been able to call his father Daddy. Looking at all the brown watercolors pooling on the counter I didn't think so.

Nate's voice came at me again, and I looked up from the brown
puddle. He looked a bit worried.

"Sorry, Ella. I guess I got carried away. All I wanted to say was
that's why you think Kitty is more beautiful than you are. The truth
is, you're just as beautiful. Just in a different way."

If I was so beautiful, why didn't others see it? So instead I tried
to think of myself as God did. Tried to appreciate what colors He
would have had to use, and how much effort He had put into make
my skin a rich, warm color to give me protection from the sun.
How much love He gave me in that covering, in my features. I
closed my eyes till I was as blind as Mr. Macabe. Closed my ears,
too, blocking out all the voices that went all the way back till the
1600s. I tried to think of what Mr. Macabe said about Africans
loving themselves so much that they didn't even think about their
skin color; it was just a beautiful part of who they were. But I still
couldn't see myself as an African saw herself. My eyes had already
been changed.

CHAPTER 34

Something frightening was happening with my face and body. My breasts had erupted, and my slender frame seemed to fill out more each day. I stared in the mirror at my face; it seemed to be expanding, and a soft fullness puffed out my cheeks. It was when my skin started itching so much that I took off, running, straight to Dr. Shepardson's house. There was his mother, still clinging to life, cocooned in a bright red-and-white blanket, lying on the old tattered chaise lounge. She had rouge on her cheeks, and I wondered whether her son did her makeup, too. I was just about to leave when the old ma's eyes sprang open and she glared at me.

"Come on in, Ella, close the door, you're bringing in a draft."

"I was looking for the doctor," I started to say, but she interrupted me.

"Well, he's not in, but since I'm his next of kin, I'm the closest thing you've got. What did you want to see him for?"

"I think I'm sick."

"Why do you think you're sick?"

"I don't feel like myself. And I'm putting on weight even though I don't eat much, and my nose just keeps getting larger and larger." I couldn't tell her about the itching.

"Come closer so I can see."

The old ma observed me for a second; then she sat bolt upright, and her bony, sticklike hands pulled my face closer. I was startled she could do this, because the doctor carried her everywhere. She looked at my nose, and then put her hands on my shoulders and felt her way down to my legs, pushing and prodding, stopping for a moment at my breasts and stomach before looking back at my face.

"Nothing wrong with you, Ella. You're just pregnant, that's all."

I was too shocked to breathe for several seconds.

"No!" I cried. "No! No! No!"

"Stop it, Ella. Stop being hysterical."

The old ma's voice was bossy and harsh, not the whispery, paper-thin voice I had heard last time. Even before I could think, my cries dried up, the response to the old ma automatic and immediate. Meanwhile, my brain was flapping around like a bird caught in a trap, many short bursts of thoughts—Ma would kill me.

Whether the doctor would tell everyone: Nate; Ma; on and on the thoughts raced until suddenly, when I looked up, I was staring at the ceiling, and I saw that I was lying on the floor.

Dr. Shepardson was peering down at my face.

"You fainted."

I tried to get up, but my legs trembled.

"You've had a shock, Ella. Lie still for a while. You're not pregnant. Just something my old ma does to scare girls straight and keep them away from boys. I keep telling her she's going to cause a heart attack instead. Just stay here awhile, and I'll bring you something to drink."

Tears of relief flowed down my face. I was still crying when the doctor returned with a glass of water.

"How old are you, Ella?"

"Twelve," I mumbled.

"Have you had your monthly visitor?"

I shook my head slowly, no. I knew what visitor he meant. Kitty had started her period at thirteen, and Ma kept a stock of pads in a cupboard near the kitchen.

"Well, have you had sex?" he asked gently.

I nodded.

"You have?"

I muttered, "Only once. And he never even took his thing out of his pants. He said it was a different way of doing it."

The doctor's eyebrows went straight up to his head. Then he shook his head, as though to clear it.

"I don't think you had sex yet, Ella. And don't think of having it. You could get pregnant very easily once you get your period. You are going through puberty and the weight gain is just your body going through changes."

I wanted to stay on the floor forever.

"What's bothering you, Ella?"

It was then I got up, not even looking at him.

"Nothing."

"Doesn't seem like nothing to me."

I kept my mouth clamped shut.

"Okay," he said finally. "You can leave but stay away from boys."

I rushed out of there and ran back to where I knew I would find Luke. He was sitting where he always was these days, behind Nate's outhouse, smoking pot.

I rushed at him, hitting him as hard as I could, blindly slapping and scratching till he grabbed and held me.

"Whoa. Wait up, Ella, what's gotten into you?"

"You didn't have sex with me," I yelled, spit flying out of my mouth and into his face.

He had the grace to look ashamed. Ducked his head.

"How do you know?"

"I know," I said ominously.

"You're only twelve, Ella. I have a sister almost your age," he protested.

He held me off as I pummeled him, my fists going one two, one two, into his chest. "Come on, Ella, why do you want to so bad? It isn't even supposed to feel good the first time. And what about God? Now, you know He'll be mad if you do, and there you are always talking about Him."

That stopped me for a second. "But I need to," I said, and then I burst into tears because I could only think of how much I had hurt God by what I had tried to do.

"Come on, Ella." Then he hesitated.

"You think Kitty is getting something good you aren't, just because she's beautiful or something. Is that what this is all about?"

I almost shouted no. But then I couldn't tell him the truth. Couldn't tell him that this was all I had to keep Leroy away from me. Keep him from trying to break me apart.

"Well, just so you know, Kitty isn't getting any either. She's too busy trying to use it to buy her way into a wedding ring with some doctor or lawyer." His lip jutted out and I could see just how much it must hurt him to tell me that.

"There you go, two virgins in the very same house."

I turned away. I was done being mad at him. All I could do was to hope Leroy still thought that I was having sex. If not, I would have to think of something drastic to keep him away.

Instead of going home, my mind, like a homing pigeon, was suddenly full of Miss St. James, full of the words she taught and spoke, so crisp and clear, like lemon in a fresh glass of cold water. I made a beeline for her house. Ran up the stairs and knocked and knocked. It took a minute or so and then the door swung open.

"I haven't seen you all week, Ella, everything okay?"

I nodded.

"If there is a problem, you know you can tell me?" She probed carefully, nervously.

I nodded even though I was lying. I would never tell her everything.

She took my arm and walked me into the house, and then she handed me a tissue.

"Go fix your face," she finally said.

When I got to the bathroom, I saw my reflection; my face was awash with dried tears and snot. When I walked out five minutes later with my face scrubbed clean, there was tea on the table along with the Scrabble board.

"Feel better?"

I nodded. The cold water had soothed my face and somehow the incessant twitching had calmed down.

Surprisingly enough, Miss St. James knew that Scrabble would comfort me, just like the pacifier that C.T. used to keep in his mouth till Leroy got sick of it and threw it away.

We played in silence, but I was off my game and she beat me easily, twice in a row. She pulled out some paper for me to do some writing.

Instead, I faced her.

"Miss St. James?"

"Yes?"

"Why did you want me to start lessons with you?"

She smiled. "You remember how I first met you?"

I nodded.

"Well, there you were, this little scrap of nothing, pummeling that big boy sitting on you, without an ounce of fear and with that look of determination on your face. I thought to myself, well, that's someone I want to get to know. Someone who is bold and fearless like that."

I smiled, and felt like I must look like a fool, grinning like that. Her words made me think I could do anything.

"Now, I used to be just like that, all the way into my teens," Miss St. James said. "Then I became more introverted. Now I've reached my great age, I've decided to try to be bold."

"What great age is that, Miss St. James?" I asked slyly.

She laughed and wagged her finger at me.

"What angles are you talking about when you say you are examining all angles of black migration, civil rights, and the murders?"

"You never do give up, Ella." She looked at me quizzingly. "I thought we already talked about this."

"Are you going to interview the people in North Ricksville?"

Miss St. James looked a bit surprised and then she said, "I hadn't really thought about it. I didn't know there was a North Ricksville when I was in New Jersey. No, I'd planned to go to Philadelphia, it's only about an hour away."

I was looking hard at Miss St. James as she spoke.

"I know exactly what they are going to say," I said.

Miss St. James shook her head. Was she disagreeing with me?

"According to Mr. Macabe," I continued, "there are three types of people: the good, the evil, and the ones in between. The ones that did the killings and all those bad things during the civil rights movement were evil, plain and simple."

"Well, if Mr. Macabe has so many theories, he should write his own book," she said.

We sat in silence. It was the closest we had ever gotten to an argument.

The silence grew. And grew. We sat apart, me glaring, she with her eyes down; a shuttered look had come over her. I was stubborn. I wasn't giving up.

"Can I read what you have?"

"No."

The word was crisp and final, but I now tried begging. "Please?"

She didn't bother to respond.

"Will black people like what you are writing?"

"Ella!"

"I want to know," I persisted.

"If you must know, it's meant for everyone, but I can't write, thinking what people are going to say or think, otherwise I wouldn't be an academic."

But that wasn't what I'd meant. I bit my tongue to stop from asking any more questions.

"You look tired, Ella," she said kindly after looking at me closely. "Go lie awhile on the sofa." She tossed me a thin blanket and went to the kitchen.

From the sofa, I could hear her taking out pots and pans, fixing things. Soon the noises in the kitchen soothed me and lulled me to sleep, and the next thing I knew, she was waking me up.

"It's late, Ella. It's six o'clock. Your mother will be looking for you."

The thought came out, unbidden. "I wish you were my mother." I caught it, held it captive, and then I was ashamed.

CHAPTER 35

Miss St. James ended up being the second person I told about Leroy. I hadn't meant to, only I was mad. The words had slipped out of my mouth and come sliding right onto the middle of her dining table. I remember her expression, too. Her mouth open in a horrified round O, as though someone had just taken a dump in the middle of her dining room.

I was shaking furiously when I said it. The kind of anger that burns a hole through your gut, causing your stomach muscles to clench and reclench. I never thought Miss St. James could make me so angry, but here she was talking about how my father, Leroy, seemed like such a nice, handsome gentleman. Why, one time he had even carried her groceries all the way from the bus stop to the house and had insisted on bringing them inside and putting them on her kitchen table.

"Do you know he is my stepdad?" I said coldly. Frigid enough for her to raise her eyebrows at me.

"I thought so . . ." she said, adding after a few seconds, "You look very different than the rest of your family, but I thought. . . . well, people often look different than their families."

"I'm Ma's child. Not his," I said pointedly, and waited for her to connect the dots.

It took her some seconds, then the slight look of surprise before she put her hand on mine.

"These things don't matter, Ella. They are best forgotten, left to grown-ups. The important thing is that you're here and loved. Fix your mind on that."

"I'm *not* loved," I cried out. "I'm hated. Leroy hates me the most."

"No, Ella, I'm sure that isn't the case." Now she looked shocked.

I wanted to hurt her, then, to pay her back for her dumb assumption about my being loved, and even more for liking Leroy. So I added, with some venom, "Leroy tries to touch me all the time."

And then she did cry out. Covered her ears with her hands, and for a moment I thought how weak she seemed that she couldn't even listen to that.

"I must think, Ella."

I looked at her. There was something appraising in her glance. I wanted to take my words back.

"Don't worry about it," I said as I brought out the Scrabble board.

But then she stopped and sat down, reached out and gathered me up and put me on her lap. I was way too big to be there, but I sat still. Soon my body relaxed into hers, and I could feel the fury melting away, like all the balled-up anger and knots were fizzling out and leaving my body and disappearing into hers. What a relief to finally say something.

⸻ ◈ ⸻

I couldn't sleep. The Ricksville Summer School Dance was my first dance ever. I had seen Kitty's dress. Ma had taken it from that endless trunk of clothes and sewed it till it fit Kitty like a glove. That dress material had cost Ma a month's paycheck. I knew because for the entire month we had eaten leftovers from Nate's till I was so sick of chicken and fries that I vowed I'd never eat either again.

The dress had pretty gold straps and gold trim at the bottom, but the rest of it was white, dipping down into a V to showcase a swelling bodice that hugged her waist before draping to below the knees. Leroy had watched Kitty sashaying around in the dress, his lips pursed in disapproval at what it revealed.

"What you giving her such a dress for?" Leroy had asked. "Isn't like she needs to impress any of these Ricksville boys."

"Not those boys," Ma had replied calmly. "It'll be Christmas before you know it, and we need a good picture of Kitty to send out."

Leroy shut right up because he knew better. That free picture, taken at the dance, would be copied and sent to wealthy families Ma knew with eligible sons from Alabama to New York, and perhaps one of those would-be suitors would be smitten. The picture had to be perfect, and both Ma and Kitty knew it.

The following morning, I woke up very early and headed to Cammy's house. I knocked and Miss Claudia came to the door.

"Hi, Ella, still growing, I see. You'll be taller than me before we know it."

I smiled, even though I was tired of hearing how tall I was getting. "Is Cammy here?"

"She's in her room."

I tapped before pushing open the door. Cammy was sitting at the foot of her bed, examining two dresses carefully laid out over the pillow. She turned when she saw me, then she gave me an odd look before her eyes turned blank.

"Hi, Cammy. Are you looking for something to wear to the summer dance?" I said.

"Yes, I have two choices." She hesitated before adding, "Can I try them on for you?"

I nodded and watched as she put on the red dress and then the green. She spun in front of me, pretending to be dancing with a real partner. She looked amazing in both dresses.

"Well?"

"I'd wear the red if you want to make people notice you, and the green if you want people to say how pretty your eyes are."

Cammy laughed, her eyes dancing in mischief. "Now you've gone and said it, I'll have to wear the red."

"I just came to see if I could borrow a dress from you. Something you don't wear often or don't like."

"I don't know, Ella, you are kind of tall. Your legs go on forever."

"I'm not that tall, no matter what your ma says, and I'm about the same size as you up top. It'll just be a little short."

Cammy went through her clothes and pulled out two dresses, a pink frilly number and a light blue one that was prettied up by swaths of dark blue ripples. The V-neck of the blue dress dipped low enough to show that I was not completely flat, and the bottom of the skirt was wide enough so I could twirl as I danced. "Take the blue, I think that will go better with your skin color."

I wasn't so sure, but after staring at myself in her mirror, I finally decided that perhaps she was right, so I put the blue dress in a bag.

"See you at the dance," I said, hurrying out with the bag before she changed her mind.

I rushed all the way home to try it on again in front of my best mirror, C.T.

"Is it okay?" I asked him.

"It's beautiful, you look like a butterfly."

A butterfly! C.T.'s eyes were so big and so shiny that I had to laugh. "I hope I get the same reaction at the dance, C.T.," I said, pulling him to me.

A few hours later, my hair was combed up neatly with a matching blue bow. I put on my blue flats and headed out the door alone; Kitty had already left. I practiced my dance steps as I walked up the road.

"I do declare, you are as pretty as you'll ever be," I said to my reflection in a passing car. Then I spotted Fats standing outside his house. He walked over and fell in step with me.

"I like that white suit, Fats."

He grinned. I could tell that, like me, he wasn't used to getting compliments, or giving them. When I saw that none was forthcoming, I twirled before him. "Don't you like it?"

"Since when did you care how you dressed, Ella?"

I rolled my eyes at him.

Fats didn't say anything more, just held that tongue in his mouth like he knew what was good for him. Unfortunately, that lasted only till we reached the school building.

"Ella."

"Yes?"

There was a pause and I suddenly got very irritated with him.

"What is it?"

"Everyone's talking about you."

"Saying what?"

"Saying that you let Luke do stuff with you."

"Who says that?" My voice came out in a squeak.

"Everybody. Luke's been talking junk. He was listing who he'd slept with and your name was on the list. He's stupid. Especially when he's on those joints or some hooch."

I stood stock-still outside the entrance of the school, not knowing what to say. What did Fats mean by "everybody"? The whole school? Was that why Cammy had given me that side-eyed look when she first saw me?

"He's a liar."

Fats shrugged. He looked miserable.

I wanted to disappear.

"Well, you coming in or not?" We were almost at the entrance of the gym where the dance was being held. Fats was still looking at his shoes, not into my eyes.

"No. I'm not coming."

"Some people already saw you. They will talk even more."

"I'm going home." I turned on my heel, but then I spotted Kitty entering the school grounds. She was holding hands with Luke. At first I thought she was going to ignore me like she usually did, but then she turned and made her way towards me, Luke in tow.

"Nice dress, Ella," she said mockingly.

Kitty had an audience. She could never get enough of the attention. I could tell by the way she began to flick back her hair—flick, flick, flick it went. Then she let go of Luke's hand and walked around me, creating a circle of onlookers as she went, till I was standing in the middle of it.

Fats broke into the circle and grabbed hold of my hand to pull me out, but Kitty came at me and pushed me down.

The crowd laughed.

"Beat her down, Kitty," I heard one of her friends shout.

With her audience watching, nothing could stop Kitty. She stood an arm's length away from me.

"You stay away from Luke, you ugly, good-for-nothing slut. Everyone's talking about you. He's just using you. He loves me. Got it?"

The words stung. Hurt as though a thousand bees had descended on me.

Kitty turned on her heel and the crowd drifted apart. It was only then I saw Luke, his lying eyes searching for Kitty, his hand already held out possessively. He glanced at me, shamefaced, just before he turned away.

I slunk away like the thief they all thought I was. Ran up that endless road, trying to get enough distance between me and the

school, ignoring Fats's calls to wait up. Ran all the way up Ricksville Road, past our house, where Ma would have had questions
about why I was back. I ran till I could run no more, and then I sat
at the side of the road and bawled.

At midnight, I got tired of the mosquitoes biting and went on
home. The front door was locked. Every light was out. I tapped
lightly, hoping that Stevie would hear and come to the door, but
no one stirred. Then I banged louder. The house was still. I looked
up at the windows, and for the first time since I could remember,
every window was shut. The mosquitoes started up buzzing in my
ear and sucking at me again. I slapped my arms and hugged myself.
Short of being bitten to death on the stoop, where could I go this
late at night? I walked up Ricksville Road, quickly ruling out Mr.
Macabe's house because he would be in a panic if I showed up this
late at night, and quickly ruling out Nate because he had once told
me that he slept like a log. I thought of Miss St. James, but worried
that I would scare her senseless if I knocked on her door at this
hour; she would probably think someone was coming to rob her,
or worse.

When I reached Fats's house, I crept around to the side, where
a single window was lit. I dashed back to the front and grabbed a
fistful of pebbles and went back to the window, hoping it was Fats's
bedroom window—I'd never stepped foot inside his house—and,
holding my breath, one by one I threw the pebbles up against the
glass. At the fourth pebble, Fats's face appeared at the window,
and I exhaled in relief. Within a minute, he was at the front door,
frowning.

"What are you doing here?" he whispered.

"Long story, just let me in, Fats."

He opened the door wide and I went into the dimly lit hallway.
The outside of his house looked like most of the houses on Ricks-

ville Road, except it always had a good coat of paint on it, never dirty or faded or peeling. But it didn't prepare me for the inside. Walking in, I was stunned. The hall light threw enough light for me to see rooms full of beautiful oak furniture that was so polished it shone, piled with lovely cushions that matched. There were also leather armchairs and chests I had no name for but knew they were expensive.

"Fats, you're rich," I said resentfully because I always figured he was like one of us.

He shrugged. "Not really. My mother just has an eye for nice things and she picks them up at flea markets and yard sales in the rich areas of Ricksville."

I kept silent. Fats's ma kept herself to herself, barely mixing with the rest of the grown-ups on the street. She was an accountant, had a car, which was rare for our street, and drove to the next town for work every day, coming home late in the evening. His dad owned the barbershop at the end of Ricksville Road, but his ma and dad weren't together anymore.

"What is wrong with you, Ella?" he asked after a while. "Why in a few weeks have you suddenly become a different person?"

"I just need somewhere to sleep for the night." Even to me, I sounded like a sulky child.

Fats looked resigned. "Okay, come up to my room. I'll sleep on the floor, you can have the bed. But you have to leave by six. My ma comes to wake me up soon after, and she will kill me if she sees a girl in my room."

What a baby. I bet his ma still tucked him in and woke him up with a kiss.

I couldn't stop looking around his room once I got there, taking everything in. Taking in all the love he had in this house. Bookshelves stacked with what looked like amazing adventure stories, the desk over in the corner with the case packed with pens and pencils, curtains that matched the bedspread . . . and, most of all, his name, the one I had never known, Edmond, stenciled in cursive lettering on a wooden board, hanging across the wall directly in front of me. Suddenly I despised him and his nice tidy house and the big bouncy bed with the fluffy pillows and matching bedsheets. I wanted to claw out his eyes at the unfairness of it all. I wanted to say something that would make him hurt, but search as I could, I couldn't find something to pin him to the ground. Thought of yelling out that he was so fat, every step was like jelly, wobble, wobble. The words were on my tongue, just ready to drip off. Stop it, I said to myself. Be grateful. You could be sleeping on the street, being eaten alive by mosquitoes.

Soon I fell into an uneasy sleep but then I started to dream of my father. I was standing at the edge of Ricksville Road, waiting. A car came roaring down the street. It was a large blue Cadillac. So large it filled the whole street. So shiny that it looked like little diamonds studded the body of the car. It slowed down and stopped right next to me. I looked down the street and everyone was there. Nate, Mr. Macabe, Stevie, Kitty, Ma, Leroy, Miss Claudia, C.T., even the doctor and his old ma. They had gathered to see this celebrity. He stepped out of the car, and he towered over us. I tried to see his face, but it seemed like he was too tall for me to see all the way up there.

"I'm looking for Ella, my daughter. I have been looking for many years now. She must be twelve years old. Will someone please help me?"

His voice rang out clear and bold, but there was a catch in it, small but just enough that I could tell he had been searching the whole state for me. I rushed at him, holding on to his leg as though I would never let it go.

"I'm Ella," I said. "I'm your daughter." He reached down and picked me up and hugged me tight and kissed me. I looked over his shoulder and saw the shock in all those staring faces. And more than shock—Kitty, green with envy; Ma, slinking away in embarrassment; Leroy, blustering and weak; Fats, mouth wide open. I reveled in it all. I looked up towards his face, still perched in his arms. I wanted to see his face. Would he look like me? I squinted up, but the sun was so bright, and he was wearing a hat that cast a shadow over his face, obscuring it.

"Take off your hat," I said loudly, so he would hear. "Take it off so I can see you."

I was woken by a rough shake.

"Stop it, Ella, you're talking in your sleep," Fats whispered. "Ma will hear you."

"Shut up," I mumbled in disappointment, before drifting into an uneasy, dreamless sleep.

CHAPTER 36

"They are all liars, Kate. Never believe them." She remembered repeating the same words diligently as her father did, trying to please him as he sat by her bed, mouthing them next to her. That's my girl, he had said when she was done. She still remembers the counselors' annoyance. "He was trying to brainwash you. Do you get it now, Kate?"

What Ella had told her about her stepfather shocked her to her core. She had seen the thin, tall man emerge from Ella's house from time to time, always well dressed and polite whenever their paths crossed, which was rarely.

Perhaps Ella was lying?

There was something about being in Ricksville that put her on edge. Whereas she couldn't hear her father's voice all the way in Princeton, being here, sometimes his voice would fly into her head and she would have to swat it away or wrestle it to the ground. He seemed so close here, almost as though his spirit still somehow lingered in the Mississippi air.

She had looked at Ella, trying to gauge whether she was telling a fib or the truth. It was only then that she saw the change in Ella's face—that open face becoming closed, her eyes shuttered, like a curtain being drawn. She forced her arms to reach out before she could think it through. She had held Ella as close as she could for as long as she could. Ella had held on.

She almost wept at the sheer enormity of being able to feel something, for Ella. She pushed her father's thoughts away, pushed Kate away.

CHAPTER 37

"Ella?"

"Yes, Miss St. James."

We were sitting at her wooden table. My feet dangled an inch off the floor and I was swinging them back and forth. I was waiting for Miss St. James to get finished with her chapter so that we could play Scrabble.

"Yes," I said again, knowing that she had forgotten what she was about to say and was back to being fully immersed in her writing. Her pen, a warn plastic blue Bic with a chewed end, was moving furiously across the page. It took her a second to register that I had spoken.

"Sorry. I want to talk to someone in the neighborhood who can give me some background information about South Ricksville. Do you know anyone who will be willing to talk to me?"

Miss St. James didn't have to say what we already knew. That she hadn't made any adult friends in the neighborhood.

"A grown-up?"

"Yes."

I was thinking, my mind running through all the people I knew. It was no, no, no, until I got to thinking about Mr. Macabe.

"Perhaps Mr. Macabe," I said cautiously. I knew she had met him before. "He's nice, but he's blind."

I expected her to say no because he was a man, but after just a second of hesitation, all she said was "Great."

I made the arrangements and a day later headed to Miss St. James's house to walk over to Mr. Macabe's with her. When I got there, to my surprise, Miss St. James was all dressed up in a long swishy dress, like she was going to a fancy party. She was also wearing perfume.

"He can't see," I pointed out when I saw how nicely she had dressed.

"Just because he's blind doesn't mean we can dress any way we please. We are going to visit, so we dress up."

"How will he know you dressed up?" I asked.

"He'll smell that perfume and know that I made some kind of effort."

I looked down at my rumpled T-shirt and shorts.

"Can I have some of that perfume?"

I didn't want Mr. Macabe thinking only Miss St. James had made an effort. She sprayed some all over me and we walked on over to Mr. Macabe's.

Mr. Macabe was wearing one of his favorite shirts, the red checked one. He had a jug of iced tea and three glasses already laid out. We sat down with him at his little table on the porch, and after saying hello and thanking him for my iced tea, I sat quietly, taking it all in, how grown-ups talk to each other, especially ones like Mr. Macabe and Miss St. James, who didn't know each other well. First, they were very polite to each other, with Miss St. James complaining about the heat and Mr. Macabe right along with her, complaining about how hot it was, rattling on about how his fan was not working, and on and on till I wondered whether Miss St. James had clean forgot why she had come. I went inside to make some more cold tea, and when I got back, they were talking about her life up north. Miss St. James talked so much I thought her tongue would fall out. She talked all about the university that she loved, the town of Princeton, her professors, and all her fellow students, most of whom could be her children, and a few of

them looked at her like she was an eccentric old woman returning to school. I could tell Miss St. James had been dying for some
grown-up company all this while. I knew Mr. Macabe was also
enjoying the conversation, because he was very still as he listened,
and then wagged from side to side as he laughed. I knew just what
it was like to have him listen so hard that way, like he was waiting
to catch every word that fell from your mouth, like a dog does
when it knows a treat is about to fall from your hand. It made you
feel like you could tell him just about anything, and that's why
Miss St. James was talking a blue streak.

I knew things were getting deep when Mr. Macabe told me to
run to the store for a bottle of cheap wine. Only he didn't say
cheap wine, he said good wine, and gave me a little wink so I knew
what he meant. "Check my pocket," he said, and even though Miss
St. James protested, I got five dollars from his pocket and left them
to it.

I already knew what Mr. Macabe wanted. The bottle with the
bright blue label called Sereum. People drank it because it was
cheap, but it could knock you silly if you didn't take care. When I
got back with the extra-large bottle, they were laughing, so I went
inside to get the glasses, twisted off the wine top, and poured them
each a glass.

"That's way too much," Miss St. James said, but I noticed that
she drank it all. Mr. Macabe sipped his slowly. After a while, Miss
St. James said, "I heard this town got its name from a man named
Rick Howard, who owned all the land but lost it in a gamble."

"You heard right," Mr. Macabe said, smiling. "I don't know
how he lost all that land, but he must have been a serious gambler.
He owned a whole lot of cotton-producing land, slaves, mansions. He was so famous that even though he lost the land, they
still kept the name. Now, mind you, he also lost all the slaves on

the land with that gamble, I am told, because they lived on that land and their homes and all of them went right along with it."

Miss St. James then asked how slaves were housed back in slavery days. Did Mr. Macabe know what their houses looked like and what kind of food they ate? This part was interesting, so I sat and listened till Mr. Macabe asked her if she knew about the custom of jumping over the broom to denote marriage between slaves.

"She doesn't know, she's white," I explained patiently.

"White is just a skin color," said Mr. Macabe. "Doesn't mean she knows or doesn't know."

Turned out Miss St. James had read all about it at the library, so I was wrong. I got up and poured her another glass of wine.

Then she asked Mr. Macabe how he viewed white people. Did he hate them for what they had done to his people?

Good thing she hadn't ever asked Ma that question. That was the kind of question that made everyone in Ricksville nervous. That was a government kind of question, and any which way you answered could be a problem. So I held my breath and waited to see what Mr. Macabe would say, but he said nothing. Just sat there for a few minutes. The only noise was the tinkling of their glasses, then a gulp as she swallowed.

When he finally started speaking, I was hanging on every word, right along with Miss St. James.

"What's white people? I'm blind. Never seen the color white in my life or the color black or blue or gray for that matter. To a blind man, color means nothing. My ma used to tell me that the world is like a glorious set of watercolor paints laid out in a handcrafted palette. Sure wish I could see what that is. She made it sound special. The only things I can 'see' are bad people, good people, and those in between. The bad ones you can easily avoid, but those in-between people are the worst, because you never know when they'll help you up and when they'll kick you in the teeth. So ask me instead if I hate people and I will tell you that some are deserving of hate, and others not."

Then he went on and on about marketing and how black people were the targets of a smear campaign to get farmers to buy more slaves. That the color difference was exploited as a marketing tool so that when people saw a colored skin tone they immediately thought that this person was only good for menial work or was a criminal or up to no good. That's the genius of marketing, Mr. Macabe went on. "It stays and perpetuates. Just as you know Tide is good for washing, they thought they knew what colored people were good for. It would have been far better for everyone if slavery was abolished because they finally realized that the whole rationale for slavery was one big marketing swindle. That way, we would have been done with fighting the battle of perception of black people on every front. Instead, slavery ended because of a tug on some people's conscience, and you know how that goes. The do-gooders feel they ought to do something, but the others, well, they still believe that same old marketing hype. We're still fighting the smear campaign today." Mr. Macabe sighed.

I looked at Miss St. James a couple of times while Mr. Macabe was having his lecture, just to see whether she was writing it all down, but her notebook stayed in her bag. She had an odd look on her face, like she was being prodded with needles and didn't like it. She nodded once or twice but didn't say anything.

"Mighty complex," Mr. Macabe said, and took a big gulp of wine. Miss St. James did the same. Then there was silence.

When the conversation started up again, it wasn't about slavery.

Over the next hour Mr. Macabe and Miss St. James finished the whole bottle between them. At one point, I'd moved from a chair to the top porch step, and I knew they'd forgotten all about me because Mr. Macabe started talking about his wife and his life before Ricksville; he never talked to me about those things. He talked about being born and raised in Mississippi, which I knew, but I didn't know he was married to a pretty young New York City fancy lady, way before I was born. When Miss St. James asked what happened to her, he only said, "When bright city lights call, makes people go running." I couldn't imagine Mr. Macabe in New York, though he said he'd lived there for a spell. Right in central Harlem, in a city that was awake all night.

"Didn't you like it?" Miss St. James asked.

"Since I couldn't see anything, all I heard was the endless noise," Mr. Macabe answered. "The noise of the cars swishing by, so close I'd swear they were about to knock me down or at least side-swipe me. The sounds of their horns, blaring day and night. Crazy sounds of a city all jumbling up in my head. That was the problem with marrying someone who could see. She could describe all she wanted, but all I could hear were the sounds clashing all around me. The one sound I appreciated was the jazz music, finding its way through all the unpleasant noise and soaring through the air; it was indeed a mighty fine thing to hear, but it wasn't enough. I could hear good jazz in lots of places a whole lot less crazy. So I took the bus back to Mississippi and planted myself back home. Grew roots, too," he said. "If anyone ever tried to uproot me, they'd have to start digging, all the way from one end of Ricksville Road to the other, and up and down Perry all the way to Main, to dig up all the roots to get me out of here." He chuckled, and Miss St. James echoed with a soft chuckle of her own.

"So when did you go blind?" she asked after a moment.

"Been born blind," he said. "My ma told me it was a punishment for having me out of wedlock, and for stealing another woman's

man, but I never thought of it as a curse. I never did meet my father but once, and that was enough. When I was twelve, he rode
into town. I was playing the saxophone because in those days that
was what most of the blind kids did, play some musical instrument
to be able to earn their living since they couldn't go do any other
learning or apprenticing. So anyway, I was sitting at home, playing
my instrument, when Ma brought in a man. I heard his voice, deep
and chesty, so I knew Ma had brought in a man, but since that
happened often enough, I made to leave the room, but the man
said, 'Sit down, fellow.' I kept to my seat then. I felt him looking
at me, and then his big, rough, sweaty palm held my face by the
chin, and I knew his eyes were looking me over. I didn't know then
that he was trying to figure out whether I was his or not. 'Hmm,'
he murmured, and then he let go. 'What am I going to do with a
blind son?' It surprised me so much that I dropped the saxophone.
Not every day that you have someone calling you 'son.' He picked
the saxophone up and put it back in my lap and then he was gone.
He left my mother a hundred dollars, which was a lot of money in
those days, but we never did see him again. Reckon I must have
looked enough like him, though, for him to call me 'son.'"

It was then that I realized part of why I felt so close to Mr.
Macabe. He didn't have a father either. But at least he'd met him
once. That was more than I could say.

I watched as Miss St. James grew tipsy, and soon another five dollars came my way, this time from Miss St. James, and I headed off
to the corner store to get them another bottle of wine. When I got
back, Miss St. James was talking about how white women had also
had a hard time with slavery. How, yes, they'd obviously benefited
from all the free labor, but then think how they must have felt when
their husbands started taking up with slave women and fathering
their children? She'd read a lot about mulattoes being fathered by

slave owners, which is what changed the color of blacks in America from their original dark West African color to a brown or lighter color, and couldn't help wondering how those wives must have felt. It must have hurt them deeply.

I expected Mr. Macabe to get mad that she was being sympathetic with the slave owners' wives but he just put his head to one side, staring at Miss St. James with those milky eyes. He was so still, like he was listening very hard. Then he nodded before replying.

"Even if that were so, you would think that they would try to stop slavery, send those slaves away, for selfish reasons, to protect their families. I don't think they did. I think white women were fully complicit, some were even the instigators because the benefits of slavery clearly outweighed the costs to the family. Couple the economic incentive of having slaves with how they felt about what their husbands were doing—well, that's a pretty explosive mix: they had to take those emotions out on somebody, and who do you think they chose?"

"I don't agree." I could see two high pink spots in Miss St. James's cheeks, showing that she was getting very het up. "I think women had no power over what their husbands did. They didn't even have rights themselves. What could they have done?"

"Hmm, perhaps. Though, if they'd really wanted to get slaves out of their homes, some women could have had a hold on their men. You know what they say about the power dynamics of a bedroom . . ."

Miss St. James broke out giggling, and I knew she was getting very silly. Then she said, "Well, some farmers didn't have it easy either when slavery ended. A lot of their labor just up and left, leaving some of them penniless. This made for a lot of poorer generations. My father, Jack Summerville, was a lot poorer than his father."

"Can't feel sympathy for the white farmers when black farm-workers were getting next to nothing. Almost like slavery back again."

Things got mighty quiet again after that, but then Mr. Macabe offered Miss St. James another drink, and she took it, sipping slowly, and all seemed fine again.

"You go on home, Ella," Mr. Macabe said. "It's late. Miss St. James and I are just going to finish up this bottle and she'll be along. Not every day I have a pretty lady up in here."

I got up to go but couldn't help asking, "Just how you know she's pretty, Mr. Macabe? She could be as ugly as a hyena and you wouldn't know it."

"Oh, I do know. All I got to do is smell that perfume and I know that I have a pretty lady in front of me."

I grimaced, but Miss St. James winked at me with a "see what I told you?" twinkle in her eyes.

CHAPTER 38

Miss St. James and I were outside having our walk. She would now come up to the entryway to my yard and I would be there waiting. She and I would walk right up Ricksville Street and walk all the way down. She said walking helped her think, and there I was, thinking right alongside her. Nobody joined us. Some stared, and I would stare right back. Stare all you like, I would say to myself. This is my friend. Miss St. James was my best friend in Ricksville, and I was hers. Sometimes on our walk we would say nothing at all and other times she would ask me about one or another neighbor. I told her all about Cammy's mother, who had jobs now and again but didn't have much money, and all about Fats's ma, who had gone to Howard and now worked as an accountant in the next town. When we went past Ty's house I told her how Ty's grandma had marched with Dr. Martin Luther King, and had been one of those people who had done sit-ins at the height of the civil rights movement. Everybody around here loves Ty's grandma, I told her. We treat her like she's a queen.

Miss St. James would tell me about Boston, saying that she didn't have many friends there, but she liked New Jersey better, at Princeton. It was pretty there, she said, lots of trees. I loved it when she talked about her school: the grand buildings, her pro-fessors, and the clubs you could join if you went there. There was even a journalism club and a hiking club. I thought about how I could get there when I was older. "Just study hard, Ella," she said, smiling. "You can get there. You're so smart."

"Can I stay with you when I get there?"

"Well, if I am still there, you can come to stay."

"Where's your family? Still in Boston?" I asked because Miss St. James said she noticed how neighbors were in and out of one another's houses, like we were all family.

"They are dead. Long gone."

Miss St. James didn't say much about that anymore. She didn't talk after that for the rest of our walk, and I wished I'd kept quiet. I thought she might be missing her family. I took her hand and we walked, swinging our hands, saying nothing, till we turned and started back down the street again. When we got near Mr. Macabe's I yelled out.

"Mr. Macabe, you on that porch?"

There was silence for a second and then, as we passed his house, I heard his voice rolling up behind me.

"That you, Ella? What you doing yelling in the street for?"

I turned to Miss St. James and told her, "People around here will tell you to mind your manners, even if you're not their child."

She laughed. "He loves you, Ella, just as much as I do."

I stared at Miss St. James, at what she had just said about loving me. She had said it casual like, and I wanted to hug her but at the same time I wanted to cry. I don't know why. I wasn't sad. I was so happy, my chest was pounding so hard I was sure she could see my heart jumping out of my chest, going pom pom pom pom, like a giant stamping on the pavement.

I love you, too.

Only I didn't say it out loud.

I just thought it.

But it did make a difference. Before, I had held back because Miss St. James was so different-looking, and she was writing that thesis that I wasn't sure about. When I'd described her to anyone before, I would say that she was a bit like a pale frosty blue. Cool to the touch but still nice to be next to, especially when it was really hot outside. Miss St. James was only cool on the outside, because when you went deep, to the very center of Miss St. James, all you would see were reds and oranges. It was only when I saw this warm side of her that I completely let go all the air that it seemed I was holding on to when she was around. It came out of me that day, all of a sudden, and I was standing there, just me, the real me. Either Miss St. James had scaled the wall that was me, or I had taken it down.

When you love someone, it sets you free. I read it in a book somewhere, or a poem, or heard it in a song. It wasn't that I hadn't loved anyone before. I loved God the most because He was always rescuing me, but that was a different love because it was God. On this earth I could say that Mr. Macabe, Nate, Stevie, and C.T. were the people I loved, but somehow the love I had for them was different from what I had for Miss St. James. The love I had for her was fuller, larger and more complete. Like a big meal you had that gave you what you had longed for—sweet potatoes, fried chicken, gravy, biscuits, lemonade, apple pie, all of it—till you were just lying there full, not able to wish for a single more thing on your plate, or even a second course. Maybe, I pondered, it was because they were men and she was a woman. I couldn't figure it out but all I knew was that with that feeling of fullness, I needed nothing more.

CHAPTER 39

The move to get Miss St. James out of Ricksville started like the wicked wind I've seen come roaring through in summer, pushing slowly at first, then pulling back so you'd relax, thinking it's gone, but all the while it is quietly waiting, building, building, ready to hit you when you least expect it. When it finally comes back, it is a gale that pummels everything in its path to smithereens.

I knew that the winds had started blowing by early August, but in a way, it was my big mouth that started it all. I had told Miss St. James the story about Nate and Mrs. Catchedy and how they had been friends till she died. Whether it was this notion that Nate was as friendly as Mr. Macabe, I don't know, but somewhere along the line, Miss St. James got it into her head that she would like to talk to Nate. But I hadn't offered to introduce her to Nate like I had Mr. Macabe.

If she had asked me, I would have said immediately, "Don't go up there. Nate's not so easygoing after what the Catchedy family did to him at the funeral and afterwards." It never crossed my mind that she would walk over to Nate's and just go on in. But she did. By all accounts she just strode in there like she went there every day. Now, I could have told her that while Nate's Diner was on Main Street, the only people that went in there were black folk, and if someone wasn't sure what Nate's was all about, all they had to do was to glance at the frames on the wall, full of black people, from movement activists to athletes and boxers, to get a clue. But

Miss St. James wasn't from the South. I don't think she knew that in Ricksville, everyone knew their place and stayed put.

I heard what happened the day she walked in there, because Mr. Graves was there at the time, and he took the story from house to house on his whiskey run, which as usual included a stop at our house to talk to Ma.

The way he told it, the diner was crowded because it was a Friday night—certainly, Miss St. James had picked the worst night of the week to walk into Nate's. There were a bunch of men, all coming off work, eager for a bite to eat, and Nate was busy, making and flipping burgers as fast as he could. The crowd was rowdy by the time Miss St. James arrived. Mr. Graves said that after she stepped in and it was clear that she wasn't asking for directions and that she was there to stay, you could have heard a pin drop. The silence lasted about twenty seconds, and when the noise picked up again, it was muted, as customers ate in silence, each wondering what it was she wanted there. Every ear was pricked up, every tone muted, eyes on the backs of their heads, watching. Not that she knew; Miss St. James was sitting in the center of the room with her face towards Nate, who was turned towards the grill, so his back was to her. When he finally turned around to take her order, he was so shocked to find her sitting there, and the very one everyone had been talking about for weeks to boot, he turned back to the grill in confusion or irritation and flipped another ten burgers.

Meanwhile, Miss St. James was getting mad about not being served. Mr. Graves said he could tell because she twisted every which way in her seat trying to get Nate's attention, and when it looked like he wasn't catching her movements, she called out for him to take her order. Mighty bad, Mr. Graves said, shaking his head slowly. After this, Mr. Graves slowed down his story.

He had drawn that story out till Ma was on the edge of her seat, waiting to hear what happened next. Then he scratched his head, as though trying to remember, till Ma remembered that, oh, she hadn't yet offered him a drink. Ma motioned for me to go, and I returned with a tot of whiskey. Mr. Graves took his sweet time savoring his swig of whiskey before finally getting back to the story. Now Mr. Graves said the way she called out for Nate to take her order, well, it was bad. She had sounded loud, shrill, and imperious. She may just as well have called out, "Boy, get me a burger." That's the way Mr. Graves said it. I couldn't believe Miss St. James would be so loud and rude, and I'd glared at Mr. Graves when he said that, because I didn't believe him one bit, but he wasn't looking my way. He was too busy basking in the glow of Ma's shock.

Mr. Graves said that words were exchanged. Not "irrevocable words"—ones that once said cannot be taken back, words that are like bullets that go in hard and stay buried, impossible to dig out. These were angry words, more like "Don't talk to me like that, not in my own diner, I'll serve you when I'm good and ready" words. And she'd answered back, "I think you're a terrible businessman, I don't know why you're still in business," or something of the like, and it got loud enough that someone stepped in and hushed them up and asked Nate to fix Miss St. James a burger. By then, though, the crowd at Nate's was irritated. A few men started telling her she didn't belong down there talking like that, and there was a lot of muttering going on in the room. It was then that Leroy, who happened to be there, stepped in with another man and quietly escorted her home.

At this point, Ma had called out to Leroy to corroborate the story. He'd been upstairs taking a nap and came down bleary-eyed. "Yes," he said shortly, "we did escort her back home, more hurried her along before she made things worse. Folks were getting riled up at the way she spoke to Nate." Then he yawned and went back upstairs.

"I don't tell lies," Mr. Graves said solemnly. "I told you like I saw it and heard it."

Ma just shook her head. "That woman," she said. "When she moved into that house, I told everyone nothing good would come of it."

I waited till Mr. Graves had left and Ma had gone upstairs and back to her bedroom, and I ran out and straight to Nate's.

"Your Miss St. James" were the first words that greeted me when I got there.

"She really is a nice person," I responded. "Very nice once you get to know her. She's just a little . . . a little . . . well, she's from Boston and doesn't know much about being down here."

"She's an ignorant, racist white woman. This is my store. Bought with my own money. I would have tossed her out on her ear if it hadn't been for the fact that every second sentence out of your mouth for the past few months has started with Miss St. James this and Miss St. James that."

Nate's shoulders were hitched up and spread out, like he was about to fight. I knew that whatever it was in Miss St. James's tone that had gotten him all bothered was still crouched up inside him waiting to spring out.

"Spoke to me like I was nothing. In my own place, too. She did everything but add 'boy' at the end of her sentences."

Nate's voice was loud enough to carry across the room all the way to the far corner, where a thin man sat, smoking a cigarette. I hadn't noticed him at all till he spoke up.

"Heap of trouble that's a-brewing," he said. "Having a white woman here. Alone, too?" He shook his head. "I heard the way she spoke to you. Folks won't take kindly to that. Why's she here anyway? Why doesn't she go on to the north side like she belong? Heard she's writing some kind of book. The Reverend said something 'bout it. All about the civil rights and the murders of those men in Philadelphia. Bet she's not writing about the way they disappeared, and all the white men that were involved in shooting them like they was dogs."

The thin stranger only helped to rile Nate up even more. Nate started talking up his father, Joe Catchedy, who wouldn't even acknowledge him even though there was no doubt in anybody's mind whose son he was. One only had to look at Joe and then at Nate to know they were of the same blood. Same nose, same thin mouth. Only difference was his shade and the ruffle in his hair. Nate carried on, talking to the stranger. "You know the only one that acknowledged me in that family was his wife. Imagine that. Was probably because Joe had me before he up and married her, but still, she and I." He shook his head. "Well, we were tight. Now, that was a tough old bird. Hard and leathery on the outside but pure good right inside. Church woman, too. Burned my ears about forgiveness. She knew what I felt about Joe not owning up to the fact that he had a son. Tried to make up for it, too. Now, that was one white woman I know was worth something." Then he turned to me: "Not like your Miss St. James."

Within an hour, another five people had come in, and soon they were all buzzing about Miss St. James. I could smell trouble coming down, the way I could smell Leroy coming before he showed up. I slipped down from my chair and left the diner to find Miss St. James.

She was at home, sitting at the dining table. The notebooks were all around her and she was typing away, turning blue cursive handwriting into ink-black block letters. I watched her for a while because she was so intent on what she was doing that she had barely nodded to me. When she came to the end of the page and was about to put another piece of paper in the typewriter, she finally turned to me.

"How's it going, Ella?"

"Fine." I shrugged nonchalantly.

She started to wind in the paper. Then she stopped, looked at me, and said, as though she'd just remembered, "I met your Nate yesterday. No idea why you like him so much, he was very rude."

"He's nice," I insisted.

"Well, he was not nice to me. He talked to me as though I were—"

She stopped. I waited. I had never known Miss St. James to not know what word to use.

Then I couldn't help it. I just blurted it out.

"Did you talk to Nate like he was nothing?" My words came out loud in the room.

Miss St. James went bright red. The tips of her ears were piping hot, just like chili peppers.

She stood up, and I took a step back. I couldn't tell what she was going to do, but she was shaking.

"No, I did not. We had some words. Well, it's his fault. He talked to me as though I was someone who should not dare come into his diner. I could tell in his manner just what he thought of me. Why, I sat there at the table forever while he just decided not to serve me. I called out, I waved my hand. I don't think he was going to serve me at all. Can you believe that? I was plenty mad, I can tell you. What a terrible man." She stood there with her face moving, like she had a tic or something.

I thought of all the times Nate had told me that people never wanted to serve him in a store, just too intent on asking what he was doing there, like he was up to no good. I knew he wouldn't do that to anyone.

"Well, Nate's gone through a lot of bad stuff in his life," I said quietly. "I think he was just shocked to see you in there, that's all."

"That's certainly no reason to be rude. I haven't done anything to him."

Miss St. James caught her breath, and then she sat down and put her head in her hands.

Was she crying?

"Are you okay, Miss St. James?"

Her head remained buried.

"You okay, Miss St. James?" I asked again, worriedly.

When she didn't answer, I said quietly, "You may want to go live on the north side of Ricksville. You could still come here to do your research. I'd meet you at the library."

Miss St. James lifted her red, streaky face and stared at me. *"Et tu, Brute?"* she said.

I couldn't make out what she meant, so I didn't respond.

"I am surprised at you, Ella. Reverend Walker, yes, he suggested it, as have quite a lot of other people, mostly white people, but I can't believe you of all people would say that."

I hung my head. "It would stop people talking about you," I tried to explain.

"Don't you think they'd talk about me also in the north side of Ricksville? Maybe do worse? I came here for a reason, Ella, and I'm not leaving till it's done."

I stared back at her. Gone were the tears, and that part of her that sometimes seemed like it would break. She wasn't the quiet lady now. She looked so decisive that I turned away, confused.

"Why did you come here?" I asked.

She laughed out loud, a hearty, chesty laugh that swooped up into peals of giggles that went on so long that I started to get scared. Then she wiped the tears that spilled down her cheeks. She had laughed so hard and so long that I thought she wasn't going to stop.

I looked at her doubtfully. Miss St. James was acting a bit crazy, I thought.

She must have read my face, because her next words were "You think I'm crazy?" She looked annoyed. "I told you before, I came to write my thesis. You are supposed to be with the people you are writing about. It's called *immersion*. What better place to do research and write about the civil rights era than in a town like this?"

Maybe not crazy crazy, like half-naked Sammy, but if I was staying in a place where I had to get information from the people I was living with, I'd be as nice as pie to them. And to make matters worse, I had the goose bumps again. If I told Mr. Macabe, he would have said something evil's brewing.

⬥

Folk around here say trouble always comes in threes, and by the end of the week, things that were already bad with Miss St. James's run-in with Nate took a turn for the worse.

I saw Cammy near my house and she looked bursting to tell me something. Before I even said hello, she started talking.

"Miss St. James sure is in a heap of trouble," she said excitedly.

"What do you mean, 'heap of trouble'?"

"She talked to Nate like he was her servant, and man, did he get mad. He stood on a chair and told her where to go. Then she spat on him. They had to pull them two apart. Your Miss St. James is a racist."

"You're just a plain *liar*, Miss Cammy Locklear," I shouted, spitting mad. "That never did happen and you know it didn't."

"Sure did, I know because Ma told me, and she heard it from Mrs. Robertson, who heard it from Mr. Russell, and he heard it from Mr. Graves, who was there!"

"That's a lie!"

"Are you calling my ma a liar?"

I didn't get to scream "YES" like I was about to, because suddenly Stevie showed up and was standing right there in the road with us.

"Hey, Ella," he said, acting like he didn't know he'd walked smack into the thick of battle.

I was still as mad as a hornet stuck in a window frame, so I didn't pay him any mind. I got right up into Cammy's face and all but spat out the words: "Your ma is *wrong*."

"Ella, stop. Calm down," said Stevie.

I stormed off. How dare he be on Cammy's side, telling me to calm down? What about telling *her* to calm down? Smart boy sees a pretty girl and all of a sudden he's dumber than a box of dirt. I turned around when I got to the front door. Cammy was talking to Stevie, no doubt happy I was gone. Well, she'd see. I wouldn't talk to her all week. I went inside, slamming the front door behind me. Seemed like everyone was against Miss St. James and me.

That was the second bad thing that happened.

The third was that Leroy, out of the blue, told Ma that I was spending too much time over at Miss St. James's and that I should stay away from her. This comment about Miss St. James was the first time he'd ever given any advice about the way Ma was bringing me up, and she stared at him, an odd, melty look on her face, like the way the cheese melts in a grilled cheese sandwich, before turning around and shouting at me, "Hear that? Mr. Johnson is looking out for you. Enough of those lessons. You need to stay away from that woman's house. Tell her we need you here for chores. There's been a lot of talk about her in the neighborhood, and I don't want you mixed up in it."

She was referring to the latest rumor about Miss St. James. She had been offered a much bigger and nicer place in the north end of Ricksville for the same price she was paying now. It was a bargain, and the man offering it was none other than Mr. Dickerson, who owned Ricksville Bank and who had declined loan applications from every black person we knew. Miss St. James had turned down the offer flat, Ma had heard. Said she was happy where she was. Mr. Dickerson's maid, Big Nellie, had heard the living room conversation herself as she set the table for breakfast, and whatever part she hadn't overheard the first time was repeated a second time by Mr. and Mrs. Dickerson over the breakfast eggs and toast. Big Nellie had said that Mr. Dickerson was so mad about Miss St. James turning down the accommodation that the missus had to keep warning him about his blood pressure.

"That's what's getting folks uneasy," Ma said to Leroy. "Now, why would she not leave when a nice place was offered to her for peanuts up in North Ricksville?"

To make matters worse, it seemed that the library assistant, who was black, had told another lady who told another lady whose maid told Ma's friend that Miss St. James was digging up all these books about the Freedom Summer murders. Not only that, she had asked the assistant to find her any book about southern farmers and the difficulties they faced after slavery was abolished. Stevie, who was so often in the library on Main Street that no one paid him any mind as they talked, said black and white people were talking about how Miss St. James would sit at the desk in the corner with a mountain of books surrounding her, many of them about black people.

Ma summed it up for Leroy: "Funny we'd all be of one mind about this thing, but I'll tell you, white and black folks alike are getting real worried."

CHAPTER 40

It had all gone so horribly wrong. Just when everything had been going so well.

He was younger than she expected, thicker and more muscular, and there was nothing kind about him. She knew they all worked and so she had decided to visit the store early in the evening, perhaps before the night rush. But everything went downhill from the moment she stepped into the restaurant wearing her red dress, black heels, and red-and-black striped belt. First, there was a sea of black faces, and the crowd was thick. Every face had looked up as soon as she shut the door, and once she'd shut it, she could hardly turn tail and run. These were the people she had to interview. So she steeled her face to hide every emotion that was rushing over her. She was conscious of how white she looked in the room. A well-dressed white woman in a sea of working-class black men. The very ones to be featured in her thesis. For a second, their gazes were expectant, almost as though they expected her to turn around and head back out because she was so out of place, but the minute she started looking around for a seat, she felt their gazes grow cold. She had stumbled, righted herself, embarrassed, and clutched at the nearest chair, which happened to be occupied by the largest black man she had ever seen. The look on his face had propelled her swiftly to the only unoccupied table, right dead center in the middle of the room, with a straight bird's-eye view to Ella's Nate, whose back was turned to her as he worked the grill. As soon as she sat, the room went silent. Not a word or a whisper or a scraping of a chair. Perhaps Nate, sensing that quiet, had turned around swiftly to find out what was happening. There was an instant where his eyes caught hers. She saw his startled look, but before she could smile or wave at him, he had turned and was back at the grill.

Out the corner of her eye, she saw a short woman, not Ella's ma but someone else, moving between the tables, bringing drinks. She waited but the woman seemed to be working only the edges of the room.

She heard whispers and knew they were about her. The glances, the bowed muttering heads. She wasn't stupid. She sat quietly. Sooner or later, Nate or the woman would get to her.

Time dragged on. She sat there quietly, her breathing now calm. The lady serving drinks had disappeared and hadn't returned. She saw Nate turn to put two filled plates on the counter and then he called out, "Max, Leroy." She thought about getting up to leave, but how would that look? So, instead, she put up her hand and waved it, high. She should at least get a drink, and if not a drink, a burger, and then she could leave. She knew Nate saw her, but he went right back to the grill. She glanced around. Had people seen him ignoring her? She thought she heard a snicker. Two men, presumably Max and Leroy, came up to the counter, picked up their plates of food, and went to sit back down.

She sat there as Samuel, Elroy, James, Little T, and a host of others were called and came up to collect their food. Each time Nate turned around to slap a plate on the counter, she would raise her hand and wave it. He barely glanced in her direction, but she knew that there was no way he couldn't see her. An hour crept by. Then another. Now the noise in the room was at full volume as people ate.

She sat there, the slow burn of indignation, embarrassment, and outrage fueling an anger that she tried to control. He had seen her. They all had. It was then she heard her father's voice, roaring in her head, *So you will let these niggers treat you like this? You, whose family goes back generations, right to the* Mayflower? *Stop being such an idiot, Kate. She felt herself getting hot. How dare he, this Nate character? Who did he think he was to ignore her? Her father would not have stood for this. They used to tremble at his voice.*

The fear she felt slid back where it came from, and suddenly she was furious now.

She finally couldn't bear it. She shot up out of her seat as though propelled by an invisible cord, and finally, she was scared no longer. What were they? Nothing but a bunch of nig— Her brain shut the word off before she had a chance to utter it. Then her voice, suddenly loud and authoritative, shouted above the din, "What is wrong with you people? Can't you see a lady trying to get your attention?"

Even as Nate turned, the entire room emptied of sound. As though someone had suddenly pulled the plug on a loud radio. Now every eye moved between her and Nate.

Nate looked at her long and hard from across the room. Then he untied his apron, set it on the counter, and walked towards her.

Her fury turned to fear with every step of his approach, his thick shoulders squared, but she willed herself not to move. He wouldn't dare touch her.

"What can I do for you?"

It was the polite, cold calmness in his voice that irritated her, because now, suddenly, she was the one being irrational. It was a trick they used in therapy, to grow quiet when the patient was loud and angry. Well, she wasn't in therapy.

"Don't tell me you didn't see me waving my hand all those times. Are you blind as well as stupid?" Her voice filled the room.

She saw that she had gone too far because his eyes suddenly narrowed and he took a step towards her.

"Don't call me stupid. You don't walk into my restaurant and talk to me as though I were a dog. If you are stupid, yes, stupid enough not to read the sign on the door that says on Fridays you have to pre-order and put your

name on a list up front when you come in because we don't have help past six thirty p.m., then it is not my fault. You could have asked any one of these people sitting here why you weren't getting served. But no, you just sat on your high horse expecting us to treat you special, like the queen you obviously think you are. I don't know what is wrong with you people. You think you own the whole earth. Well, this is my place and if you don't like my rules, you can just get the hell out."

She could have sworn she heard someone begin to clap.

Well, she wasn't going to be talked to like that.

"How dare you. How dare you talk to me in that manner. I am the customer, so when I try to order, you have to damn well take my order!"

"Well, I dare. This ain't slavery days!"

Nate was interrupted by two men who stood up and came around him and put their hands on his shoulders.

"Just let her be," one of them said. "You don't want the police coming over here and making trouble. They'll try to shut this place down."

The other man, who was tall, with very light skin and green eyes, spoke. "It's all a big misunderstanding. Nate here will fix you a burger and then we'll walk you on home, make sure you get in all right."

It took her a minute to place him. Ella's father. Stepfather. That one.

Nate suddenly shrugged their hands off.

I'm not cooking anymore.

She felt weak, like all her energy and bravado had just evaporated. Her legs were suddenly shaky, but Ella's father held her and eased her to her chair and she collapsed into it. Within ten minutes he was back again, and before she knew it, she was being led out the door by him and the other man, a plastic bag containing a burger and fries clutched between her fingers. She had no idea who had cooked it or where it had come from. She trembled all the way, but whether it was because these two men, one perhaps Ella's molester, the other goodness knows who, were walking with her at night, or because of what had happened, she had no idea.

They saw her to her front step, waited patiently while she fumbled with her key, and said cheerful goodbyes as she propelled herself through the door.

There she sank to the floor and cried, partly because she felt her father in that restaurant, next to her, applauding her, but also because of what it meant for her work. When this got around, nowhere, nohow would she be able to interview anyone. She knew how they all talked. Every door would be slammed against her.

CHAPTER 41

No one had a good word about Miss St. James. The thought that she might leave Ricksville completely and head back north was keeping me up at night. It was then that I went to see Mr. Macabe. As usual, he was sitting on that front porch, and the minute I put my foot on the first step he called out, "That you, Ella?"

"How do you always know it's me, Mr. Macabe?" I called up to him.

"Just feel that ray of sunshine you bring with you, warming me up. Just feel it the minute you put your toe on that bottom step."

"How's you doing, Mr. Macabe?"

"Right as rain, Ella. How's things?"

"Okay."

I went up the stairs to look at him, just like I always did, to see how he was doing. He was still too thin, but he was wearing a good shirt and he'd had a haircut.

"Your ma? How is she?"

"Fixing to drive me crazy."

Mr. Macabe roared at that one.

"Who's been taking care of you so well, Mr. Macabe? That Mrs. Robertson still after you? You know she's on the lookout for a replacement."

Mr. Macabe threw back his head and laughed again, showing white gleaming teeth. Then he gave me a sly smile. "You go back in there and open that fridge of mine and then come out here and tell me what you see."

When I got back, "You—you—" was all I could sputter before we both burst out laughing, because there in the fridge, piled high, I'd seen at least half a dozen casserole dishes, all neatly labeled Monday to Sunday, and all signed "A.R., Augusta Robertson," just in case another woman came by and peeped into his fridge.

"Is the food good?" I asked, once my laughing had trickled into chuckles.

Mr. Macabe leaned forward and whispered, as if Mrs. Robertson might be lurking behind a tree or at the side of his house, "No." That set us off again.

"What you going to do with all that food in there?" I asked after we'd recovered again.

"Would you empty as many as you can into the trash and take the bag out with you? She'd be sure to notice it in the trash when she comes. I've been giving some of the food to Reggie, but even he don't want it no more." Reggie was an old, single, retired vet who walked over from his house on Perry every week to pay Mr. Macabe a visit.

"So why don't you just tell her you don't want it?"

"Just because she's bad at cooking doesn't mean she's bad at every-thing else," he said, with a twinkle in his eyes and a smile on his lips.

I gave him a side-eyed look, not that he could see it. Wasn't sure he meant what I thought he meant, but I wasn't about to ask. "Mr. Macabe, you're giving me the heebie-jeebies," I warned.

Mr. Macabe went right on smiling.

"I'm worried about Miss St. James," I said quickly, changing the subject.

"Why?" His smile immediately faded.

"Well, everybody hates her."

Mr. Macabe kept quiet for a while. Just stared sightlessly straight ahead. Finally, he leaned his head towards me a little and said, "Well, Ella. Maybe they think they have good reason. Everybody's heard about what happened at Nate's."

I shook my head. "She doesn't understand the way things work around here. And all those lynchings and things white people did, well, that was a long time ago and had nothing to do with Miss St. James. She's from up north, and she's nice. She's a bit afraid of black people but you would be, too, if you were white and came from a place without many black people."

"Ella, never make excuses for people. They are what they are."

"Don't you like her?" I cried out. "I thought you did."

Mr. Macabe didn't say anything for a moment. Then he said, "I'm just saying, Ella, I don't want to see you get hurt, if she isn't what you think."

If I didn't get Mr. Macabe on my side, Miss St. James would have no chance at all.

"Mr. Macabe, please," I pleaded.

"What do you want me to do?"

"Can't we get people to like her somehow?"

"So you want to roll back the whole tide of history to somehow make this town like Miss St. James?"

"Yes!" I was louder than I should have been.

"Don't get all het up, Ella. Mighty hard for some of us to trust people like her, especially after what just happened at Nate's, but I'll tell you, she sure seems to like you. I'll give her that."

"So why don't you help?"

Mr. Macabe was quiet.

"You said we shouldn't judge people by their color and that there are only good people and bad people and those in between. Well, Miss St. James is good people, Mr. Macabe."

"That's called using my words against me. Well done. You should be a lawyer. Well, Ella, I can't tell you what to do. Fact of the matter is, no good comes out of trying to play God. Things will happen as they are meant to happen."

"Mr. Macabe, please."

"Does it matter so much whether she's here or not, Ella?"

I thought of Ricksville without Miss St. James. Without the word games, without the hugs, without the questions and answers, without the way she laughed at the silly things I did, and without the freedom of running around in her house the way I did. She hadn't said anything else to me about Leroy, but just being at her house made me calmer. Then there was this other thing. She was the only person who had ever said she loved me. Suddenly I knew I would do anything to keep her here.

Mr. Macabe's voice broke into my thoughts. "We're not enough for you, Ella?" He said this softly, and I wanted to cry out, *you are.* But the words died in my throat.

"Well," Mr. Macabe said a bit sadly, "I can't tell you anything much except you'd better guard that heart of yours a little better."

I gave Mr. Macabe my meanest look, but of course he didn't see it.

"Please, Mr. Macabe," I said again.

"I don't think you should meddle in all this, Ella. People are going to think the way they want to think. Now, to change what they think, something has to happen that will make them think of Miss St. James in a whole new light. She'd have to do something mighty special, I tell you, because once folks have made up their minds, they don't change them too often."

CHAPTER 42

As I walked back home, I kept thinking of Mr. Macabe's words. The more I thought about them, the more I realized that Mr. Macabe was probably tricking me. Like giving me a math problem to which there was no solution. What special thing could Miss St. James do that would change people's minds about her? She could bake, play Scrabble, and put together outfits, and she had mentioned being good at tennis, swimming, and horse riding, but none of those would impress anyone I knew.

It was Stevie's mention of the annual Ricksville Picnic that evening that got me thinking. The picnic was South Ricksville's largest gathering—one big party with music, food, and dancing that celebrated the end of the summer. Nate would close the diner early and head down to the river with as much chicken as he could carry in his truck. Ty's ma had been the head of the picnic committee for as long as I could remember. Could I get Miss St. James down there to help the committee set up? I pondered. Maybe if I could get her to apologize for what happened at Nate's, they would begin to like her? Even as I thought about it, I realized how terrible my idea was. Miss St. James didn't believe she had done one thing wrong, and the ladies, well, they would be mighty stubborn in thinking Miss St. James was a racist. Still, it was the only idea I had, so the next morning I headed up Ricksville to Ty's house.

"Hey, Ty." Ty was throwing a ball against the side of his house and catching it.

"Hey, Ella."

"Isn't your grandma going to get mad that you're doing that?"

"She isn't home. She's at the church."

I watched Ty make his catches and tried to talk while the ball was in the air.

"So, what time they start to set up for the picnic this Saturday?"

"Dunno."

"Well, is it at three or four because everyone comes 'bout five?"

"Dunno, Ella." Ty swooped past me to catch the ball as it fell in a plop next to me.

"How many people help your grandma set it up?"

"Guess about ten ladies, old ladies from the church." Ty threw the ball again and this time it hit the siding with a loud crack.

"You going to bust up your house and your grandma's going to kill you."

Ty ignored me and went right on throwing.

"So if I got there about three, your grandma and about ten people will be there setting up?"

"Said I dunno, Ella." He caught the ball niftily in the palm of his hand and finally faced me. "She sets up when the time seems right, no one's looking at a watch, you know."

I gave up then. "Okay, see you around. You going to be at the picnic?"

"'Course, I'll be eating through all those burgers and chicken wings. So long as I stay away from the water, my grandma says I can eat as much as I want, dessert too."

And there it was: the idea, like Ty's ball, had flown right out of his mouth and landed at my feet.

"Want to earn a couple of dollars?" were my next words.

◦◈◦

Saturday was hot and sunny. One of those scorchers that would light our backs aflame. Rows of tables and benches already lined the grassy mound by the bank of the Big Black River. I had arrived early, with Ty in tow. Now I glanced at the grown-ups. About twenty people, some from the women's committee, were there putting the final touches on the tables before the rush.

I glanced at my watch. I had told Miss St. James to come at 3:30 to meet two women who were interested in being interviewed for her work. I had crossed my fingers behind my back as I said it, and watched her face flush with pleasure. She had been so excited. She'd be even happier when it was all over, I reminded myself.

I ran through the grass, up the bank, and onto Ricksville Road. Miss St. James was right on time, walking towards me.

"Oh, there you are, Ella, do I look all right?"

I glanced at her. She was wearing a long pale blue skirt and a white blouse that went with her white flats. She looked like she was going for a casual stroll.

I nodded and took her hand.

We were about twenty feet from the spot next to the river that I had marked out when Miss St. James stopped short and stared out ahead. I knew what she was looking at. Maybe the scene reminded her of Nate's, because she had this look on her face, like she would rather be anywhere in the world but here. I pulled at her hand, but she didn't budge.

"I thought you said we were having a meeting with two people," she said. "People that might be willing to be interviewed. This looks like a lot of people, and it looks like there's going to be a picnic."

"The picnic is later and that's just the women's committee doing the setup. We are meeting with two ladies over there." I pointed a few yards ahead, at the grassy spot I had saved, right beside the river. I pulled at her hand again, but she was still staring at the women, who by now had started to stack the paper plates into piles.

"Ella, this isn't a good time. Everyone's busy."

"No, they. . . ."

Out of the corner of my eye to the left, I saw a movement in the water.

I turned and saw that Ty was already in the water.

"Miss St. James, we have to hurry, they are over there."

Two seconds later, I saw Ty go under, once, twice.

My brain fumbled around. That wasn't a part of the plan.

The water was still. Ty wasn't jumping up and screaming and flailing like he was supposed to. Then I heard a scream. It was Ty's grandma shouting by the edge of the river.

It took seconds for my brain to make sense of what my eyes saw.

"You've got to help save him, Miss St. James. Ty's drowning!" My rehearsed words came out easily, but the reality of it had me trembling.

Miss St. James's eyes were on the river, seeing the horror unfold, the women crying and shouting for help at the river's edge.

I felt Miss St. James's hand slip from mine.

A wave of relief followed.

Miss St. James was moving quickly. She was leaving, but in the wrong direction. There was no way she was headed back to Ricksville Road.

But she was.

I ran and grabbed on to Miss St. James's blue skirt and pulled so hard that it started to slip down around her hips. She glanced at me, but her eyes were far away, as though I was no longer there.

"Please save him. Nobody here can swim well."

I heard a ripping sound as my fists tightened around her skirt and pulled on their own accord. The skirt swung down her hips.

It was the moment she saw me. Mouth open, bawling at her, tears and snot running down my face, fists clenched so tight around her skirt that it ripped as she yanked it out of my stiff fists.

As she finally recognized me, she pushed me out of her way, and ran, towards the river. After that, everything was a blur. I saw a flash that was Ron arrive at the water's edge. Peering in. Then he jumped in and disappeared, and then came up in a rush, gasping for air.

Ty's grandma in the water. Ty was her favorite grandchild, and she was going to drown for sure.

Finally, Miss St. James reached the edge of the river. She dove in, her skirt ballooning like a giant inflatable before she went under. She came back up once for air, and then we didn't see her. It seemed like she was down there forever, and when she finally came back up, she was holding Ty, limp and still, in her arms. She carried him to the bank and laid him on the ground and started pushing his chest in and out, while I prayed, prayed like I'd never prayed before, promising God everything and anything. I would never skip church; I would give every cent I ever made to the church. Begging and pleading and bargaining for Ty's life.

When Ty gave a little hiccup, it seemed like a miracle. And when the water came streaming out of his mouth, we expected him to sit up in a moment or two and be okay. But his eyes were still shut and his body limp, lying like a rag doll on the grass. Miss St. James shouted, "He needs to get to a hospital fast."

The nearest hospital was at least eight miles away. Most of us didn't have cars, but someone had the sense to race off to Dr. Shepardson's, and within five minutes the doctor had arrived. He seemed to kiss Ty's face twice, then pushed and prodded and did several more things that looked like mumbo jumbo before bundling him in towels and placing him carefully in the back seat of his car. He got in and sped off, taking Ty's grandma with them.

I was still standing there alone when Ron came back. Looked me straight in the eye and stared for a long time.

"Ty told me about your plan for him to pretend to drown just so Ms. St. James could save him. You killed him for her," he hissed. "You ugly wannabe Uncle Tom bitch."

I knew they were the most hateful words he could think of.

The weight of guilt made my lips heavy. I could not respond.

Why hadn't she moved faster? Why had she tried to run away? She'd hesitated. If she had been faster, Ty would be okay.

CHAPTER 43

She was shaking by the time she got to her front door, partly from the shock of what happened, partly because her clothes were still damp. She had jumped in the river fully dressed. Then it came in a flash again—the memory she hoped she had carved out of her mind—she, at fifteen, jumping fully dressed into the same river, an hour downstream. The old memories that should have been buried were resurrecting, pulling at her, causing her to stumble. She blanked them out, like turning off a switch, and focuses on today. She savors the fact that she just might have saved a boy's life. Why, he'd be dead if it weren't for her. It was indeed providential that she came to Ricksville, and was there at that precise moment that she was needed. What she would do to be a fly on the wall when they told that terrible man, Nate. He would have to reflect on how dismissively he had treated her. She was still sore about that. She ran herself a piping-hot bath, put in some bath salts, waited for the slight cooling, and then immersed herself. She sank beneath the water, to let the warmth infuse her face as well.

It was only later, as she lay in bed writing in her old journal, the one that had stayed shut for so many years, that she remembered Ella's distraught face. For a second all she could picture was Ella's eyes wide and big, mouth open, those fingers, grabbing and pulling at her skirt. She quickly dismissed the image. She was a bit shocked to see all those people there. That was all. It had taken her longer than she cared to go out there and help them.

She slammed the door shut on any lingering unease. The only thing that mattered was that she had saved a life. A life her father would not have saved.

A life for a life, she wrote in her journal.

CHAPTER 44

It was shocking to me how, in a matter of days, Miss St. James became the South Ricksville heroine. All talk about who she was, how she had spoken to Nate, her very whiteness, just disappeared. It was as though, by saving Ty, she had been folded right up into our Ricksville community. Miss Claudia, who had once warned me about Miss St. James, now smiled amicably at her from her front porch, and sometimes even called out, "Morning, Katherine," as she walked by. The older folks, the ones who were there when Miss St. James dove in the river, started to invite her to church, hoping that with her rare acceptances, her salvation would be complete.

Even Mr. Graves was smitten. He would now say on his whiskey walk, "She just went in there and gathered little Ty up. See how she jumped in with all her clothes. Now, that's a brave woman, right there." Ma wasn't so easily convinced, nor was Nate. Ma would snort disdainfully, and the whiskey Mr. Graves craved would remain hidden. But the whole street would have lined up for her to interview them.

Miss St. James, in response to all the admiration, seemed to change. Observing her, unseen, through the foliage of the sycamore tree as she walked to the library, I would note, with the detachment of a scientist, that she now walked slower, her slight hips moving with a little more sway than usual. Her voice, normally clipped and fast, was now slower, warmer, and with a little more singsong accent than before. She was also tanned, and with her windswept hair, now sometimes braided, she seemed to have relaxed into the South.

The happier Miss St. James seemed, the cooler my heart became.

Inside I was seething. Boiling with a bitterness that was as sour and acrid as chewing on hickory root. I couldn't swallow it down, nor could I spit it out. It sat there, curled up, gnawing in my belly, growing larger each day. No one knew the truth. Knew how Miss St. James had stood stock-still, unmoving, and then tried to run away while Ty was out there drowning. But the worst of it was that I couldn't tell them.

Then there was the other thing burning me up inside. Ron had blabbed, and the kids blamed my plan for Ty's almost drowning. Every day he was not released from the hospital filled me with dread. I knew they wanted my blood. Could feel it in their eyes as they glared at me, their hostility ripping into me up and down the street as I walked. All they had to do was to accidentally on purpose let it slip to Mr. Graves that I was the mastermind behind the horrible plan, and I would become as unwanted in any house as gum on the bottom of a shoe.

I took it. I knew what I was. A traitor. I had sold out Ty for Miss St. James. The opposite of love is hate, and as much as I had loved her, so my heart wanted to stamp out every trace of her.

If only Miss St. James had moved when I told her to.

If only. She was really the one to blame.

I went to see Mr. Macabe, to tell him how much I now hated Miss St. James. I hadn't seen him for a while, and just as I started up the porch stairs, I realized he had a visitor, and it was Nate up there, talking loudly. Nate didn't visit Mr. Macabe very often. I'd never seen him there before. I stopped on the second step because it seemed like Nate was angry. Then I heard Miss St. James's name. I didn't hear Mr. Macabe at all, just Nate saying, "What I suggest you do . . ." I missed the rest of the sentence because Nate, for some reason, lowered his voice. Then I heard Mr. Macabe say something, and Nate replying, "Yes, okay, if you have the money."

The rest of the conversation was lost in the wind.

I stood on those stairs for a while longer, but they were now talking too low to hear.

Suddenly it didn't matter anymore and I turned on my heel and walked back home. It didn't interest me, whatever they had to say.

It wasn't a long walk from Mr. Macabe's house to mine, but it felt like I had walked a mile. I sat on our stoop, playing the scene back in my head. Miss St. James, scared—no, terrified—of everyone out there. If I had let her, she would have run right out of there and down the road. What was it about all of us by the river that scared her so much? I thought of all the folks that were there. They were kindly natured, most of them, except maybe the ones that shook their fingers at us when we were too loud. Most of them would never hurt a fly.

◈

I got to see Mr. Macabe the next day. After hardly sleeping during the night, I was miserable and tired.

He was not at his usual place on the porch, so I opened the front door and peered in, and there he was, sitting on his living room sofa.

He didn't move.

"Sit down, Ella, right next to me."

When I did, Mr. Macabe turned to peer at me with those sightless eyes. He just kept looking at me. It was then I realized that he wasn't really staring at me; his face was cocked, so his ear was closer to me, the better to listen. He was listening to the sounds, the inflections in the breaths that I took.

"What's wrong?" were the next words out of his mouth.

My chest felt tight.

"Why can't anyone love me for real?" I burst out.

Mr. Macabe just stared blankly out, his eyelids fluttering ever so slightly. Then his voice was a calm rumble.

"She's just human, Ella. Bound to make mistakes, as wonderful as you think she is."

"She's not wonderful at all. I hate her."

Mr. Macabe was silent for a moment. Then he said, "Things change so quickly. You were just trying to get people to like her the last time I saw you. Now what she do?"

I kept quiet, wondering whether I should let out the secret curled up in me. I trusted Mr. Macabe with it, so I took a deep breath and let it out. "She didn't save Ty on time. I don't know why. It's like she saw all those people out there and didn't want to be anywhere near them."

Mr. Macabe didn't say anything. Instead, my words sat between us, like a heavy boulder, taking up all the air in the room. In the silence that followed, a sudden unwanted thought, always there but hushed, snaked back through my head. *Didn't Mr. Macabe tell you not to get involved?* My mouth opened and closed in shame. More thoughts came at me. *You started it. It was you that decided to make up that plan. You are also to blame for Ty's accident. Mr. Macabe told you to let it alone.* I shook it off, but the words returned, louder. I gasped, out of breath. I was suffocating with guilt. My shoulders began to shake and my breath started to come in gasps.

"Breathe awhile, Ella. Let it out. Take a deep breath in and let it out very slowly, as though you are trying to flutter a candle flame but not let it go out." Mr. Macabe's voice came from around me, calm and unruffled.

He took his hand and felt around till he found my face, and the tears, and then he blew slowly into my face.

"Like that."

I took in a breath and let it out slowly, just like he said—like I was causing a flame to flicker but not letting it go out.

"Do it again," he said.

And I did.

"Do it again," Mr. Macabe repeated each time I was done. By the time I had done it eight times, the knot that was boiling inside me and seemed to take over my whole body began to feel smaller, blown out into the air. I continued breathing like that till Mr. Macabe stopped me.

"Have you heard of the African continent?" Mr. Macabe suddenly asked.

My head jerked up. It was a weird question. Of course I had heard of Africa. "Africa is poor," I said.

"Africa is rich," Mr. Macabe responded. "Let me tell you a story told to me by an African man I met. You just sit back and listen and resume that breathing."

I breathed out over the imaginary flickering candle and listened.

"Africa, the man told me, is blessed by God with an abundance of gold and diamonds and oil in the ground. Why do you think so many people try to take it over? Carve it up like it was a cake, sliced so much that each separate slice cannot easily survive on its own. Africa is what made Europe and America great. Gave them that edge they needed and almost killed the continent in the process. That's what the man from Africa said. He said that it's like the American South: there are poor people, and there are rich, but they have cities and roads and lights and houses that are as fancy as those on the white side of Ricksville. The continent of Africa and its people once ruled the world, their kingdoms in West Africa and Zimbabwe of worldwide repute in learning, architecture, and trade. Those kingdoms fell and the world now tries to hide that this even happened, but there is written and architectural proof. But Africa is rising, growing and getting stronger. Some countries are doing very well. In other countries, however, corruption is like a cancer, spreading blight across the land. Once that cancer is cured, Africa will flourish. It will once again take its place in the world, back to the glory days of Mansa Musa and its great civilization."

My chest felt so much lighter. I leaned farther back into the sofa cushions.

Mr. Macabe's eyes seemed to look out into space. I couldn't tell what he was thinking.

"I think the continent of Africa envelops you, holds you up strong," he said. "Gives you pride and identity so that when you do enter the adult world—and you will, Ella—you can hold your head up. Be who you are, and proudly. The world outside of Ricksville is very, very different. You will have to deal with different kinds of people that are not your own people. You will need to be proud of who you are to survive and thrive. You should go to Africa one day, Ella, before you are grown. Visit a few countries. See if it will help you find your wings. But not today, Ella. Today you belong in Ricksville, among your people. You have to become proud of who you are here first."

Then, with his hand still on my shoulder, he added the words I would never forget.

"Africa. That's the continent where your father is from." Then he added, "The words I just told you about Africa were his words."

I whipped around and stood up and stared into those milky eyes, willing to go into them and see what he saw.

"Well, what did he look like?" The words were out of my mouth before I remembered that Mr. Macabe couldn't see.

Mr. Macabe shook his head. "I don't know, child. Just heard him talk about how wonderful the continent was. Your father . . . well, he up and left Ricksville not long after the day I heard him talking."

I had so many questions bursting to come out, but before I could ask even one, Mr. Macabe stilled me by putting his finger to his lips.

"Hush, child, before you drive yourself mad with questions. I know very little, but I'll tell you what I can. Now, as you know, I'm not much of a drinking man, but I met your father for all of one hour in the Fox bar, which is no longer here. I had gone for a doctor's appointment with Cecee, and she was late for work, so when we got as far as Nate's, which was Catchedy Groceries back then, I said I would walk the rest of the way home. I had my cane and knew the way. I crossed Main and had just passed the Fox when I heard a voice that wasn't from around here. It was such a distinct voice that it stopped me. I had heard and spoken with our African brothers in New York City, but this voice was different. I don't know what made it different, except the deep voice stopped me. It rang out into the street. It drew me closer, and out of curiosity I walked into the bar and sat about three seats away from the man whose voice had compelled me. Didn't even introduce myself, I just sat listening. He had a group of men around him, and they were hanging on his every word. He was telling them about the African continent, and he mentioned West Africa. When he got to the end he said, 'Just so you folks down here know, we aren't that much different from you, just the same people, sometimes poorer, sometimes richer, but we draw our strength and pride from the land. It will change you,' he said. 'You got to come live there a few years and find yourselves.' Then he invited everyone over to his country to see him, saying they could stay with him. Some laughed and went back to drinking, and a few said they would certainly make it down there in their lifetime. Then, before I could ask a question, he was up and gone.

"I heard them talking after he left. Seems he was tall, handsome, and well-dressed, wearing a suit and tie. He was 'blue-black' according to one fellow. He'd never ever seen a black man so black he looked almost indigo blue, like a trick of the eye or something. Wish I could have seen it. They seemed to think he had plenty of money in his pockets. Didn't look broke, they said. Definitely well educated, the way he spoke and carried himself. I later heard that he had stayed in town for a while, and your ma was taken with him, real taken, for your ma's a picky woman. In any case, the rest is history. That's all I know of your father. Wish I had my sight and could tell you what he looked like."

"What else you hear, Mr. Macabe?"

If there was anything else, Mr. Macabe wasn't telling.

A father from somewhere in Africa, I thought. Why couldn't he have been from Arkansas or Mississippi where I could get to him? I looked at my pitch-black skin. So that's where it came from. That's why its hue was so strange in Ricksville. It was a color that reached way back from a history that I couldn't even begin to know about.

Then my thoughts wandered even further. What was the African continent like? There must be something special about it if it produced men like my father, like Mr. Macabe had described. Something inside me gave a flutter of joy. I had a father. It filled my mind with something else to think about other than Miss St. James.

Mr. Macabe's voice came at me: "You need to love yourself first, Ella. Don't go searching for love in other people's eyes until you love yourself first. You come from somewhere beautiful. West

Africa and Ricksville. The best of both worlds. I'm sorry I don't know which country in Africa. It could be Senegal, Ghana, Liberia, Sierra Leone, or Nigeria."

I leaped up and in a second I was in Mr. Macabe's arms, holding so tight. His arms were just as tight.

"Thank you," I said. Mr. Macabe just nodded.

"Why didn't you tell me before?" I was thinking that, all this time, I would have had something. Something special that was just for me.

Mr. Macabe didn't say anything for a minute. "I didn't know you needed it till Miss St. James came into town. I'm a mighty fool, a blind fool, that's what I am. Holding it in my pocket till I felt you needed it, when you've been needing it all along" was all he said.

I reached out and hugged him again like my life depended on it. I felt like I was hugging my real father.

"You're no fool, Mr. Macabe," I said into his neck.

Mr. Macabe just hung on to me, not saying a word. His face scrunched up like he was about to cry.

Mr. Macabe's words about my father were like trying on a coat that was too big to wear, so I put it around my shoulders like a cape. It made me feel snug and secure.

I danced all the way home wearing that coat, right through the door and upstairs. It made me feel so free and alive. Then I wanted to tell someone, and apart from Nate, my next thought was Miss St. James, but I squelched it. Friends would tell friends things that happened to them. Big things. But she wasn't my friend anymore.

CHAPTER 45

Ma's sickness came out of nowhere, with the stealth of a thief in the night. But unlike a thief, it lingered, casting a shadow on everything and leaving havoc in its wake. It happened about two weeks after Ty's almost drowning, in the third week of August, and completely washed out any thought of Miss St. James.

I had arrived back from choir practice on Wednesday night to a dark house. I hadn't seen Ma at church, so she should have been back home.

Didn't we pay the bill again? I wondered. I moved to switch the lights on. There was a reassuring flash, and then light flooded the room. Leroy was lying on the couch and Stevie was sitting next to his feet, bent over with his chin resting in his hands.

"Where's Ma?"

Leroy barely lifted his head off the couch pillows. "Your ma's real sick. Dr. Shepardson left a few hours ago. Looks like she's going to be sick for a while. She will need you here to help. Tomorrow morning, I will take C.T. to your aunt's in Baton Rouge." That was Leroy's sister.

"I can look after him," I said quickly.

"You can't. Your ma will need you. Dr. Shepardson says she can't be left alone."

"What about Kitty?"

It was only then that Leroy raised his head, cutting his eyes at me. I saw the scowl on his face, and it shut me up. It was Stevie who answered.

"Dad's sending her to Uncle Jerry's in Atlanta to finish her last two weeks of summer school."

Stevie was being Leroy's puppet again and talking for him. I scowled at him in turn. So Leroy had gotten Kitty out of doing any work, I thought angrily. Ma would be happy, though. Uncle Jerry was her brother. But wouldn't Ma want Kitty around?

"What's wrong with Ma?" I asked nervously. "Is she going to die?"

Leroy didn't answer. Instead, he swung his legs off the couch, put on his shoes, and tousled his hair into place. By the time I put a foot on the staircase, he was already on his way out the door. Stevie stood up as soon as the door closed.

"Look, Oreo, I have to get a book from the library. I'll be back soon." Then he, too, was gone.

I went upstairs and paused outside Ma's bedroom door. Then I knocked lightly. There was no response, so I pushed open the door. A stench, putrid and rancid, blasted into my nostrils. I struggled to push the odor far from me by covering my nose with my hand, and then with my T-shirt. This distracted me for a moment, but when I looked up, I saw her—a bulky frame on the bed, wrapped in a blanket, an oddly covered hump. It was only when I drew closer that I saw her head was rolled to the side. Her eyes were open and burning with a flame that came from something. Was it anger? Pain? Her mouth drooped to one side, and I couldn't tell what was worse, seeing Ma so twisted and helpless or the sudden realization that she was the source of the horrible stench.

"Ma?" I said. "Ma?"

She didn't answer, just watched me with those burning eyes, drool coming from her mouth.

I grew scared. "Ma? Can you talk?"

A blur of sounds, like muffled curse words, came streaming from her mouth. Almost as though someone had stuffed a handkerchief in her mouth and sewn it shut.

I backed out of her bedroom and turned and ran into mine. I stayed on my bed till I heard Leroy calling me to Ma's room about an hour later.

"Oreo. Now, you're supposed to stay in here with Ma. Keep her comfortable."

I looked at him nervously. "What's wrong with her?"

"She's had a stroke."

"What's that?"

"Something to do with the brain not working well."

I filed away the new word. I would look it up later. "Why does she smell like that?"

Leroy quickly looked away, and in that instant, I knew. Ma couldn't even control herself.

Leroy's face turned reddish. "It'll be your job to make sure she's clean." He glared at me, as though it were all my fault.

I asked whether Aunt Sandra was coming to stay. She was Ma's sister and very nice but we never saw enough of her. She lived in South Carolina.

"I went to the Reverend's to call her. She's looking after her grandbaby, so she can't be here until after a couple of weeks."

"What am I supposed to do?"

"Doctor says feed her. Soup. She can't eat properly. Can't swallow well. Whatever it is, it's affected her throat muscles. The doctor said it would get better with time."

"I can't do it," I said, and I heard the whine in my voice, but before I could say anything more, Leroy slapped me. Hard enough to silence me momentarily.

"Your ma has done a lot for you. You'd better stay here and help look after her."

"What about school coming up?" I whispered nervously.

"When your aunt gets here you can go to school. If she's not here when school starts, Stevie will bring you your homework."

I didn't say a word. Just listened as Leroy said he would go get the bus tickets to Baton Rouge. That he would leave with C.T. that very night. He would come back in a week to take Kitty to Atlanta, and from there, he'd figure out how to get some money because all the doctors' bills couldn't be paid in paper. Besides, Ma would need a nurse to look after her when Aunt Sandra left. Leroy wasn't looking at Ma as he talked. Seemed like he was talking to the air. Certainly wasn't talking to me. I watched him pace, two steps to the right, one to the left. He was jittery. I could tell that Leroy wanted out of there so fast. I could see Ma's eyes flickering between us. She was alive in there, hearing everything we said, knowing that Leroy was going to take off again, just when he was needed. If she'd been able to, she would've jumped up and begged him to stay.

Leroy started pulling his clothes from the rack and from drawers, slamming them into a suitcase, folding, pressing, mashing them together. Too many clothes for just a week. Ma became agitated, making gibberish noises and flailing her good arm. She didn't want to be left with me. Leroy ignored her and finished stuffing the suitcase until nothing more could be jammed in. He snapped the suitcase closed, lifted it up, and walked out of the room into my room to get C.T.'s clothes. Then he was gone. Not so much as a peck on Ma's cheek.

That evening, Dr. Shepardson returned, carrying some things with him. He put down medicines on the counter and wrote instructions for everything that Ma had to take. Stevie and I had to crush the pills, mix them with any liquid, and feed the mixture to her with a syringe. Since she couldn't swallow properly, we had to put a thickener in her liquid food so she didn't choke. He said he would send someone to wash her once a day till she started to recover, but we would need to pay the lady.

"Will she get any better?" I asked.

Dr. Shepardson's answer was not reassuring. "It's a pretty bad stroke. We pray there isn't another. If not, there will be improvement perhaps to her left side, but as to whether she will walk again, I don't know. The first few weeks are the worst to get through."

I thought of Ma dead. Sprawled out, and then trussed up like a turkey and put into a box and into the ground, forever. Suddenly I didn't want her dead. Didn't want to think of being left alone with Leroy for even one day. I would run away for sure. Maybe go live with Mr. Macabe. The doctor's voice pulled me out of my thoughts.

"Come here, both of you. I want you to listen carefully." Dr. Shepardson explained how to pull Ma up into a sitting position and feed her, and how to give her a sponge bath every night. He told us what to do in case she choked on her food, and how to mix the thickener into the soup.

After Dr. Shepardson left, Stevie went to pick up some groceries for the soups Ma would have to eat.

Ma and me. Me and my ma. This was what I had always wanted. Only those eyes of hers were glaring at me with such fury that it made me writhe. It took me a moment to realize that she couldn't hurt me. Couldn't pull out the Ma O whip and tear into me. Couldn't ask for Kitty instead. Couldn't act like I didn't exist. I put on a face of maddening glee and rubbed my hands together.

"Now I have you where I want you," I said. "Now I'm going to eat you up."

I pranced around the room like a mad person, watching Ma's expression change from fury to horror to fear, and then I burst out laughing. I laughed till my sides hurt and I could laugh no longer. I went right up to her and stared into those now confused eyes. "You're lucky you have such a forgiving daughter, Ma, because right now I could treat you very badly, and no one would know. I'm only twelve, but I could pinch, slap, and swear at you, just like you do me, and you couldn't do a thing about it. I could even refuse to feed you."

The panic in her eyes almost started me laughing again, but then immediately I felt wicked. I hoped God wouldn't strike me down.

I learned how to pummel Ma's back to get the food to go down, and push the pail into her lap when it could only come back up. I took over the kitchen, becoming an expert on how to mix and grind so that no morsel of food would stick in Ma's throat. I swept, mopped, and cleaned, and saw more than my fair share of soiled underwear, not to mention what I had to do for Ma to wipe her down. It was just like taking care of a baby, Dr. Shepardson had told me, and by the end of that second week, I was convinced that I'd never ever want a baby.

Dr. Shepardson would ask, "Where's Kitty? Too beautiful for this type of work?"

But after a week of seeing just Stevie and me, he had stopped asking where she was.

Kitty was gone, already in Atlanta. The few days she was home, she had spent barely more than fifteen minutes at a time in the house, saying that the stench was making her nauseated, and besides, she couldn't study, what with Ma grunting. I was sure it was because she thought she would catch something and ruin her looks. If only she would catch chicken pox, I had thought.

Dr. Shepardson just shook his head when he heard she was gone, before saying, "That girl's been spoiled. Don't hardly know what type of wife she'll be."

I could have told him that Kitty would hardly have to be the type of wife he meant because she would be married to a rich doctor, and he would hire someone to do all the work she didn't want to do. She'd only have to worry about looking pretty.

By the end of the second week, Dr. Shepardson taught me how to get Ma to pronounce certain words. This was the part I loved best, because then I could be the boss of Ma.

"Say *Stevie*," I would command, and she would say, "Ve."

"No, more slowly. Try again. 'Ste' first, then 've.' Hold your tongue steady and try to control your mouth." I felt like a grown-up and never got tired of this. Thus we would sit for hours practicing, just as Dr. Shepardson had taught me, till finally, after two weeks of this, a clear word rang out of her mouth.

"No."

"No?" I repeated in surprise. I stared at her droopy, sloppy smile. How proud of herself she was. It was the first time she had smiled since she'd taken sick, and I jumped up and did a jig about the room.

That small success spurred me on, so I went to see Dr. Shepardson and learned all about muscle strengthening and toning. "Ask Stevie to get her out of bed as much as possible and get her moving, as the feeling is coming back into her legs," he instructed. So two evenings that week became our moving days when Stevie filled the house with O. C. Smith, the Temptations, Ray Charles, Aretha Franklin, and any other record with soul and a beat. I watched while Stevie worked the routine that Dr. Shepardson had given us, stretching and pulling to make those muscles work again. Often, I jumped and danced along to the record as Stevie worked, twisting and turning.

It was the most fun I'd ever had with Ma. She had taken to looking at me, and I kind of swelled up when she did that. It wasn't a kind look, more a curious one. Like she didn't know where I came from or whether she liked me. I didn't mind. At least she was looking at me. She kind of had to, since I was teaching her words, but it made me feel like a real person. And with every improvement she made, I felt triumphant. Then one day, after a difficult speech session, Ma reached out her hand to mine and just held it in hers. As far back as I could remember, she had never once reached out to touch me in kindness, and it stilled me. Made my heart race and my eyes widen in shock. But before I could even tighten my hold, her hand fell away. I took that brief touch as her way of thanking me, and it made all the work I had done feel worthwhile.

One bright sunny day, I set off to pick up her prescriptions, and since it was only a few seconds away from Nate's front door, I stopped in to say hi. Nate was cooking as usual.

"Hey, pretty girl," he said. "How's your ma?"

"She's a lot better but not like she was."

"Make sure to tell Leroy to shell out some of that money he is always claiming he has and hire someone to help. He back?"

"No," I said. I couldn't keep from grinning.

Nate looked at me seriously. "You really can't stand him, can you? Here's you doing all that work, and you're still happy to be doing it as long as he's away."

I nodded.

Nate came up to me, bent to my eye level. Put his hand on my shoulder. "Nothing lasts forever, Ella. You know that, right? Not the good times and not the bad times neither. You hang on to that and you'll be fine." He straightened. "Your ma's really getting better?"

"Ma's fine. Now she can move her left hand a bit, and she can walk on her own. Not fast, but she isn't falling. She's put back some of the weight she lost, too."

Nate laughed. "Listen to that pride in your voice. You would make a good mother."

I made an "ugh" face but still smiled back at Nate. I felt all grown up.

"Miss St. James? Are you still going by her place?"

"No." I didn't want to explain.

"Good" was all Nate said.

"Now, when's your aunt coming so you can start thinking about school. It's started up already, right?"

"Yes. She'll be here next week," I said.

I couldn't wait. It was mid-September and school had already been in session one week.

◈

It was lucky for me that Ma's sister, Aunt Sandra, arrived when she did. It meant that I could finally go back to school.

I liked Aunt Sandra. For one thing, she couldn't stand Leroy. Her first words when she arrived at the door with all her suitcases were "Is *that* man here?" When I grinned and said no, she threw back her head and hollered "Thank the Lord" so loudly, I was sure Mr. Macabe had heard her up the street. I had heard her telling Ma that she was a fool to be taken in by that good-for-nothing man. "Handsome, I'll give you that. Nice-looking, strong. But that man's all smoke and no fire."

She took over feeding and looking after Ma as soon as she changed her blouse, all the while talking nonstop. As she folded the sheets and towels in Ma's room, she was still talking about Leroy.

"Thelma, where is he when you are laid up in bed? It isn't right of him to disappear like that. In sickness and health, you know. Now, my Ned, I know he has his faults, but he'd be with me day and night if I were sick."

Ma, now talking hesitantly and slowly, to get the words out, said that Leroy was working, that he had been fixing to make enough money to get her a nurse. Aunt Sandra just shook her head and said, "So whatever happened to that nurse? You're getting better, and now he's going to show up with a nurse . . . three weeks late?" Ma didn't say a word.

Aunt Sandra looked just like Ma: tall, on the larger side, with a big bosom and long, straight, glossy hair. She had a big behind, too, which Ma hadn't inherited but which Aunt Sandra was all too proud of. She talked a lot about her husband, Uncle Ned, whom I'd never met but who she said took one look at her behind and declared that she would be his wife. She had turned around to give him what for, and then stared down into the most beautiful eyes she had ever seen. Beautiful, puppy-dog amber eyes. And that was that. Even though he was at least four inches shorter than she was, and not as handsome as she would have liked, all she had to do was look into those eyes and it made up for all the rest. Even all the rest of it that marriage brought—the cheating, the whoremongering, the stealing of her checkbook . . . Ma interrupted her and flapped her good hand in my direction to swoosh me out of the room. I hightailed it out of there, glad I didn't have to hear about whatever else Uncle Ned's eyes made up for.

CHAPTER 46

Ma slowly got better, and, after a couple of weeks, she could use her left leg and arm a lot more. So much so that she could now get herself off the bed and use the cane to get to the bathroom. Aunt Sandra stayed another week after that and then said she had to go so that Uncle Ned would remember where he called home. I would leave a tray for her in the morning, and Stevie would come home in the afternoon to leave her a tray for lunch.

Nate stopped by to see how Ma was doing. I was in the kitchen and near enough to hear what they were talking about. All Ma seemed to talk about was Leroy.

"He took Kitty to Atlanta, and then went off for three weeks and got back last week. All he did was drop C.T. back home, but then he was off again. I know he's in Ricksville but he hardly stops by. He hasn't done that before. In the past, if he was out of the house, it was because he was on one of his road trips, looking for whatever work he could find. But this is just odd. I thought it was because of Sandra—you know they've never seen eye to eye—but she left a week ago and he's still not back to stay."

"Well," Nate responded, "it certainly wasn't right for him to disappear when he was needed the most."

I sat perched on the kitchen chair, listening hard. I didn't care about Leroy's stupid excuses anyway. I was just glad he was keeping away, even though I could tell that Ma was hurt. I didn't hear anything for a while, so I got off the chair and went to peek around the door. Nate was leaning closer towards Ma, talking and talking, and I grew worried. What was he telling Ma? How to get Leroy back? I tried to hear some more but it was impossible.

That evening, Ma was in a better mood. She had gotten a letter from Kitty, and by all accounts she was having an amazing time, which pleased Ma to no end. Ma's brother, Uncle Jerry, had launched Kitty into black society by holding a party to end all parties. He had invited every eligible bachelor between twenty-five and fifty. I didn't think Kitty had done much summer schoolwork, because what she said in those letters was that she had gone to so many parties she had clean run out of dresses. Uncle Jerry only had sons, and his wife was so excited about having a girl to dress that they had bought a dozen more for the fall. Apparently, Kitty was going to spend her final year of school in Atlanta.

"Almost worth it I got sick," Ma muttered to herself as she read the letter. She'd read it over and over again, and the page that mentioned the new dresses and a certain Dr. Morgan was still tucked under Ma's pillow.

"Do you know where Leroy goes?" I asked Stevie just before bed.

"I don't know. I don't keep track. I thought I saw him near Nate's earlier this week." He looked at me, frowning. "What do you care, anyway?"

"I don't. I just like to know where he is and if he is going to be coming back."

Stevie didn't ask me why. So we sat in silence, each pondering.

"Do you like it when he's here?" I asked very softly, hoping he didn't hear me but wanting to know anyway.

Stevie didn't answer.

"Did you hear me?" I said louder.

"Why do you keep pushing, Oreo? Leave things alone."

"I can't," I said simply.

"Okay, fine. When he's here all the time, it's nice but I don't want him to come back only to go away again, but at least I have a dad." Then he realized what he'd just said and added quickly, "Sorry, Ella, I didn't mean you, I meant compared with some people I know without dads."

Then he muttered, "I never know what to say around you. Stop asking, okay?"

"Okay," I said.

I found out where Leroy was quite by accident. I was walking towards Main Street when Fats came over to me and asked, "Is Leroy living on Tucker Lane now?"

I was as surprised to hear Fats speaking to me as I was to hear about Leroy. He and the rest of the kids were still giving me the silent treatment and a wide berth.

"I don't know . . . is he?" was all I could manage.

"I guess so," Fats replied.

Turned out Fats was taking trumpet lessons with Mr. Graves, who lived next to Mr. Frazer, who was renting out rooms on Tucker. He had seen Leroy going into the basement apartment and asked Mr. Frazer, who was only too happy to share a piece of gossip: Leroy had rented out the one-bedroom apartment two weeks ago and paid in advance through the next two months.

So that's where Ma's nurse money probably went. To rent that apartment. Ma would go mad if she found out. It was partly because I was so relieved that Fats was talking to me again, and partly because it meant that I would see a lot less of Leroy, that I flung my arms around Fats. He quickly pushed me away in embarrassment.

"None of that, Ella," he said. And for a second, I saw his skin turn yet another color, one I hadn't seen on him before.

"Is he living alone?" I asked.

Fats shrugged and said he didn't know and hurried off—I think he suddenly remembered he wasn't supposed to be talking to me. Still, the ice was thawing, and I was glad.

I thought of Ma, and how she would feel. Without Leroy and Kitty, the two people she loved best in the world, who did Ma really have?

—◇—

Two days later, I could hear the storm raging all night and the wind howling, rattling the windows in their frames and pummeling at the door. I buried myself under my bedsheets and pulled the pillow over my head to block out the noise. C.T. was now sleeping in Ma's bed, so my bed was all mine, but it felt a bit lonely. It was almost 3 a.m. when I finally managed to get to sleep, and when I woke up and went outside, the front of the house and the road and the other lawns were all awash with leaves. The October air was fresh, cool, and clean.

Stevie had not come home during the night, but Ma, still preoccupied with Leroy's disappearance, said she was tired and had gone up to bed early. I was not really worried. Stevie had done this before; fallen asleep in the library, not waking as the librarian had switched out the lights and locked the door, but because I couldn't imagine how he could sleep through the storm, I went into Ma's room to tell her that Stevie had been out all night. She was getting C.T. ready for preschool, and she stopped for a second to mutter, "That boy, I'll skin him when he gets back," and asked me to check in with his friends at school. No one had seen him, but when I got back, Stevie's books were on the kitchen table.

I rushed up to his room.

"We were worried about you."

He was lying on his bed, facedown, but I knew that he was awake, so I sat on the edge of his bed and poked him. "Ma's going to beat you to death when she sees you."

Stevie didn't answer. He rolled over to face me. His eyes were red, as though he'd been crying.

"What's wrong with you?"

"Leave me alone," he said.

"Did you get locked up in the library again? Come on, where were you?"

I heard the front door open and shut. Ma was home. Then we could both hear the slamming of cupboards and drawers downstairs.

"Where were you?" I persisted.

"I saw Dad with her, you know."

"With who?"

"Some young woman down on Tucker Lane."

That stopped me dead.

"I was coming back from the library last night when I spotted them together."

"Well, maybe she's not Leroy's girlfriend. Maybe he doesn't like her that way and they're just friends."

"Does not liking involve kissing him?" Stevie shouted. "Does that involve putting her tongue down his throat and rubbing herself against him?"

Could it be true? I wondered. Had Leroy really found himself someone else?

"So what happened after that?"

"Nothing much. She left, and I followed him to Tucker Lane and knocked on the door a few minutes after he went in."

"Did you tell him you saw them together?"

He looked defeated. "What difference would it have made? I heard she's rich, too." Stevie's face told me everything else I needed to know. He would have wanted to be big enough to yell in Leroy's face, but he was still this skinny kid with big ol' buck teeth who was just plain nice.

"Does Ma know where you were? Does she know you spent the night with Leroy??"

We heard pots banging now, slamming down hard on the stovetop.

"I'd say she knows." He looked so forlorn.

I tried hard not to feel hope in Stevie's pain.

Fats had said that Leroy was living in a basement on Tucker Lane, and Stevie had confirmed the street, so that evening I went down to the lane and peered into each basement. I saw lightbulbs glowing from three of them, so I sat quietly by the side of the road, waiting to see if anyone went in or came out. A large elderly black woman emerged from one, so I crossed that one out and moved closer to the other two houses. Both basements had drawn curtains, so I couldn't tell which one Leroy was in.

It was about 10 p.m. when I heard the sound of laughter. Leroy's laugh. Then I heard the jangle of keys and more laughter.

Then I saw her; she was slender, and I could tell she knew she was pretty just by the way she swished her hips as she walked. She didn't fall over in those tall shoes, instead they seemed to be just another part of her. Her white pants and sheer white long-sleeved blouse looked expensive, as did her matching red belt and handbag. Ma wouldn't stand a chance, even if she ever became fully well. Leroy was laughing, his hands around her waist, and her head was flung back, leaning against him, laughing in response. The top button of her blouse was undone, and for a second she seemed a bit unsteady, but then Leroy pulled her up and kissed her. I could feel my face coloring in shame for her as she pressed herself against him. I watched as he fumbled with his keys in the door before he drew her in.

It was only then that I turned away, satisfied.

CHAPTER 47

Quiet. Muted. Hushed. Silenced.

I stood by my locker. I could hear the raised voices in the hall-ways at school, the laughs, the yells, the excited chatter.

But no one spoke to me. It seemed that gossip about me had hopped, from person to person, like lice.

I imagined what they would say: "Ella made Ty just about drown. All for Miss St. James."

I felt my disgrace with every withdrawn glance, every withering look.

Out the corner of my eye, I saw Cammy. But she sailed by, nose in the air, talking nonstop to Lucinda.

I was as unseen as the *Walk, Don't Run!* signs that dotted our school's hallways.

Then I saw Fats, and for a second the happy sensors in my brain fired, and I opened my mouth to say hey, because he had talked to me before. But then I saw his shifty look. His glance just before he turned away, hunching his shoulders so he looked smaller, no doubt hoping that he had somehow become invisible.

I scowled at his sloping back.

Ty was back from the hospital and was put one grade back on account of his fuzzy memory.

"I'm sorry I ever thought of that plan," I said to him when I saw him.

"It's okay, El . . . la. I was ex . . . ci . . . ted. Jumped too far in."

At least he was the one person who had spoken to me. But it only made me feel worse.

I might have just given up and told Ma that I was never ever going back to school, but then Ron made me change my mind just a week later. He was so mean to me that I could only think he was trying to set a world record. I tried to ignore him the first week, and when he shoved me or tripped me I just got up and went right back to what I was doing.

The next time he pushed me, I was quick. As his hand shoved me from behind, slamming me up against my locker door, my outstretched hand reached up, grabbed my *History Through the Ages* textbook, all six hundred pages of it, and hurled it fast and hard at his swaggering back. It hit him with a resounding whack, so hard that he stumbled, the shock of it making him trip over his feet and fall to the ground. It took him seconds to get up, but when he did, he was furious. He came up on me, his mouth all ugly and twisted, and I stood there, waiting for the hail of curses that I would have to answer.

And then . . . nothing.

That was when I realized they must have made a blood pact not to talk to me.

I taunted him then, knowing that he couldn't respond, jabbing like Muhammad Ali around him, floating like a butterfly and stinging like a bee, talking all kinds of junk. "Come on, you want to hit me? Come on."

Ron turned on his heel.

It was my first realization that I could survive this.

Walking home from school, I still saw Miss St. James. And she was having the time of her life. My eyes would glimpse her ponytail bouncing in and out of homes. Her satchel was always strapped across her body, bits of paper sticking out. She would walk right up to a house and knock loudly and confidently at the door. She seemed very sure of her welcome. Saving Ty had guaranteed her a place on everyone's sofa. Once I stayed to watch her go into Mrs. Robertson's house. She didn't stay long. Within forty minutes, she was out, letting the screen door bang shut, never stopping to close it slowly.

To me, she seemed different. Less worried. Happy. From the pleased look on her face, I could tell that she was getting exactly what she wanted.

Where was all that fear I had seen before at the river? Did it evaporate? If I hadn't seen Ty with my own eyes, as living proof, I would have thought that I had dreamed the whole thing up.

Maybe as long as the people you fear are doing what you want, when you want it, and how you want it, there is no reason to fear them.

I now knew that I was dumb. Dumber than a brick. 'Cause if I knew Miss St. James wasn't quite what she seemed, then why did I make friends with her again?

Cammy would have said stupid is as stupid does.

I would have looked her right in the eye and said, like I meant it, "Well, that kind of talk is not even original, Cammy Locklear! Stupid is not stupid when you know what you're doing!"

"So what are you doing, Ella? You got another one of your plans?"

That would have shut me right up, so perhaps it was good that Cammy still wasn't talking to me.

I hadn't planned on being friends again, but then I hadn't reckoned that Miss St. James was as cunning as a fox, and, like a rabbit falling into a trap, I fell right in, and all she had to do was to be kind. It all happened about a month after school. I was walking back home as usual and spotted Miss St. James stepping out of Ty's grandma's house. She looked funny because her lips were raspberry purple. She saw me and waited till I was right next to her.

"Ella, I haven't seen you for ages. Where have you been hiding?" Her eyes were warm, and she put her arms around my shoulders and tugged my heavy backpack off. "You're all bent over, like an old man. You need to leave some of these books at home."

She took four books out of my backpack and held them as we walked down the road.

When we got to my driveway, she handed the books back to me. Then she said simply, "I have missed you."

That was all it took.

My mouth started talking even as my brain told it to stop.

I looked at her purple tongue and said, "Your teeth gonna fall out, from all that Kool-Aid."

I wanted to slap my loose lips silly.

She laughed, with her new laugh that now showed all her purple teeth. "It's all part of being social. What's a few teeth?"

I wanted to keep that smile in my mouth, but it finally peeped out and I put it right back in.

She wanted to be friends again, but I wasn't having any of it.

Miss St. James bit her lip. "I don't know how to tell you how sorry I am, Ella. I don't know what came over me at the river."

I stared up at her. I knew just what had come over her, but I wanted to hear it from her own lips.

"Ella, I'm trying. It's . . ." Then Miss St. James stopped.

I didn't say a word.

She picked my chin up and bent towards me. "Sometimes it's just that the old me slips through, but that is not me. Trust me on that?"

I thought about it for a minute. Thought about what I had done to make Ty stupid. Thought about how Fats, Cammy, and everybody wouldn't forgive me. Didn't I deserve a second chance? Didn't Miss St. James?

I felt a quiver of a smile twitch in my cheeks. I let it settle all over my mouth and finally I was smiling at her.

"Friends again?" she asked.

I nodded.

And that was that.

—◇—

The new relationship between Miss St. James and me was different from what it had been. I couldn't put my finger on it, but just like the chair in her dining room that wobbled that tiny bit, so our friendship was that bit off. Miss St. James would stick paper under the one troubling leg, folding it up different ways to try to make all the legs the same length, but there was always that wobble, sometimes so slight you would think you were just imagining it. It wasn't only that I didn't quite trust Miss St. James the way I had, but we were both changing, evolving, becoming something other than what we were. She was all wrapped up in her work, still interviewing people left and right, and I was starting to fully wear that big old African coat, getting used to the way it fitted around me.

From the library, I had taken stacks of big picture books on

Africa. I opened them up slowly, with trepidation, and then let the pictures spill out before me.

I had seen pictures of thousands of black people together, but there was usually a specific reason for the gathering—sometimes for things we had to fight for, like the March on Washington, or things we cried over, like Martin Luther King's death. But here were throngs of people, thousands, just doing everyday things. They were walking, riding on buses, laughing, cooking, selling things in the market, dancing, watching a soccer match, a boxing match. I had never seen so many black people all clumped together just being themselves. It filled me with awe.

Then there was the shock of seeing their faces. What were my wide nose, lips, and smile doing on their faces? I couldn't stop looking, turning page after page after page, peering into their deep black and brown faces, wondering at the high cheekbones, the rounded cheeks, the generous mouths, the high brows. I could never get my fill. I turned a page and the colors splashed out before me. Vibrant reds, gold, greens, yellows, and every color in between. It was a market scene, filled with mostly women selling their things. They were dressed in every color and pattern under the rainbow, while their children ran amok through the market. They looked happy, their smiles peeking from beneath wide-brimmed straw hats.

I closed my eyes and imagined I was there. That I had stepped across the continents and landed in an African country. The one where my father lived. All I had to do was step into the pages of the book and I was right in the heart of the market. I looked around. There were throngs of people with things on their heads. Baskets of oranges, piles of bananas, cooked food with exotic names like kenke and banku and okra stew, and piles of cloth, and jars of nuts. There were people selling dog chains, shoes, fruits, clothes—

everything you could think of—to their customers. To my surprise there were also market women selling to people stuck in traffic, on buses and in their cars. I saw goods exchanged through windows and doors—sachets of water, juice, pies, even a pair of sandals. I saw the cars, carts, people, dogs, and buses, all jostling for a place in the busy road. The noise was loud, full of car horns and sellers shouting their wares. My senses exploded.

But my father was right there. Perhaps he sensed how overwhelming it was, because he held out his hand. "Come on, Ella. Let me show you the beauty of being here. Feel one with the crowd, join them in the market."

"I can't," I shouted above the din. "There are too many people."

"You've got to. You can't be an observer, looking in from the sidelines. You need to be one with them."

"Am I going alone?" I asked worriedly.

He nodded.

"Where will I go and how will you find me?" I looked so much like them that I was worried he might not be able to spot me in a crowd.

My father laughed. "You are my daughter, you look like me. Of course I will recognize you. Wait here." He got some books from a passing seller and put them on my head. "You need these to feel part of the crowd. Hold on to them and don't think. Just feel. Feel the crowd, the rhythm of the city."

I had to be brave. I took a step forward and immediately tripped over a seller. I stood staring at the throng of moving black bodies and finally I felt bold enough to join them. I put one hand on the pile of books on my head and held on tightly so they wouldn't fall off. Then I took one step, and then another, and finally I was in the road with all those people. It was odd how quickly I disappeared into them. Became invisible, swallowed up whole.

How graceful they were, and how tall they walked, with backs so straight, perfectly aligned, as they walked swaying, unhurried, even as cars dodged around them. I straightened my spine and held my head high and tall. I looked around and there was a girl about my age that passed me with a pail on her head. She was as dark as I was, and her big eyes stared ahead serenely. She knew where she was going. I took off after her, dodging sellers, trying to stay as close as I could. Then we were out of the market, going along a narrow pathway on the side of a main street. At some point she must have sensed me trailing behind her and turned her head quickly to see who it was. Some of the water sloshed out of her pail and onto her neatly braided plaits, but she smiled broadly at me. Then she raised her hand and beckoned. I smiled back and gave a little wave.

As we walked, I found that the balancing act I was forced to do to keep the books on my head had changed the rhythm of my walk, and to my surprise, we were suddenly in step, and the high arch of her back and neck, by some type of transference, had become my walk. For miles I followed her, swaying the way she swayed, moving like a slow meandering river, just like a couple of sisters on the way to draw water at a well, looking so regal, so proud.

It wasn't surprising that I was back in the library almost daily. Today I was going to Miss St. James's, so I took one last look at the picture book. Underneath the picture were the words in small print, "Market Scene from Accra, Ghana."

"Accra," I mouthed. The book was on cities in Africa. I would be back again tomorrow to visit Dakar, in Senegal.

Miss St. James was already at home when I arrived, making herself a dinner that I was sure to taste. She was normally home by four, and I timed my arrival for just after that. I would do my homework while chatting to her till about seven, and then head home for dinner. Ma no longer asked me where I was because she was too tired and preoccupied with Leroy's absence.

Miss St. James and I would still do many of the things we used to do, like play Scrabble, but now we mostly talked about the neighbors. Miss St. James would tell me about some piece of gossip she had heard, like how Miss Claudia's ex-husband was coming into town and she was apprehensive about it, or how Mr. Graves's son was moving in with him to try to keep him away from the bottle. It was a new side of Miss St. James I hadn't seen before. In a funny way, I missed the old her. She used to measure out her words so carefully, so as not to offend. Now she spoke without hesitation, without that careful, appraising look that I took to be how she measured the impact of her words.

I thought that if I was putting on that great big African coat, then Miss St. James was already wearing her own new Ricksville coat—one she had tried on and believed made her belong.

All this should have made me relax, because surely Miss St. James was becoming one of us as she moved in and out of everyone's houses. But instead, her new open way of talking meant that ever so often she wasn't as careful with her words, and some of those very words put me on edge. One time I asked her about what she had written down from Miss Claudia's interview. She replied that the most interesting thing Miss Claudia said was that she still thought that former slaves should have been given forty acres and a mule. Miss St. James had laughed about this, as though Miss Claudia was just being silly.

I thought about how I might feel if I had just been given my freedom, and then handed forty acres and a mule. It wouldn't have compensated for four hundred years of work without pay, not to mention the tearing apart of families. But it would have been something. That meant ex-slaves could have farmed their land, especially if they were given good land, and they could build themselves a home. Families could have stayed in one place. Why, they could have added homes on other parts of the land as their sons and daughters married. They could even have sold parts of it, if they needed money. I thought of how we still had to rent and how sometimes Ma had to call the landlord to say the rent would be late because Leroy hadn't made it home yet and she just didn't have enough. Wouldn't it have been nice to just have a place of your own to have something to fall back on?

"I think that was a great idea," I said to Miss St. James.

She had this look on her face, like I was a kid who didn't know what I was talking about.

"I'm not saying it isn't a good idea, but farming is more complex than you think. You need skills to manage a farm to make it successful, Ella. It's not just about planting and harvesting crops. There's farm finance, there's management. I know, my father was a farmer."

It was then my stomach did this funny turn. Like I had swallowed something bitter I didn't like. How come it was okay for Miss St. James's father to be a farmer, but it was too complicated for us? I couldn't figure out how she could spend all that time with the neighbors, talking like she liked them, and yet, in the very same breath, she would make it seem like we couldn't do anything on our own.

I faced Miss St. James. "They already knew farming, and they could learn whatever else they needed to learn. It's not that difficult."

She looked surprised at my outburst.

"Ella, you didn't understand what I meant. I just meant that being handed forty acres was not really the solution in the long term. The solution was jobs, which brings income, real cash. Many moved north to get jobs, others stayed and worked on farms."

Wasn't having and working forty acres a job? One where you were your own boss? Didn't have to rely on anyone for food or housing? What happened if your boss fired you? Or the factory closed? But I didn't know much, so I just kept quiet.

That was the last time we talked about Miss St. James's work. It was as though she'd decided to avoid all the things that would make us quarrel. So instead we talked about Ty's grandma's recipe for collard greens, which we later tried, and I liked, and Miss Claudia's cornbread, which was a disaster when we finally made it.

Not long after this, Miss St. James surprised me. When I arrived at her house, she handed me a copy of her house key.

"I volunteered to teach Ty in the afternoons, and because of that I will be late most days. This way you can just come in and make yourself at home."

It was the best gift in the world, that key. It unlocked the door to my own home away from Leroy, who would ever so often just turn up, to grab a sweater or something he had left, sneaking off before Ma realized he was home. Miss St. James's place was where I could relax and feel safe.

From then on, I would never stay at the library. I would check out my Africa books and head to Miss St. James's, and there I would feel at peace, lying or sitting on her couch and reading as many of those Africa books as I could get through in a day, or doing my homework at her dining table until it was time for me to go home. I had discovered something new in those books. No matter which country they wrote about or whether the pictures were of poor people or rich people, everyone looked so confident. It amazed me. The way they wore their clothes, braided their hair in all sorts of styles. They didn't worry about how anyone looked at them. They knew they looked good. They could just be themselves.

Then I would sit with one of the books in my lap and continue to daydream of really meeting my dad and spending time with him.

It was a new kind of bliss.

CHAPTER 48

I was in my new home, which was Miss St. James's house, when I spotted a thick notebook next to the typewriter. I picked it up and flipped it open. By the time my conscience told me to stop, it was too late: I had read the words *June 1967*, and then underneath was the word *Carl*. It was in Miss St. James's handwriting, and seeing that just made me more curious. I skimmed over the words, but by the second line, I was riveted.

She remembers Carl's blood, even though she has tried to forget it. Most of all she remembers its color, a deep maroon red, gushing out, emptying itself in spurts onto the floor. Seeping into the wood. The stain left behind is etched in her memory.

She doesn't remember much, but they say she cut herself over and over again with anything she could lay her hands on—a fork, a pencil, even the edge of a piece of paper. She picked at her arms with her nails, teeth, anything, till she was as bloodied as she could get. They had finally cut her nails, and when that was not enough, they had bandaged her hands till they looked like boxing gloves. After that, she was fed by the nurses. She still tried to use her teeth to inflict as much damage as she could on herself, and so, as a last resort, most of the day she had to wear a mouthguard. It was one old black nurse who had told them to swaddle her in cotton, to calm her down. They had wrapped her tightly in layers of white cotton strips till she lay inert, unable to move. The bizarre treatment had calmed down her body and stilled her hands, but not her mind.

She remembers back to the day, two weeks before the wedding, when

*her father came home with the terrible news from his network down in
Louisiana. She could not believe it at first. Her Carl was a nigger. No
different than the niggerboys that picked cotton and worked on their farm
back home. There was no calming her father down, even as she reeled at
the news. How? It had to be a mistake. He was blonder than she was, as
white as she was, and his eyes were such an unusual sky blue that her
mother had said over and over again that she hoped her grandchildren
would inherit those pretty blue eyes.*

*She hadn't believed it at first. She had first spoken rationally, trying to
convince her father that Carl was just as white as they were. Then she had
fallen to her knees before him, pleading for him to be reasonable. Whatever
he heard was likely a misunderstanding and all this mess could be cleared
up if they asked Carl and his parents about their origins. She was pretty
sure they were Scottish and English. It wouldn't be awkward; they had a
right to know because of the children that would surely come. It was then
her father had thrown the evidence, ten sheets of paper, in her face. The
painstaking work of his network down south. They had started with Carl's
mother's name, then his father's, and worked their way back generations.
There, plastered on one of the sheets, was a record of sale for Carl's paternal
great-grandmother.*

*She had never seen her father so crazed with rage. A nigger, trying to
dip a spoon into his bowl. All he wanted to know was whether that nigger
had touched her. Had he touched her lips, kissed them? Had he slept with
her? He bellowed at the embarrassment—he had sent wedding invitations
to his network down south. She had grown afraid then, terribly frightened,
because she knew what her father, in that state, could do to her. What he
had almost done when she was a child.*

*But her father had not struck her. He had turned on his heel. She had
heard the door slam shut, but seconds later, another one opening. Then she
was on her feet and running, screaming, out the door, just as she heard the
gun go off. Carl had opened his apartment door and her father, cold sober*

that day, had shot him right through the chest wall. She had seen Carl's look of terror, those blue eyes turning to her in shock, still holding hers captive, even as he crumpled to the floor.

She hadn't touched Carl as he fell. Hadn't gone to him as he lay crumpled, the blood gushing in spurts onto the wooden landing between their two apartments. Her father, standing over Carl, had looked triumphantly at her and smiled.

For seconds, she saw what he saw. A lying nigger on the ground dying at her feet, right before he became Carl again. Even then, she had thrown up, over and over again, while her mind collapsed into itself.

She had walked down the apartment stairs and just kept going. At some point she had started to run, without a single thought in her head. She wasn't wearing shoes, nor did she have a coat, and it was freezing outside. A few people had tried to talk to her, to help her, but she was in a daze, and had pushed them aside as she ran. Eventually, a few days later, still in bare feet, she had been stopped and bundled into a police car. They had taken her to the hospital, and then to the mental ward when there was nothing they could do for her. There, they had assessed that she'd had a mental breakdown, caused by her beloved father killing her fiancé in a family argument. She had never corrected their assumption, based on the Boston Globe *newspaper, that Carl was white, and that he had died because of an argument.*

How could the father have murdered Carl just because he was black?

My mind whirled around in confusion at the words Miss St. James had written. They made me angry. Serve that woman right that she ended up a crazy person. I hoped she stayed crazy forever. I couldn't think why Miss St. James would write such a story unless she was writing a novel. I flipped to the beginning of the notebook to find out if there was more. I was so engrossed in what I was doing that I didn't hear the door open and close, but when I heard a movement and looked up, there was Miss St. James, standing right over me, her face an angry red that flushed clear down to her chest.

"How dare you? How dare you read my journal! I trusted you enough to give you a key to my home, only to find that you are nothing more than, than a ni—"

She hurled her words with such a fury that if they were flames, I would have turned to ash in an instant. I stood up and tried to slide past her, but Miss St. James towered above me, and she was quick, boxing me in on both sides, as angry as a raging lioness whose cub has been disturbed. I cowed before her, using my elbow to shield myself from what I thought she was going to do. Her python-like arms came around me and squeezed and shook me as I fought her off. She grabbed my hands and twisted them as I screamed in pain. It was only when she lifted me off my feet that I realized I still had her journal in my hand and she was trying to get it. I dropped it like it was a hot potato. As she swooped to pick it up, I slid under her arms and ran to the door. I heard her yell out my name as she scrambled up, and I almost passed out with fear. She caught up with me and those arms closed around me as tight as a handcuff.

I struggled to get out of her embrace, but her arms were bands around me, and I was scared. So scared, I started to cry.

It took a second. Then ten seconds. Then she was still.

Her hard hands became softer, and her face melted back into the Miss St. James I knew.

She was trembling. "I'm so sorry, Ella. So sorry. I didn't mean to scare you. Sorry, Ella," she said again.

She loosened her hold and said, "I'm sorry, I should never have reacted like that. I see I scared you. I overreacted but only because that journal is personal. Did you read any of it?"

I didn't answer and suddenly her voice was an urgent whisper in my ear.

"Did you read it?"

I shook my head, no. I was too scared to tell the truth.

She let out a breath before she smiled, finally.

I wanted everything to be how it had been between us, so I stayed in her arms, trying to pretend to myself that nothing had happened at all.

But this time it didn't work.

I had heard her almost use that word.

CHAPTER 49

She couldn't believe Ella had taken her journal and wouldn't give it back. She had almost lost it when that happened. She was so furious. It was those scared eyes that kept her hand from knocking that child backwards. The anger she felt has shaken her and for a minute she knows what it reminds her of—Kate would have been this furious.

She feels betrayed. She trusted Ella not to pry in her things. Had actually thought of adopting her. She even imagined what it would be like to return to New Jersey with a rescued black child in tow. She had so carefully constructed herself as Katherine St. James, a liberal northerner, concerned about justice and the plight of black people in America. But it hadn't stopped there. She had championed every poor community, taken many classes on Native Americans, Jews, poor whites, and others. It fit her lifestyle up north, and it was this person that everyone welcomed, praised, and admired. She regrets revealing so much of her background to Dr. Livenworth, but it was a calculated trade. She needed to get a passing grade in her class. So bringing Ella back would not have raised any eyebrows. She would have been congratulated. She loves herself as Katherine. It is this version of herself that has propelled her out of the ashes, into NYC, and now into Princeton. No one on the lauded campus of Princeton University would have welcomed her old self, Kate.

There is no doubt that her new persona has worked. Her success seems unending. Her time in Ricksville can only be said to be another success. Her plan to use Ella to aid her acceptance into the community has worked to perfection quite inadvertently. They have accepted and trusted her.

Yet she can't quite trust Ella's words that she hadn't read any part of the journal.

It is unsettling.

Then she remembers something. The pages that should not be in this journal. The ones she had written in the early days when she was quite mad. She panics and flips over the pages until she finds the section. Three pages, still blacked out. She can hardly read the words, and therefore hopefully neither has Ella. She takes her pen and blacks them out over and over again. Now she is worried, and that worry brings fear, and that fear brings on the anger again.

She cannot allow Ella's nosiness to mess her up. She won't stand for it. She thinks of everything she has built over the last twelve years. She has resurrected herself.

She cannot let Ella ruin this.

CHAPTER 50

She paced around the house, thinking. Ella had been sitting in her house since she came back from school. That would have been about 3:15 in the afternoon. She had arrived late, at about 6. This meant that Ella could have had close to three hours to decipher the scribbled words in her journal. The thought that her life was in Ella's hands made her want to scream. What would Ella do with that information if she had it? She was always talking. She would tell Mr. Macabe. Maybe even Nate. They were the two people in Ella's life who stood guard over her, who would believe everything that she said. She wasn't worried about Mr. Macabe, he was old and blind. But Nate was just the type of man her father would have enjoyed subduing. She knew black men like Nate. He reminded her of the last time she saw Curly. Insolent, cocksure, needing to be brought down a peg or two. What would Nate do with that information? She doesn't have to think it over. Nate would go for her jugular and enjoy every moment of it.

She wished she had her father's anger, because it rolled off his tall, strong body in shock waves, pummeling the person at the other end of it. But she is not over six feet tall, nor is she intimidating. Instead, her anger is like a coiled venomous snake, ready to strike when the need arises. She tried to rein it in, temper it, but fear about what Ella might have read and said to Nate causes it to escape, like steam rising from a pressure cooker.

CHAPTER 51

I was late for work and ran up Ricksville Road. I spotted Cammy as I ran. I wanted to yell to her, I'm not friends with Miss St. James anymore, to see what she would do, but I couldn't because she still wasn't talking to me. But I could tell she wanted to.

I got there, breathless, and swung open the screen door quickly, to get a bit of warmth, and who should I see right up there, next to Nate, but Mr. Macabe. Now, Mr. Macabe is hardly ever at Nate's, just as Nate is rarely at Mr. Macabe's, yet this was the second time I had seen them together.

"How's you, Mr. Macabe," I called out, just to let him know I was there. He was up at the counter, sitting as close to Nate as he could, the two of them looking as though they were up to something. "How come you're here?" I asked suspiciously.

"How come you're here?" Mr. Macabe countered. "Can't a body come and get hisself something to eat?"

"I work here," I said indignantly.

"Oh, right, Ella. I forgot. Just came to get something from Nate."

I got out the broom and started my cleaning routine, but out the corner of my eye I saw Nate slip Mr. Macabe a brown envelope. I wondered what was in it because unless it was in braille, Mr. Macabe couldn't read it.

Then there they were, talking low again. Before long, Nate had handed Mr. Macabe his cane and helped him past the tables to the door. Mr. Macabe had trouble with his legs, so the cane was for walking as well as for seeing.

Mr. Macabe just said, "Bye, Ella, come by and see me sometime," and he was gone.

"How's he going to make it back home?" I asked. "What's he doing here? He never comes here."

"He'll be fine. People will watch out for him. As to why he's here, well, why wouldn't he be here? Just because he has all those women fighting over making his meals for him doesn't mean he can't pop in now and then."

I was just about to cry out that they couldn't fool me, like I was eight or something, but for some reason I didn't say another word. Perhaps I didn't want to know, so I just shut my mouth and went back to sweeping.

I was surprised when, just before I hefted the trash bag out of the can, Nate seemed to change his mind and came over and said, "It was just about a trip I took to Philadelphia. Mr. Macabe wanted to know how the trip went."

"What's Philadelphia like anyway?" I asked.

"Well, it's bigger than here, for one, more shops and such. I guess you already know it's right around there where those election workers were killed, right?"

I nodded.

"Yes, but do you know what really happened that night?"

I nodded. "They were chased out of town and killed."

"Well, Ella, it's more than just getting killed. It was premeditated murder, that's what it was. There were three young men in their early twenties, two white boys from New York, and one black boy from Meridian, which as you know is not too far from here. Well, these boys were working with the Congress of Racial

Equality to help black people register to vote in Mississippi. In 1964, these boys were working alongside other organizations, including the Students for Non-Violence Coordinating Committee on the Mississippi Freedom Summer Project. Now, you know a lot of all that, but did you know that without those types of organizations, black folk would never have had a chance to vote? They were there to convince black folk that it was in their interest to vote and to help them get through all the requirements. And I tell you, black folk were scared because they knew what would happen if they tried to actually go and vote. So those boys sure had their work cut out for them."

I knew how important it was that they got out the vote. But I couldn't imagine what it was like to put your piece of paper in the ballot box, knowing all the while that someone could kill you for that. Just because you were black.

"So if the three men knew how dangerous it was, for themselves and for black folk, why did they do it?" I asked Nate.

"Are we going to do the right thing, or we going to let fear take over?"

"We are going to do the right thing," I said.

"We sure are. It was a risk those three boys decided to take. A risk every person who registered was prepared to take. But it was not easy. The KKK was active in the county and their members were everywhere, in the government, in the police force, in the army, the sheriff's office, you name it. In fact, in the town of Philadelphia, one of the Klan leaders was having meetings every week to plot how to stop the black vote. By the time those three boys rolled into town to investigate the Klan burning of Mt. Zion Church, one of the locations of the registration, the leader, Jack Summerville, and his boys had been planning for their arrival for a while. It wasn't surprising when the three boys were picked up in town and hauled to jail on some pretext. But then surprisingly they were released a day or so later."

"Why did they release them if they were just going to kill them later?" I asked. "They'd already got them. Why did they let them go?"

"People are tricky, Ella. It was just a plan to make it seem like the police and the county sheriff's office were not involved. That their deaths were something that happened on the road out of town. But they knew all along what they would do. Those men in the county sheriff's office and in the police force, as well as others, got into their cars and followed the three boys out of town. The rest of it, the murder and the disposal of the bodies, is something you know about already."

There was dead air swarming around us, heavy and cloying, holding thick around my chest. I was thinking about those three civil rights workers. They must have been so happy to get out of jail. They were probably laughing in the car, so relieved. But then down the road, they must have noticed some cars following them. There were police cars, the deputy county sheriff's car, and a whole bunch of trucks. I can just imagine their fear when they looked behind them. Must have made them start to panic. Ask themselves what on earth they had done. I imagined them looking in the mirror, driving slowly, checking, then slowing down and stopping.

I thought of the young black man they had killed, James Chaney. He was one brave Mississippi man. He knew the danger he was in the minute he saw all those cars and trucks because he'd had to deal with it all his life, being a Mississippi man, but he was just like a soldier, going into battle for his people. He must have seen death coming the minute he saw those cars.

Then I thought about those two young white men with him, Michael (Mickey) Schwerner and Andrew Goodman, both from

New York City. Michael was the leader of the group, and it was Andrew's first time in Mississippi. It wasn't even their fight. They could have stayed at home, worked and did what most people did, closing their eyes to everything. But they didn't. They had risked everything to fight for what was right. If they were here, alive, I would have reached out and hugged them just for that. I'm sure they never imagined that white folk would kill them just because they were helping out black folk. That was how far the hate had gone. It had even painted white folk black.

I looked up at Nate. "Those were brave men. They need to give them a medal, or something."

Nate was somber. He nodded. "We're riding on the backs of these heroes."

I thought in my head of all the heroes who had died. I thought of Dr. King, Malcolm, and Emmett. Then I added the ones I had just learned more about, James, Michael, and Andrew. It didn't matter what color they were. They were all heroes.

After a while Nate said, "We've come so far, but there's a long way to go. We need young people like you. People with heart who know what is right. They don't have to bend the truth or make excuses, they just know what's right and act on it."

I nodded. I knew what he meant.

"So anyway, where was I?"

"I think you were done."

"Almost. There is an ending. They eventually caught some of the killers thanks to a tip-off. The FBI was called in and they put up these posters all over town with those three boys' faces on them, asking people to call in a tip if they knew something. As soon as they were up, they were torn down, but someone kept putting them up. Racists don't want their evil deeds staring them in the face."

"Who did the FBI say killed them?" I asked. "Did they know it was the police and the Klan?"

"Yes, but most got away with it. Only seven of about fourteen who they were able to place at the scene were sent to jail. However, they spent less than six years in jail for murder, imagine that. The one they wanted the most, Jack Summerville, whose barn they all met up in, disappeared right before the FBI showed up."

"Do you know who gave them the tip-off?"

Nate smiled, and when he did, it was a broad grin. "I sure do. I met the lady because she's still living and is now quite famous among black folk in Philadelphia. Her name is Bessie, and she was Jack Summerville's cook."

On the way home from Nate's, I thought about what I had heard. I wondered why some people hated black people so much when they had gotten so much out of them. Worked them to the bone in slavery and yet called them lazy. That didn't make sense. If one sat back and made someone else do all the work for free, who was the lazy one? Didn't pay them for four hundred years for all that work and still tried to stop them from getting more.

Before long, I realized I was right opposite Mr. Macabe's house.

Mr. Macabe was sitting on his porch listening to his tape recorder. Some jazz was playing, and it filled the air. It took away the bad feeling I was feeling from hearing all about those three election boys. It drew me up Mr. Macabe's stairs to hear some more. I danced and shook my feet climbing up.

"Hello, Ella, it must be my lucky day. Twice in a day."

"See you're listening to jazz today."

"Yep, I'm just in a jazz kind of mood. It's not like the blues, it can make you feel all kind of up, even when you're feeling low inside."

"You in a low, Mr. Macabe?"

"Well, a bit. You can say today I got some news I didn't really like."

"That got to do with the brown envelope Nate gave you?"

Mr. Macabe didn't say anything for a second. Then he shook his finger in my direction but he didn't tell me anything.

I told him the story Nate had told me about Philadelphia and the three young election men, and he just nodded and said yes, that was a real bad time. Then I told him about the story Miss St. James had written in her journal—the story about the father killing his daughter's fiancé because he was black.

"Now, why would she write a story like that?" I asked.

"Don't know, Ella. You said she was mad you had read her journal?"

"Yes, real mad." It felt good to get it off my chest, but I didn't tell him that she was scary mad, like one of those cartoons where someone is so mad their head explodes, starts shooting off rockets and everything.

Mr. Macabe didn't say anything more. Another jazz piece had just started. Charlie Parker. Mr. Macabe just leaned back, taking in that music. I remembered then that he used to play the saxophone. So I also sat back on the floor by his feet. The notes of the sax were so high and so sweet. We listened as Charlie weaved his magic, soaring higher and higher till I was holding my breath with it, my heart full of the beautiful notes as they danced and thrilled high above us. I wished it would never end. And it didn't, because this was Charlie live, and he was putting on a show, and so on and on it went, a solo without pause. Finally, from the highest, clearest note, the notes began to descend. We listened to the descent, the notes thrilling, then getting deeper, and soon we were back down to earth.

Mr. Macabe sat up.

"Wasn't that something, Ella?"

"Yes." It was all I could manage to say.

I sat there and imagined Charlie playing his sax out there in the park. Mr. Macabe said that he was always out in the park, walking around in that grass, playing, practicing, and refining his notes—so much that they called him Yardbird, and later they just called him Bird. He never saw the civil rights movement coming, he died long before, and he must have faced all kinds of terrible things in Jim Crow time, and yet there he was playing his heart out in that park, for a little while free from everything that put a label on him and tried to pin him down. Just soaring with those notes, just playing to the sky, the birds, and anyone who stopped to listen. Made me realize just how strong black people were.

How strong I already was.

CHAPTER 52

I ran from Mr. Macabe's back to my house. Ma must be back home, I thought. Ma was now working three days a week on account of Leroy, who hadn't brought in any money over the past month. She was also trying to save up to buy a bus ticket to Atlanta to see Kitty. She wasn't fully recovered: she had to sit and rest more often, and she had a limp, which meant that she had to use a cane and rest a lot, but Nate didn't seem to mind. He was just glad to see her up and about. However, he refused to let her eat any of his buttermilk fried chicken, explaining that Dr. Shepardson had been in and told him that he should cut down on the salt and lard and make sure Ma ate more vegetables. There was a new menu item at Nate's called Nate's Healthy Fried Chicken. It had pepper with just a pinch of salt and was lightly fried before being put in the oven to finish cooking. Nate didn't want to call it "baked" chicken. He didn't think people would take too kindly to it if it was called that, but even so, the new "healthy" fried chicken wasn't very popular. Nate had used Ma as an example for why people should try the new chicken, but few people wanted to shell out good money for this new type of chicken when they were already happy with the old. One customer was as blunt as could be, telling Nate, "It just don't taste the same. That finger-licking good is gone. Your food is turning into my wife's cooking." Regardless, it stayed on the menu, but the only people who ate it were Nate and Dr. Shepardson.

The moment I pulled open the front door, I almost passed out with shock, because who was sitting right there on our brown sofa, talking with Ma, but Miss St. James. I almost ran out again, but Ma was sitting there with a stern look on her face.

"Come in, Oreo, and say good evening to Miss St. James." Ma's face was a stone mask, frozen in rigid politeness.

I approached her tentatively. What was she doing in our house, sitting on our sofa, with a smile on her face? Had she come to interview Ma? That wasn't possible, because Ma had said right off the bat that there was no way she was answering those nosy questions she had heard all about.

I shook her hand. But before I could turn around and leave, Ma gestured for me to sit down.

Clearly, this had something to do with me.

"Miss St. James was telling me—" Ma's voice stopped. She was having trouble getting her words out, and I knew she would hate Miss St. James to see her like this.

"Telling me."

"Telling me." Ma had forgotten what she was going to say.

We waited and the seconds went by, and all this while Miss St. James didn't jump in and rescue Ma. Just sat there, waiting, while Ma struggled.

Finally, Ma said, "You took something. Wasn't yours to take. Stole her journal."

My voice was as shrill as could be when I forgot myself and yelled at both of them. "I didn't take anything! I never stole her journal. She's a liar!"

Ma was so angry, I could see her shaking, right from her feet all the way to her bosom. All hell was going to break loose. But she couldn't. Not in front of Miss St. James. I could tell by the way Ma clenched her teeth as she spoke, and by that evil eye she laid on me, that my life was going to be over the minute Miss St. James left.

She was going to switch me up. I just hoped the stroke had made her weaker and she couldn't hit as hard.

Meanwhile, Miss St. James just sat primly.

"You need to make it up to Miss St. James. What do you suggest?" Ma asked Miss St. James. "Ella could use her Saturday money to help you get another journal, unless it was something very expensive. And don't worry, if she has it here, we will find it and return it to you."

Miss St. James cocked her head, considering.

"The money is not important because the journal cost so little. But I think it will be a good lesson for Ella to learn how to keep her hands to herself. Why doesn't she come over and do chores for me for a week? I think that is punishment enough."

I could tell Ma was so relieved that the journal wouldn't cost her anything because she nodded in agreement so fast that I didn't have time to yell that I was never ever going back to Miss St. James's. Seconds later, Miss St. James popped off the couch. Then she stopped and said abruptly, "I almost forgot, Ella, I need my spare key back."

Ma glared at me. All I felt was shame as I walked upstairs to get the key from my dresser. That would only bring more switches with the cane because now I'd made Ma look even worse because it looked like I'd taken advantage of Miss St. James and then robbed her.

I got back and placed it in Miss St. James's outstretched hand.

"Ella, you have taken advantage of Miss St. James's kindness."

If a tone could kill, I would have been lying on the ground, spread out, dead, blood seeping from my veins.

As soon as the door closed, letting Miss St. James out, all that embarrassment that Ma felt went into her hand, and even though her left side was weak, her right side must have gotten even stronger to compensate. She didn't say a word, just held that cane gripped in her right hand and brought it down, over and over again, till I almost passed out.

I think Miss St. James must have wanted me dead.

—◆—

I missed school that week, but the next week, when I showed up at Miss St. James's house right after school, the seed of bitterness had spread, like a rash, all over my body, just like the marks of the cane, which I hid with jeans and a long-sleeved shirt. Miss St. James opened the door and said, "Oh, hello, Ella," as though what she had done had never happened.

"What do you want me to do? The laundry? Clean up the kitchen?"

Miss St. James handed me a broom and I began to sweep her floor. As I swept, I thought about all the parts of the Miss St. James that I knew. All the parts did not add up, like puzzle pieces that did not fit. Sometimes she was so nice, but now, now I saw a side to her that made me want to run. I finished sweeping.

"Now what do you want me to do?" My tone was insolent.

"Ella, come here for a moment."

I reluctantly went towards the table where Miss St. James sat.

It was then I saw the journal in front of her. She'd had it all along!

"You said I had stolen it! You are the liar!"

"I want to know if you read it."

I went quiet.

"I said, did you read it?"

There was something in Miss St. James's voice that made my chin jerk up and my eyes stare at hers. I saw something in there that I feared. As much as I feared Leroy.

My brain started to work, even before I told it to, looking for an escape. In my glance around the room, I calculated how many steps it would take to get me to the door. How many seconds it would take for me to yank the door open as I ran, picking up speed.

"I did not read it."

I would have said anything, told any lie, even as my conscience bit me again. I knew what I would get if I told the truth. I could already feel it, the way I have always felt it when Leroy's anger builds up and surges.

"Did you look at this page?" She shook open the pages and all I saw was nothing but blacked-out marks covering the page. There was nothing there to read. Was she crazy?

This time I did not have to lie.

"No, I did not read it," I said quietly, ridding my voice of any insolence or anger, trying to placate her by my voice, the way I sometimes have to with Leroy.

I knew it before she even knew it. Saw the disbelief in her eyes even before it descended from her eyes to her lips. Saw her rage and disbelief unite into a powerful force, the way they do in Leroy. Saw the fire light up even before it kindled.

Then I was gone, running, even as she took her first step to catch me, maybe to hurt me like Leroy always wanted to.

Five running strides to the door, three seconds to pull if I twisted fast and pushed out, one second to stumble over the door post.

I could feel the wind at the door as I opened it. It was pushing me forward, and I was gone, caught up in its force, swept up in it.

I knew Miss St. James was standing at her doorway, looking rattled, annoyed.

She didn't know how much practice I'd had.

CHAPTER 53

A few days later, I was sitting with Mr. Macabe at his patio table, having just stopped by on the way from school, when I heard a tap, tap on the porch steps, and then in a second Miss St. James's head emerged. I had just been teasing Mr. Macabe about the long woolen scarf Mrs. Robertson had knitted for him. It was red, with gray polka dots. It looked hideous but he said it kept him warm. I immediately got up to leave but then Mr. Macabe heard me and motioned for me to sit down, so I did, moving to one of the deck chairs in the corner, with my eyes fixed on Mr. Macabe, not even bothering to glance at her polka-dotted shoes and her long white skirt.

"Hello, Miss St. James. Welcome again." Mr. Macabe sounded jovial, as though he had been waiting for her to show up all day. I wanted to mutter to him, don't let her fool you, but I bit my tongue to hold it from flapping.

"Hello, you two," she answered cheerily, as though she hadn't caused me one of the worst beatings in my life and as though she hadn't tried to wipe me out. "I've come to conduct the last interview. Thanks for agreeing to do it. I'm almost done in Ricksville, can you imagine it? I will be taking off in about a week."

"Where next?" Mr. Macabe asked. "Back to Princeton?"

"Oh no, not yet. I have another town to pass through, but I won't stay as long."

Mr. Macabe sat back down at the patio table and patted the chair next to him, but instead Miss St. James said it would be better if she faced him, so she walked around to the other side and sat down. She brought out her notebook and a thick stapled package.

"It's about thirty questions, I hope you won't get tired. Just talk as fast as you want, I can take shorthand."

I pulled Mr. Macabe's deck chair into a lounging position and lay down so that I wasn't looking at them at all. I was staring into the blue sky.

"Ready for the first question?" she asked. "Here it goes. The civil rights movement was supposed to give blacks the rights that they felt they deserved. How did you participate in that movement, and what do you feel that it accomplished, looking back from today?"

I didn't hear Mr. Macabe respond so I glanced at them. Mr. Macabe was facing her and yet he was so still that I thought he'd fallen asleep. You can never tell with his eyes being the way they are. Her notebook was out, her pen poised, waiting.

The silence grew. She looked uncomfortable. Probably wondering whether he was fast asleep and whether to prod him or not.

I closed my eyes. Let her figure it out.

"How do you feel about your father's involvement in the KKK and the fact that he helped kill those election workers turning out the black vote?" Mr. Macabe's voice seemed to come from nowhere.

My mouth fell open. I sat up quickly and stared at Mr. Macabe. Had he gone mad? Then I glanced at Miss St. James. The pen had slipped out of her hand but her fingers clenched as though she still held the pen between them.

The silence lasted seconds and then Miss St. James moved and pointed at her ears.

"Can you repeat what you just said, I don't think I heard right?"

"I said, how do you feel about your father's involvement in the KKK and the fact that he helped kill those civil rights workers?"

Mr. Macabe's voice was so deep that it was like an engine rumbling.

Miss St. James worked her mouth till some words fell out. "Did I tell you that when I had too much alcohol, because if so, I do get quite silly and say anything when I am drunk. Thankfully, that is rare."

"No, wasn't that. You only told me your father's name, Jack Summerville."

Now it was my turn to turn to stone.

That name. I remembered it. Nate had said that the men plotting the murder of the three election workers used to meet in Jack Summerville's barn. I looked at Miss St. James as my brain tried to make sense of what I'd heard, but I was distracted because Miss St. James started to freak out. She jumped up and started to gather up her bag and her papers and pens, but they kept slipping through her fingers, spilling out onto the porch floor. She scrabbled to pick them up and stuff them in her bag. Then it seemed that she changed her mind, because she gave up and started talking.

"My father did belong to the KKK but all the rest of it was never proven."

Her words were hard, she was now annoyed.

Mr. Macabe didn't seem to have heard her, because he was now talking in that strange rumble I had never heard before, like an engine about to take off.

"Also put two and two together and figured that your father killed your fiancé. Your black fiancé. Guess you never did tell anybody that Carl was black? Nate read me some newspaper articles about the trial he found on microform in the library. Seems the judge convicted your father to twenty years for killing a white boy." Mr. Macabe began to chuckle. "That's the Lord's justice right there because your father would likely have gotten a shorter sentence if they knew Carl was black. However, he was so white looking your father got a very stiff sentence for manslaughter. The lawyer could have produced the document showing his ancestry to try to convince the jury that this was a black man. But of course if he did, the prosecutor would have said it was premeditated murder, and any publicity could have tied him back to the earlier murders. Now, that's what you call being stuck between a rock and a hard place, and the lawyer must have chosen what he thought was the easier path."

She didn't react at first. I could see her brain working in the stillness of her body. She was just realizing that I had lied. That the reason Mr. Macabe figured out what really happened to Carl was because I had read her journal and blabbed.

She turned and looked square at me for the first time since she had come. It was an appraising look. I thought she going to go crazy and come at me for lying about reading her precious journal, but instead, the fire in her eyes dimmed and it seemed like her eyes softened at the sight of my face, trying to hold my eyes captive.

When she spoke, it was to me alone.

"That was my father. All that he did was wrong, and I am not him. My father's sins are not mine, just as Leroy's sins are not your fault."

I heard her words, and they sank deep, because Miss St. James was the only one in town who knew my secret. And because of that, she was sending me a message in code. A code that Mr. Macabe would not understand, sure to bind Miss St. James and me together, as friends with evil fathers.

Her eyes held mine, and they were so kind that I was swept back to the time we spent playing Scrabble in her house, and how she had taught me all those new words, and all the fun we had had. I thought of the love that I had given her, and that she had taken. I had spoken up for her and been ridiculed. Even when everyone else wanted her gone, I had still stood up for her. But then I looked at Miss St. James's smiling face and thought of Ty's almost drowning, and the thesis she was writing. Everything was falling into place, and I was building the jigsaw puzzle that was Miss St. James with a sure and steady hand because now I knew where most of the pieces were. Most people in South Ricksville had shared their hopes, dreams, and disappointments with her because she had carefully hidden who she was. She may have wanted our views, but now that I had all the puzzle pieces, I also knew why she sat day and night typing in her living room. She was trying to make her crazy murdering father sane. Yet being poorer than other generations did not make people go out and kill other people. Only racism and hatred did that.

I was guilty because I had not told anyone, not even Mr. Macabe, about those other interviews she had planned—the ones that would have kept everyone's tongue fastened in their mouths. I had kept silent because I thought she was my friend, and by doing so, I was no better than she was.

But no more. No more would I be silent when I was supposed to speak out.

I tore my eyes away from hers, even as she tried to hold on to my gaze. I knew about evil fathers, and what they tried to pass on to their children, but they didn't have to learn it. I already knew that Stevie would be different from Leroy.

I took a deep breath and spoke my words.

"You could be different from your father. Maybe you want to be different, but you're not. On the inside, you are almost the same."

She stood there for a second, in limbo, her eyes vacant, no longer fixed on me. She already seemed like someone I never knew.

I was not sure whether she'd heard my words.

But then I realized she had, because she snatched the rest of her papers and things from off the floor and straightened up, indignant and haughty. Miss St. James was leaving. She was hurrying down those steps.

Mr. Macabe was not done. "Don't even try to use that information you collected from everyone. You cannot be trusted to tell our stories and we will write to the university to complain about you. I want you to leave this town by tomorrow or you will find the entire neighborhood on your doorstep. That I can promise you."

I knew how boiling mad she was by the sound her shoes made as they slammed down hard on the wooden steps.

Mr. Macabe went to sit back in his chair, cool and easy, like he did this every day.

We sat there for the next few hours without saying a word, till it turned to dusk and fireflies danced above our heads, zipping back and forth. Me with my thoughts and he with his.

Finally, I asked, "How did you get all that information about her family?"

Mr. Macabe smiled. "You know when Miss St. James had all that red wine? Well, she mentioned her father's name, Jack Summerville. I noticed right then that it was different from her last name, St. James. The other odd thing was that when she was drunk, she started talking with the strongest Mississippi accent I had ever heard. Never heard anything like it. After you told me about what happened at the river, I decided to look into things. I paid a man I know to do the background check and told him that he had to track her father down. Best two hundred dollars Nate and I ever spent. Didn't take much to find out her family came from Philadelphia, Mississippi. Her father was very well known. Man, they had some tales to tell. He led the killing of those three election workers, as you now know, but some even said he used to track down other black people and kill them. We didn't find any evidence of that, but the detective found their old cook, Bessie, who is still living. I asked Nate to go down to Philadelphia and see if she would tell her story on tape because I can't read the report. That was what was in the envelope, a copy of the tape."

"Bessie. Nate mentioned her. He said she had given the FBI a tip-off."

Mr. Macabe nodded. "She's a very old lady, but she sure had a tale to tell."

"How did she know who the killers were?"

Mr. Macabe felt around for his tape recorder. He opened it up, made sure a tape was in there, and then kept pressing back and forth till he got to where he wanted it to start.

"It's a long story but I just wanted you to hear the end of it." Then he pressed the play button. "Listen, Ella. This is history in the making right here."

I made up my mind. I was gon' do it. I was scared but I walk all the way to Main Street. Now when I get there, I done look around and found those FBI posters askin' people to call in an' tell 'em about those boys. People been tearin' them down, but I find one, nailed to a tree. I pull it off really quick and stuff it down my blouse. I was right scared 'cause if they sees me, they'd have known somethin's up and before I knows it, the Klan be after me. But I look around and people ain't payin' me no mind. I walk to the phone booth, pull that paper out a bit, so I can see the number. Then I put in my coin. My hands were all shakin' and the first two times I dialed, it didn't go right. Then I stop. I close my eyes and say, Lord, please help me. Then I try again, and you know the good Lord always answers, and I hear that phone ring. Lord, how sweet that sound. Then I hear a voice, a man's voice. "Hello," he says.

I say it real quick. "Is this the number for those dead election boys?"

"Yes, ma'am," the man said.

I say, "Jack Summerville, Alton Roberts, Billy Posey, Cecil Price, Alton Roberts, James Elder, Sam Bowers, Edgar Killen, and more o' them have been plottin' to kill them boys in Jack's barn for a long time and now they gone and done it."

I wait. I hear someone clear their throat, then they say, "Excuse me, ma'am, where are you calling from?"

I put that phone down. I feel real good. On the way home, I eat that paper, one bite at a time. Chew and swallow that paper with the picture of the boys till it's all gone——in case they stop me on the street. After that, it's like those boys are my boys, 'cause now they in me. Think of them all the time. That's why no one can keep me from voting, rain or shine, legs good or no legs.

My mouth was now open. "Wow," I said finally. "That's some lady."

"She sure is. She said those FBI men came soon after and searched the barn, but before they got there, Jack Summerville had gotten wind of it and he and his family had fled up north. They caught some of the other men, but they never got him."

"Mr. Macabe, how come you're always looking out for me?" I asked in wonder.

He was smiling. "Love you like you were mine, you know that."

I always thought of Mr. Macabe as my grandfather, but that evening, sitting right there, it came to me. I was always saying I needed a father on earth, too. God had held one right in front of me, and I was too blind to see.

CHAPTER 54

The unthinkable had happened.

She can't believe that she let her father's name slip out. In Mississippi of all places. Once they had the name, the rest would have been easy. He had been so well known in Philadelphia. She is angry, but now mostly at herself, at her own stupidity for revealing that much.

She rushes about her house, dragging out her suitcase, emptying closets. She is worried that Mr. Macabe will make good his threat, and the neighborhood will be at her doorstep, wanting to smoke her out, demanding her interview sheets and notes. She hopes they don't write to her university. That her departure will be enough. But she is worried that Nate will make sure of it.

They can't! She has worked so hard.

She panics for a second, trying to find all her notes, and when she finds them, she stuffs them into her bag.

She goes to pack and the journal falls on the floor. It lands on its side and the pages fan out. She bends to pick it up, and when she flips it over, the pages open up to the scribblings that are blacked out.

She slams the pages shut and packs it away. She was crazy enough back then to write the words on paper, yet somehow just sane enough to blacken them out. They are a constant reminder of how, at fourteen, Kate had found out that her father killed niggers for sport. His own brand of hunting. Why had Kate lifted up the tarp that was tied over the flathed of his truck, thinking that he had killed a buck? The next day the sack was gone, the knives and guns back in their place in the locked cabinet. Kate had kept quiet then, even though she had nightmares for weeks. Then, when Kate was fifteen, he had told her the truth. "Niggers are like vermin," he said. "Like mice, or rats or foxes. Got to get rid of them any way we can. Trick them, be nice to them, whatever. Uncle Billy and his deputy just pull them over for a broken taillight or something made up, and then before you know it, they are dead. Don't have to be too smart about it. It's easier than shooting ducks. Don't tell anyone," he had said casually, "it's what we do. A war on the quiet."

She felt so important to be entrusted with this secret. After he told her what they did, her voice, clear as a bell, rang out—I want to come and get one, too. It wasn't that she meant it. She just wanted to show him she was with him in this. That she could handle all he threw at her. He had called her his girl, chip off the old block. Then she had become a decoy, and just once, a little more than that.

It was about five in the evening, and the sun was going down over the Pearl River. Daddy was charged up. They were just driving along the edge of the river, not a car or person in sight. Then Daddy spotted one, alone, separated from the pack.

"Kate," he had said excitedly, "go on by that young man over there. He will be dazzled by you in that pretty dress."

She had come up on the man by the edge of the river. She had smiled prettily at him and he, instead of looking enchanted, had only stared at her, bewildered. Up close she could see that he was just a boy, close to her age, about fifteen or sixteen. He was wearing shorts and an old T-shirt. She was wearing a long summer dress that her father approved of, with a satin purple cloth belt, and as she walked, she swished the bottom part of it back and forth, as though she were about to dance. For all he could see, she was walking along the river edge all alone. She had sauntered past him, done a loop, and turned around to walk back. When she reached the spot where he was, she stood next to him and said that she would like to be rowed to the middle of the lake, just because it was so much cooler, so she could feel the breeze and watch the sunset. Did he have a boat? The boy, easygoing and doing nothing but skipping rocks by the river, had said, "No, miss, but there is one over there." He had half run, half jogged over to it and brought it through the water, his hands pulling it along as he walked barefoot in the water. Kate had gotten into the boat and seen his sandals tucked into a corner. Worn but obviously precious shoes that he didn't want to get wet. He had rowed strongly to the middle of the lake, and there they had sat in silence, she looking at the sunset, he resting on the oars. She waited till she knew her father was there, with them, treading water on the other side of the boat, out of sight. Then she had stood up, arched her back, and dived into the murky brown water. As Kate swam to shore, she looked back and saw her father come up silently from under the boat. He reached out and rocked it, and finally tipped it over, emptying its contents like one would empty a bin of trash.

The boy had come sliding out and landed with a plop in the middle of the lake. He had not screamed. Kate remembers his desperate scrabbling, pulling at the air, trying to reach the boat, which was just out of his reach. The water covered him up, and then there was nothing, just his sandals bobbing on the surface of the river.

Her father had laughed about that for weeks. "Don't know why these niggers can't swim," he said. "Living by the banks of the river and only as many as I have fingers can swim." Even back then, her conscience was not completely dead. At times it kicked out, protesting. But then she'd tell herself it was just like a war, it was them or us. We are allowed to do bad things in wartime.

She knows why her father smiled at her in triumph after he killed Carl. He knew that she could not possibly object.

She wants to hate him, yet she cannot. She wants to be the opposite of what he was, yet she has failed. She and her father are one, conjoined by the *deaths that hang over them, as though they are Siamese twins. At Princeton his voice was muted, and she could imagine that she was different, but in Mississippi he is here, fully alive again, trying to reattach to his living twin.*

This killing is what she thinks Ella has deciphered through the blacked-out words, now that she knows Ella has lied about reading the journal. She knows that Ella has told Mr. Macabe, and Mr. Macabe, in turn, may have told Nate. She imagines the news spreading, like blazing wildfire, eating up and destroying the life she has built.

She goes back into her suitcase, snatches at the journal, and rips the blackened pages out, tears them into little pieces, and flushes them down the toilet so that no evidence is left.

She stands there, watching as the bits of paper disappear into the gurgling hole.

She is not guilty. She was a child. They cannot convict her of something that happened when she was fifteen. Besides, she has saved Ty. The score is even.

A life for a life, she whispers into the bowl.

The freedom from her crime that she craves does not come.

She can still feel Kate on the inside, usually small and hidden, but now emboldened, and she can still hear her father's voice.

CHAPTER 55

Ever since I can remember, God has been close by. My first memory at four years old was of me walking up the driveway with the sun on my face, and the wind blowing kisses on my cheeks. I remember seeing colors everywhere—in the leaves, in the sky, and on the birds. I remember being surprised and delighted by everything. The world was so colorful.

Ma used to leave me outside by myself all day. "Stay outside," she would say, and she would shut the door hard. I knew never to come inside before she came out and yelled for me. So I spent hours outside looking at the brilliant world, and God would play with me during that time. Sometimes the green leaves would rustle near me and I would run to them and they would snap back and hide from me and I would giggle and giggle. We would play hide-and-seek for hours. I remember lying on the grass, an endless green carpet that caressed me. God would open His hand, and a black beetle or yellow-and-green caterpillar would crawl out, and I would follow it wherever it went, dazzled by its movement and color.

I looked down at my skin. Since hearing about my father and reading and looking at all those pictures of Africans, I had slowly begun to notice how supple it looked, how gleaming, how beautiful. A few days ago, I had run to the mirror and looked at my face, expecting to see my usual ugliness but all of a sudden there was someone new looking at me. Someone whose curved lips matched her nose and eyes and whose cheekbones gleamed in the mirror. My hair, its black, tight coils, like caresses framed about my face. It was a shock to find how beautiful I was. How could that possibly be?

Stevie walked in while I was in there and caught me staring at my face.

"Come on. You, too? We don't need another Kitty in this house."

I didn't budge. I was still staring at the mirror.

"I don't know how I suddenly became so pretty."

Stevie looked at me, appraisingly. "I never thought you were ugly" was all he said.

Now it was my turn to look at him in wonder.

For the next three days I stared in the mirror, seeing myself with my new eyes. Taking in all that I liked till Stevie told me he liked me better before, when I thought I was ugly. It was then Mr. Macabe's words came to me, startling me with their clarity. "To a blind man, color means nothing. But if you happen to have your sight, look beyond the plain wrapping and instead see the world as a glorious set of watercolors laid out in a handcrafted palette." I stopped staring at the mirror then. I was behaving just like C.T. when we gave him a present. He always played with the box, too enthralled with it to open it up and see what was inside.

As I walked outside heading for Nate's, I pretended that I was blind since birth and that I had just miraculously received my sight. I fixed my eyes on the partially blue, partially cloudy skies and the trees' green leaves. I saw the brilliant arrays of reds and golds in the trees, fruits, insects, and birds. My skin had a dark hue, but in comparison with the array of brilliant colors outside in nature, it looked so plain. How plain the world would be if it were only painted in brown, black, and white.

I now knew the secret of color. It was a gift for us, like God kiss-

ing us on the forehead, because he not only made the world in colors, but he also designed our eyes to see those colors. I now knew
why God had made us in such ordinary colors like black, brown,
and white, unlike the greens of the grass, the blues of the oceans
and sky, and the rainbow colors of birds and insects. He wanted us
to look outside, at his paintings, not at ourselves.

For the first time in my life, I saw my skin for what it was. The
world of slavery had put labels on it, but it was a beautiful covering.
Nothing more than a soft supple cover that hid the amazing poten-
tial and strength that lay beneath.

And in that instant, I had a glimpse of how a girl from Cameroon,
or Uganda, or Ghana, or Mali, or Ivory Coast viewed her skin.

Wouldn't it be wonderful if everyone thought like that? If the
only color we saw was the array of colors outside in the world
and not on our skins. Then, as Mr. Macabe said, there'd be no
judgment based on skin color. There'd only be good people, bad
people, and those in between.

I thought of all the good people I knew of—Mr. Macabe, Nate,
James, Andrew, Michael, Bessie, and so many more. Then the bad
ones like Leroy and Miss St. James's father who you never wanted
to meet.

But it was those in-between ones that you'd have to watch out
for because you never knew whether they were going to help you
or kick you in the teeth.

It is funny how one simple word can make the world fully right
again, and that word was *gone*. Leroy was gone, moved to Baltimore with his rich girlfriend, whose family owned a number

of hair salons and laundromats. Ma's divorce, no contest, had just come through, and with Leroy gone for good, Ma was a bit nicer to me. By all accounts, Leroy was planning to get hitched up again very quickly. Stevie was slowly coming around after the shock of Leroy's sudden move, and he seemed even more into his studies than before. Although I still bothered him, he had developed a better sense of humor, perhaps because he was now dating Cammy's older sister, Laura, which irritated Cammy no end. Kitty and Dr. Morgan had sent out an engagement notice, and Ma had breathed a sigh of relief because surely that meant she would get help with the bills, and with Stevie's college fees when the time came.

When Mr. Macabe had asked, aren't we enough for you? I should have answered, *you are*. I was right where I wanted to be.

Suddenly all I could think of was that Nate would be waiting for me like he always did, every Saturday. It had been a while since I had worked my Saturdays, and I missed just being around him for hours on end, watching him roll those biscuits.

I got off my bed and walked down the stairs, and then I was outside in the cool, fresh air. It would be a fifteen-minute walk to Nate's, but much shorter if I ran. I took off, running faster and faster until my breath came in puffs. Finally, I was there, at Nate's. I swung open the screen door to go in, but then something caught my eye.

It was a cloud dancing across the sky.

I stepped back and let go of the screen door and it slammed shut in front of me.

I stood there, looking far up into the blue sky. Searching. The silvery puffy clouds glided open and suddenly there was God, filling the whole sky with His amazing brilliance, always waiting patiently for me to remember that He was right there.

It was then I knew. Knew who had always protected me, and who had made my world right side up.

I laughed out loud, full of joy.

Then I threw out my arms and jumped as high as I could, up to meet Him, just as He reached down and folded me up in His embrace.

ACKNOWLEDGMENTS

It has taken a miracle—and a village—to get to this point. Thanks to God for providing the miracle. To my village . . . To my amazing agent, Charlotte Sheedy, the biggest thanks for being there for me every step of the way, mentoring, sharpening, encouraging; I cannot thank you enough. To Ally Sheedy, thank you so much for edits and probing questions that propelled me to go deeper. I would also like to thank Amistad, and Patrik Bass, for wholeheartedly believing in this story. To Keisha Lindsay, my lifelong friend and an author herself (*In a Classroom of Their Own: The Intersection of Race and Feminist Policies in All-Black Male Schools*), thanks so much for your brilliant and insightful comments on the manuscript. To the staff at the Bethesda Writers Center, for continuing to provide writers with excellent workshops and creative space; to my DC Ladies book club members, who provided years of good reads, friendship, laughter, and of course great books for us to dissect; to Rev. Lydia Dailey and members of the Historic Mount Zion United Methodist Church in Philadelphia, MS, for their kind hospitality and historical materials, thank you! A special thanks to Mouhamadou Moustapha Ly; you probably never knew how much your encouraging inquiries about the progress of "my book" at work inspired me to keep writing over the years! A special thanks to Aunty Helen Odamtten, who never stopped believing in my writing, and who opened the door to my first creative opportunity way back when. For family who have always had my back . . . To my amazing mother Margaret, who was erudite, witty, and strong, thank you for the example you are and for filling our childhood with novels, and my wonderful father Francis, who could not wait to read this book. Thanks also to my dear sisters Nana and Mansa. Mansa, I cannot believe you have read practically every draft I have written; thank you! Nana, thank you for putting me in touch with those who have walked the path before. Thank you, Jeff Horn, also Bisi Adjapon and Mamle Wolo! For my other "sister" Magdalene Baffour, thank you for your support, friendship, and prayers over the years; and Jennifer Robertson, thank you for years of friendship and for that needed bed to attend the New York writers conference. Finally, last and definitely not least, to my family—David, Imani, and Micah—who have seen and heard so much about this book, thanks for being a wonderful part of the process.

ABOUT THE AUTHOR

Nyani Nkrumah was born in Boston and raised in Ghana and Zimbabwe. She developed her love of reading and writing from her mother, who taught English literature and language and encouraged her children to recite poems and Shakespeare soliloquies. After graduating from Amherst College with a dual major in biology and Black studies, Nkrumah received a master's degree from the University of Michigan and a PhD from Cornell University. She has lived in the Washington, DC, region for the past twenty years.